Munday told himself that this house was the object of his return home. It made him uneasy —restless, exposed like a blunderer to staring cupboards and walls. It was as if someone in all that strangeness knew him and was hunting him. . . .

Also by Paul Theroux available from
Ballantine Books:

SAINT JACK

THE GREAT RAILWAY BAZAAR: BY TRAIN THROUGH ASIA

The
Black House

Paul Theroux

BALLANTINE BOOKS • NEW YORK

Library of Congress Catalog Card Number: 74-6135

ISBN 0-345-25753-7-195

This edition published by arrangement with
Houghton Mifflin Company

Manufactured in the United States of America

First Ballantine Books Edition: May 1977

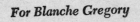
For Blanche Gregory

"Thus I; faltering forward,
Leaves around me falling,
Wind oozing thin through the thorn
from norward,
And the woman calling."

—THOMAS HARDY, *"The Voice"*

1

The Times, Tuesday November 9

The Bwamba

From Dr. A. B. W. Munday

Sir, It is to be regretted that your correspondent ("Tribal War in Western Uganda," 25 Oct.) did not trouble himself to probe more deeply into the conflict between the Bwamba and Batoro peoples, and saw fit only to repeat the confused observations of a generation of misfit District Commissioners.

The wisdom of comparing the Bwamba to other quarrelsome African peoples is questionable; to publish this comparison is folly. "A repetition of the Ibo adventure," he writes. On the contrary—colour is conceivably their only common denominator. This is not a great deal different from comparing an Englishman with, say, an Italian. An exercise in derision, but dangerous as well. A report such as his can be of no possible benefit in understanding the nature of the issues or the lapses for which both sides may be held accountable.

As it happens, I have recently returned from a long residence in Uganda and am presently engaged in writing a social history of the Bwamba. Without going into further detail, may one simply hope that when this study is published it will afford access to the sources of conflict and put paid to the notion that "civilized" society has nothing to learn even from so small and remote a people?

Yours faithfully,

ALFRED MUNDAY

Bowood House,
Four Ashes,
Near Bridport,
Dorset

Nov. 2.

2

THE STILLNESS of the country bedroom sealed their privacy and prompted them to continue the argument they had begun that morning on the train from Waterloo. But no sooner had he said to his wife, "Damn you"—saying it in the casual unemphatic way of the married person who has repeated it often without meaning it—than in the ensuing silence that had an unusual purr of safety, there was a human mutter against the wall. They were alarmed and disappointed —they were not alone, they could not explain that what had surely been overheard was simple exasperation. Then Mr. Flack was at the door, and Emma Munday at her open suitcase; and her husband placed himself across the room, at the window, pretending he had not meant anything serious.

"It's so green," said Alfred Munday, recovering his

voice. He looked out the window. It was the "guest" wing of The Yew Tree. He and Emma were the only guests. He stopped himself from speaking the next thought that occurred to him, that it was the kind of open landscape—there, out of the English window—that might have held groups of grazing zebra, or a distant regatta of tall white egrets, or some swart-sniffing wildebeest.

It was silly, but his eye, used to Africa, alert for the remarkable or strange, would not be quieted. In some places visions were interchangeable for Munday, and the comfort of a familiar detail often inspired an absurdity: once, he had woken in a hotel room in Kampala, and, chilled by the roaring air conditioner, looked sleepily out at the gray lowering sky; for seconds he believed those woolly clouds were about to release a blizzard of snow. That was on the equator, at sea level. Now he looked again at the human curves on the shoulders of the Dorset hills and wondered at their emptiness. He said, "It's as green as Africa."

"You should know, sir." That was Mr. Flack, the landlord of The Yew Tree. He said it as a friend, but he was positioned like a stranger, just outside the door of Munday's room, in his overcoat, with his fists clenched at his sides.

"Should I indeed?"

"Seeing as how you've been down there."

So Mr. Flack knew. Munday was cautioned and guardedly he said, "Quite."

"I was there myself," Mr. Flack went on. "During the last war. In the desert—I was at Tel el Kebir. Later on I was laid up in a hospital in Capetown. Malaria. That's how I lost my teeth—they had to pull them all out. Part of the cure. When my teeth were gone I was right as ninepence." He worked his mouth reflectively for a moment. "Had some blacks in the regiment, too."

Munday became interested. "Africans?"

"Hindus," said Mr. Flack. "Beautiful little chaps they were. Tremendous fighters. They had these dirty great *kukris*." He blinked and looked at Emma to explain. "That's a type of knife, sharp as anything, and they knew how to use them. Oh, we had some times."

Munday had turned to the window when Mr. Flack said, "Hindus." He said, "I didn't go in—I was getting my doctorate." He felt an explanation was required: he had no war stories. "In any case I have a bad heart."

"My ticker was none too good," said Mr. Flack, and it sounded to Munday like a rebuke. "I had these dizzy spells and went all cold in me hands and feet. They gave me six months to live."

"You look fine to me," said Munday.

"That was thirty years ago," said Mr. Flack. He leaned forward into the doorway to confide, "You're looking at a man of seventy!"

"I don't believe it," said Munday. He spoke what he felt; Mr. Flack's round figures sounded like lies. But Munday took a closer look and changed his mind.

"I'd be a lot stronger if I hadn't come down with double pneumonia during that hard winter—that was 'sixty-three. We were snowed up here for six weeks— no bread, no papers, and most of the cattle died. It was over the top of the pillar box. I'll show you the snapshots some time. That's what gave me my chest." He coughed; a rich deep wheeze traveled down his throat and slowed and thinned to a whistle. "I hope you and the missus like walks. There's some lovely walks here. And masses of history."

"We're quite looking forward to the walks," said Emma.

"I'll lend you my maps," said Mr. Flack. "I was a great walker once, but I don't do much of it these days what with the pub and my chest. And my missus has arthritis. Still."

Hearing the whiffling accent, Munday said with encouragement, "Why, you're a Londoner."

"Born and bred in Tulse Hill," said Mr. Flack, pronouncing it "Towse Hew." "I had a pub there for years, The Anchor, near the station. That's going back a bit—twenty years ago."

Munday said, "What made you choose Dorset?"

"Same reason as you, I fancy."

"And what reason is that?"

"Retirement, sort of. This is a good place for a retired gent."

"Of course," said Munday, but he was looking out the window again, past the thick black-green trees that gave the inn its name. "That's our house, isn't it?"

Mr. Flack excused himself and entered the room. He peered over Munday's shoulder and said, "That's the roof. Any idea when you'll be moving in?"

"Just as soon as our sea freight arrives. It's already in London, so it's just a matter of getting it off the dock and down here in a lorry."

"Could take ages," Mr. Flack said gravely. "I can tell you've been away for a little while. You don't know these dockers and their go-slows."

"We'll hope for the best," said Munday. "In the meantime we're counting on your hospitality."

"It's so kind of you to put us up," said Emma. "We were told you don't take many lodgers."

"Not these days," said Mr. Flack. "But years ago The Yew Tree was packed out with guests. Came from all over. We did lunches, cream teas, the lot. After old Mrs. Clissold died—she was a tower of strength—there was no one to clean. My missus can't manage the stairs, you see. It's her legs. Still, you're very welcome to stay as long as you like. You'll find it cheap and cheerful. The bar opens at six. Come down and have a drink if you're free."

"We'll just finish this unpacking," said Munday.

"Right you are," said Mr. Flack. He smiled at Munday, made a slight bow to Emma and walked stiffly out, shutting and latching the door.

"He thinks I'm retired," said Munday in a whisper.

"Aren't you?"

"No," said Munday, "and I don't like the word."

Emma opened her suitcase and took out a sponge bag. She said, "He's quite a talker."

"Six months to live!"

"And he knew you'd been to Africa," said Emma. "He must have seen your letter to *The Times*."

"Must have." Munday was encouraged. His letter corrected an inaccurate news story; it also announced that he was in England again. It was why he had used the house's address rather than The Yew Tree's. He hoped old friends would notice that he was back and settled, that he hadn't changed; but he had frequently written letters to *The Times* from Africa, reviving issues three months old, beginning, "I hope it is not too late for a distant subscriber to add a few words, as I have only just seen the copy dated—," and he ended with his address, "The Yellow Fever Camp, Bundibugyo, Bwamba District, Uganda."

He was anxious for his old colleagues to know that he was working on the book he had promised. In the letter he said, "presently engaged," which was not true. The book—all Munday saw of the future—was not written, it was not started; it was a valise of unsorted note cards and partially-filled copy books, kept over a period of ten years in Africa. Some were in Emma's handwriting, his rambling dictation, a method he had begun when the mission doctor cautioned him about his blood pressure. Dictation hadn't worked; he couldn't speak and think clearly at the same time, and anyway his blood pressure had continued to rise. There was part of a diary, too, the observations of a new arrival, a beginner: enthusiastic paragraphs entered the first year, celebrations which succeeding years of repetition had turned into commonplaces, for what had seemed unique was only strange, and when, with familiarity, it ceased to be strange—the plant life, the sunlight, the smells—it was beneath notice.

He had also said, "a social history." Not that. It would be anthropology, as travel and discovery—not a study, but a record of a people and an account of his own movements and changes in attitude, his experience of the climate and language, the kind of book that had once been written by learned and opinionated explorers. Munday had not taken his long residence lightly, and he had biases. He would risk what errors of judgment were unavoidable in such circumstances and write as a man who had lived closely with an alien people; his responses would be as important as the behavior that caused those responses. He had entered the culture and assisted in practices whose value he saw only as an active participant; witchcraft and sorcery had almost brought him to belief in those early years because he had been more than a witness. That was at the core of the book. It was the kind of book that had ceased to be attempted except by amateurs and hacks; all the excitement had gone out of anthropology—he had been away when the attitude changed; his eagerness to explore was no longer fashionable. His early paper, "Hunger and The Uncanny," was dismissed as tendentious, gullible, and anecdotal. Now he was refuted more cold-bloodedly with sociology—statistics, models, punched cards, computer verdicts, and young men crouched with clipboards at the fringes of villages. Anthropology, the most literate of the sciences, whose nearest affine was the greatest fiction, had degenerated to impersonal litanies of clumsy coinages and phrases of superficial complexity, people of flesh and bone to cases or subjects with personalities remaining as obscure as their difficult names, like the long Latin one given to the pretty butterfly. He did not use those words.

He intended his book to redeem those people. Redeem was not too big a word: they were in every sense lost. He had once described the Bwamba in a paper as "witch-ridden semi-pygmies," and privately as "tricky little bastards," but they were his, he had been the only person to study them—and by accident, for he had thought in London that they lived in the mountains, and it was only when he got there that he discovered that they were a lowland people who preferred the concealment of swamps and the isolated copse in the savannah. So he had stayed at the Yellow Fever Camp from the first and had the Bwamba to himself. Once, an American anthropologist had come to the district with plans for a study and many boxes of supplies. Munday ridiculed the man's electric typewriter and tore up the letter of introduction, written by a classmate who had gone to California—"I know you will give him the advantage of your wide experience," the letter said.

"You're poaching," said Munday to the stunned researcher. "Do you know how the Bwamba deal with people like you? Poachers? They ambush them and flay them alive. You'd better leave while it's still light. It's a long drive back."

It was partly this obstinacy that had earlier earned him the respect of many people in his profession, several of them eminent; he was said to be cantankerous but incorruptible, but, never giving in, he developed what was almost a grudge against his own honesty, and he was thin-skinned to criticism, responding to the mildest doubt of his methods with merciless personal attacks. Nearly everyone agreed that he had stayed away, among those people, for far too long; it had affected him, and when his name was mentioned in the Common Room of an English university, men who had praised his work would say, "I like *her* well enough—" But he had come home. That was his regret. He had planned to write the book in Africa, to note on the last page the name of the African Village, the Yellow Fever Camp, and the date of the book's completion, as proof of the authenticity of his remoteness, the severe distance from any library; the bush tombstone of the missionary, saying simply that he had died in that place, proved sincerity. It would be different now, a village name, perhaps his full address, but an English village in Dorset. If anyone asked why, he could say, "Doctor's orders."

"I hope he's wrong about our sea freight," said Emma.

Munday was filling a bureau drawer with his underwear and socks. He said, "Flack? He's making that up. Like his malaria, and that business about having his teeth pulled. Did you ever hear of such a thing!"

"Part of the cure," said Emma, using Flack's clinical tone of voice.

"I saw you smiling," said Munday. He shook his head. "I was afraid I was going to burst out laughing. He's incredible."

"He seems very sweet all the same." She stopped speaking and smiled at the wall, and shortly she saw her face, the mirror frame, her husband's head behind her shoulder. She tried a new expression and patted her hair. "I'm glad we're here."

"The Yew Tree," said Munday, continuing his unpacking.

"England," said Emma. She spoke it with a passion Munday doubted, enunciating it like a word in an old hymn, with a sob of relief in her throat. It was the way people said it in plays staged by amateur drama groups in Uganda, and it made Munday uncomfortable.

He went over to his wife. He was going to touch her shoulder, but thought better of it. He faced her. "You're glad the doctor sent me home."

"Don't put it like that. You make it sound like failure."

"It was, for me," he said. He had never thought he would return home except to lecture at one of the institutes on the progress of his research. His return he saw as a defeat, a partial failure of which not panic but annoyance was one symptom. He would still lecture at an institute but it would not be the same as flying to London for a conference, reading his paper, and then returning to the African village.

"You know how much I hated it," said Emma, and added her correction softly, "Them."

"We could have discussed it."

"Yes, Doctor," she said, trying not to smile. Then, "I didn't want to sound pathetic—I thought it would bore you."

"You had your painting."

"I had my painting," Emma said, and now she did smile; she saw the water colors she had forced herself to make, *Native Hut, Tulip Tree in Blossom, Rhino Camp*—the perfect reflection of the promontory in Lake Albert that had been hung upside-down at the British Council Library in Fort Portal, *Humped Cattle,* and that mess, *Sunset over the Congo.* She looked up at Munday, "And you had your people."

"You're ridiculing me."

"Because sometimes," said Emma, "you are ridiculous."

"Don't start again," said Munday, remembering that sudden voice against the wall, and Flack at the door.

"Your people. That's what you called them."

"That's what they were."

" 'Lapses,' " said Emma. "That's what savagery is when you call savages people."

"We've had this conversation before," said Munday.

"So we have," she said, her tone going from hostility to gentleness as she turned her head.

"Savages, savagery. I daresay the people around here will agree with you," said Munday. "As if any of you know the first thing about it!" He went on emptying the suitcase with angry vigor, and slapping a stack of clean shirts said, "I've got a surprise for them."

"What's that?"

"You remember Silvano, the Bwamba chap who's at the London School of Economics? I'm planning to have him down here one weekend, as soon as we've moved into the house. Introduce him to all the locals, show him around." Munday's face became amused. "Should be interesting," he said with satisfaction. "They don't see many Africans around here."

"So you're going to inflict Silvano on them, is that it?" Emma saw a cheetah, teardrop markings down its jowls, the wild thing on a leash, being taken to tea at a grand house, causing awe-struck stares and nervous conversation, then curled and panting loudly by the feet of a scared guest.

Munday smiled, and snorted with pleasure.

"Like some strange pet," Emma said. She saw the cheetah pawing the air, frightening strangers with its teeth and claws and bright fur.

"Let's not argue about it," said Munday. "Look, it's almost dark."

The husband and wife looked at the window and saw their reflections staring in at them, though it was not yet four. The insubstantial gloom of the afternoon which had made the view such a deep African green, had become night during their short talk, giving them a reason for ending it and further emphasizing the familiarity Munday felt about the landscape, for that velvet dark, the liquid windows and the overbright yellow bulbs of the room circled by one dusty moth —all of it, with the smell of floorwax, reminded him of African night and African seclusion. He wondered: Have I carried Africa here?

"We should finish this unpacking," he finally said. He turned his back on the window and walked over to the bureau where a drawer sagged open.

"Your letter to *The Times,*" Emma said. "Do you really believe all that?"

"Emma," he said, warning her with her name.

"Because *I* don't. I want you to know that. I'm glad we're here—home."

"This isn't home."

"It's England," said Emma.

"A corner of it."

"We're English," she said.

"We're strangers here," he said; his voice was gruff. "What were we in Africa?"

"English," he said.

Emma said, "You know nothing."

Munday was annoyed; he couldn't reply to that. But he remembered something else. He said, "What do you mean by saying I'm ridiculous?"

Emma resumed her unpacking. She did not say anything immediately. She took a wool dress out of her suitcase and sniffed it, then found a hanger for it and put it in the wardrobe. Then she said, "That little charade at Waterloo."

The incident had upset him; it was something he had tried to forget, but Emma's words made a picture of the furry white erasure on his mind, and he saw the obliterated portion and finally the mistake.

They had been late, it was raining. He had lugged the heavy suitcases into the station—cursing the taxi driver who had made no move to help, the huddle of porters who were unloading a coach—and past the newsstand he spotted a porter wheeling an empty baggage carrier. Munday dropped his suitcases and waved to him; the porter did not see him. Munday moved closer in a spurt, jerking the cases, calling out, and when the porter hesitated, Munday ordered him sharply to hurry up. The porter, squinting, stood his ground, for both times Munday had spoken in Swahili.

Munday was berating the porter in Swahili, furious at the man's hesitation, when Emma cut him off— "Don't be a jackass, Alfred," she said—and walked away. The porter, sensing that he was being mocked, wheeled his baggage carrier in the opposite direction. Alone and fearing for his heart, Munday dragged the suitcases onto the platform.

"I was confused," said Munday. "He was black."

"That explains it, of course," said Emma, looking at her wrist watch with an indifference Munday believed she was pretending simply to anger him.

3

At half-past six, leaving Emma resting, Munday went down for a drink. He pushed open the door of the bar and set a bell jangling. It startled him, he touched his heart; and it jangled again as he closed the door. He carried his pain across the room.

"Good evening," said Mr. Flack. He was at the bar, still in his overcoat, rubbing his hands. Behind him were shelves and shelves of bright candies in large jars, wine gums, mint humbugs, mint imperials, boiled sweets, wrapped toffees. Behind that nodding aged head a sign reading *New Tooty Aniseed Chews!* "How are you getting on?"

"Just about finished," said Munday, and he turned to take in the whole room, the bar billiards table, the hunting prints, the color print of the old brewery, *Cobnut Sliced,* the dusty blue sign *Briggs Empire Shag,* the high yellow walls, a trestle table with the ring marks of glasses, a dart board set in a scarred rubber hoop that had been filleted from a tire, the brass bell above the door, and three old men, motionless as sticks of furniture.

Two of them sat on stools by the fireplace where a low fire glowed under a smoky heaping of coal, a white-haired one in a threadbare jacket, another in a thick dark coat which reached to his ankles. The third, in a suit jacket and clean bib-overalls, and wearing a too-small crushed felt hat, sat on a bench by the front window. Munday smiled at them, but only the third reacted: he tugged his hat brim in a negligent gesture of recognition. He might have been straighten-

13

ing the hat. The other two shifted on their stools, but
continued to study the fire, the smoke curling from
between the lumps of coal.

"What will it be?" asked Mr. Flack.

"Is that cider?" Munday pointed to a plump white
barrel resting on a rack. Lettered on the barrel was
the name of a brewery and *Cyder*.

"That's your dry."

"I'll take a half of that."

Mr. Flack bent to the barrel, twisted the wooden
spigot, and drew off a plopping glassful. He placed
the cloudy liquid before Munday and said, "Four-
pence."

"Very reasonable," said Munday. An arrogance in
Mr. Flack's manner, different from the civility he had
shown upstairs, urged Munday to say curtly, "Have
one yourself, Flack."

"Cheers, sir, I'll have a tickle of this." He took a
bottle of Glenfiddich from under the bar and poured
himself an expensive measure. "To your very good
health."

The two men by the fire had begun to talk between
themselves. Their mutters filled the room; Munday
heard "buggers." He addressed the nearest one, the
man swaddled in the long coat, "Will you have one
with me?"

"Thank 'ee," said the man, and placing his glass of
beer on the floor next to the hearthstone, said to Mr.
Flack, "I'll have a short."

"And you?"

The white-haired man, who had been looking abstractedly into the fire, turned to Munday. "A Guinness, thanks," he said gently, and brought his glass
to the bar.

Munday nodded at the man with the felt hat.

"A large light," said the man. He showed Munday
his empty pint glass.

"That looks interesting," Munday said to Mr.
Flack. He had poured a tot of rum into a schooner

and was now uncorking a green bottle with an en-graved label.

"A short," said Mr. Flack. "Rum and ginger wine."

Munday passed it to the man who had been drinking beer; the others collected their drinks, and they all drank to Munday's health.

"That's ninety-four pence," said Mr. Flack. He had put on a pair of loosely-hinged spectacles to search out the figure on a dog-eared Decimal Conversion Chart.

"I don't think this is going to cover it," said Munday showing Flack the coins in his palm. "It'll have to be one of these." He unfolded a pound note and handed it to Flack. Receiving his sixpence change he could not hide his disappointment.

"How do you like your cider?" asked Mr. Flack.

"Drinkable," said Munday. He was still frowning at the sixpence.

"Careful, mister," said the man in the felt hat.

"You needn't worry," Munday joked. "I know my limit."

"You don't know that scrumpy," said the man, turn-ing grave.

"Poison," said the old man in the long coat, sipping at his rum and ginger wine.

"Rots your insides," said the man with the Guinness. He spoke as the others had, out of the corner of his mouth.

"I was under the impression," said Munday, "that the local people drank a lot of this muck."

The men were silent. After a few moments the white-haired man sipped his Guinness loudly and spoke up. "The local people," he said, "sells it."

"Some folks drink it by the gallon," said Mr. Flack. "Tourists and summer people, that is. Don't have much taste for it myself."

Munday finished his cider, a bitter mouthful, and toyed with his glass. He waited and hummed, but convention was not observed, he was not offered a drink. He turned his back on the three drinkers and ordered a gin and lime.

"You'll have to meet Mr. Awdry," said Mr. Flack. "He was in Africa, too. Your part." For the others Mr. Flack said, "Doctor Munday's lived abroad for quite a few years."

The man in the felt hat said, "I *thought* he looked a bit stunned."

The white-haired man said, "I don't hold with abroad."

"I should be very pleased to meet him," said Munday. "What is Mr. Awdry's business?"

"This and that," said Mr. Flack. "He's retired, like yourself."

And now Munday was going to say, to Mr. Flack and for the men to hear, that he was not retired at all, and that he had only come to rest his heart and write his book. He had no further interest in the village; indeed, he planned to leave the rented house when his book was finished. But he had taken a dislike to them all and objected to offering them any candor; he nodded, accepting the status Mr. Flack had assigned to him—knowing that thereafter it would be hard to dispute—and he said, "I see you've got a billiards table."

"Snookerette," said Mr. Flack. "Do you play?"

"A little," said Munday. He believed he played well, and he was eager to beat the men on their own table. "Played on one like it in Africa."

"Makes a change," said the white-haired man.

"Bit of fun," said Mr. Flack.

The old man in the long coat came over to Munday's side, close enough for Munday to smell the coat's damp decayed wool. Munday thought the man was going to propose a game on the table, but the man reached into his deep pocket and took out a bone-handled clasp knife. He showed it, weighing it in his hand, then opened it and said, "That there knife's fifty-six years old."

"Older than me," said Munday, and sought a reaction on the men's faces.

"Look how sharp he is," said the man. "Workmanship."

Munday tried the blade with his thumb. "Like a razor."

"He cost me a shilling," said the man. "The same knife today would cost thirty bob at least." He returned the knife to his pocket, patted the pocket, and went back to his fireside stool, his two drinks.

"The missus resting?" Mr. Flack asked.

Munday, annoyed that Mr. Flack had guessed correctly, said she was not.

"You'll be stopping up at the Black House, will you?" asked the white-haired man.

"Bowood House," said Munday.

"We calls her the Black House," said the man.

"I see," said Munday.

"Queer place, the Black House," said the man.

"Haunted, is it," said Munday.

The man didn't smile. "I've heard things."

"Ghosts," said Munday, biting on his smile. "I must tell my wife."

"Not ghosts," said the man in the felt hat, seeing, as Munday did, the white-haired man grow shy under Munday's ironic smile. It was the smile more than the words that mocked.

"Strange creatures, then?" Munday's voice was sharp.

"Queer noises," said the man in the felt hat.

"Noises you can't account for, that it?"

"Not in the normal way," said Mr. Flack.

Munday saw that he challenged them all. "Funny," he said, "Africans say the same about things they don't understand."

He had gone too far, he could see it in their reaction, which was withdrawal, more extreme than silence, a tightening and thinning of the dry air. He felt assaulted by their indifference. A lump of coal in the fireplace snapped, a stool creaked, the front door rattled in the jamb.

"I'll tell you who died," the white-haired man said

suddenly, and Munday turned to listen. But it was a local matter and he was not admitted to the conversation about the man's age and the speculation about the sickness which Munday knew was not fatal. This led to stories of an ailing farmer, a missing cow, a broken fence, and an extensive aggrieved tale, offered by the man in the long coat, of a laborer's humiliation by a farmer's rude and wrong-headed wife.

"They never learn," said the man in the felt hat who had been addressed as Hosmer; he said it with what Munday thought was unwarranted fierceness, and there was silence again. Silent, the room seemed empty, the men like old chairs, and Munday, alert, alive, attentive to his gin, excluded. He wondered: Who are these people and why did they tell me that about the house? He briefly despised them, saw them as a ridiculous senate of pensioners who, younger, might have been his enemies, and he understood that his irony had mystified and angered them. The men grew audible again, they coughed with force, one inhaled snuff deeply from the knuckles on the back of his hand, another smoked a rolled twisted cigarette, and the drawling was renewed: the price of apples, the cost of living, a lunatic in the next village, reckless drivers, a pair of vicious dogs Hosmer said should be put down (And I know how to do it").

"You could write a book about this place," said Mr. Flack, who took Munday's silence for attention.

"Me?" said Munday.

"Anyone who knew how," said Mr. Flack.

Munday's laughter was harsh; the four men stared at him. He waited until they began another private conversation—this one about a dead badger—before he went up to his room.

4

THE BOWOOD HOUSE described in the letter the land-lord's agent had sent when requesting a deposit for breakage and the first month's rent was not the Bo-wood House the Mundays carried their suitcases into —baggage tags fluttering from the handles—that dark rainy day towards the middle of November. In Uganda, and in the cramped London hotel, Munday had read the letter aloud to Emma, and he had pored over it alone many times, relishing the phrases that were used so casually by the agent. The description interested and excited him, generated a feeling of expectancy, a foreknowledge of comfort, that was some consolation for the disappointment he had felt on being told he would have to leave the African village and move out of the bungalow at the Yellow Fever Camp. ("That heart of yours," Father Dowle, the mission doctor, had said.) And having used the address of Bowood House on his letter to *The Times* he had committed himself, before moving in, to a fixed image in his mind. He had a settled feeling about the place and its dimensions, as if he had already lived in it and knew its separate warm rooms: there were four bed-rooms and a box room, a "snug" kitchen with "units," a "sunny" breakfast room, a studio (where he saw himself at work), an inglenook. There were "power points" in every room ("Imagine, Emma," he had said, "power points!"—but the joke was wearing thin). Outside, there was a "courtyard," and part of the house was "rendered." There were "outbuildings" on

19

the "grounds" and trees at the bottom of the garden which, the agent promised, bore soft fruit.

Mr. Flack said, "You're not seeing it at its best."

He had put on his peaked cap and, hunched over the steering wheel, driven the Mundays to the house in his old black Humber. That morning a letter had come from the freight forwarders saying that the nine cases were on their way to Four Ashes.

Mr. Flack said, "The rain." He leaned back and squinted at the gray pouring sky as if to determine how long it would last.

"A Bwamba would call this rain a good omen," said Munday. But he felt differently about it. He looked at the house. He did not want to go inside.

Mr. Flack said, "It's got bags of character."

Emma agreed. Munday heard her say, "Charming."

"Thanks for the lift, Flack," said Munday, and, already feeling let down, quickly sent the old man away so that he would not be able to report on their disappointment. The wind blew the rain against the trees and knocked shriveled leaves into the shallow courtyard puddles where some stuck and some floated. Behind them on the far side of the road the limbs of a stripped tree howled; the wind came in gusts, rain in rushing air, emptying the trees and pulling at their branches and blackening their trunks.

Even when Mr. Flack had gone the Mundays remained on the roadside, trying to make sense of the agent's letter by comprehending the house. The sight of it was like an incomplete memory, the sort an adult has, faced with his childhood house: unfamiliar details were intrusive and disturbing, the size, the color, the position, some black front windows with drawn curtains, the chimneys—absurdly, Munday had imagined smoke coming from the chimneys, and these cold bricks with empty orange flues depressed him and spoiled the memory.

The house looked small. Munday had not expected that nor its unusual position, directly on the narrow road; one long wall was flush with the road (leaves collecting at the foundation where it formed a gutter), and a high bushy bank, the edge of a field, rose up behind, dwarfing the house. It gave the impression of having once had some definite purpose on the road: the stone shed might have been a smithy's or wheelwright's.

"I don't imagine it made any difference when the only traffic was a wagon passing once a day—" Munday continued speaking but his words were lost in the engine roar and hissing tires of a truck which passed just then, its green canvas bellying on top and flapping at the back. Munday finished hopelessly, "—stand this."

The house was of stone, and squat, with a slate roof, the black slates shining in the rain; a sharp scalloped ridge on the roof peak was its only elegance. It was set plumply against the bank and looked older than that bank, as if the back pasture had risen, the verge at either end lifted in a grassy swell, sinking the house into the earth. The walls absorbed the damp differently, the pale new stone moistened like sand, the dark and almost black old stone, the brown hamstone extension at the back which was the bathroom and toilet ("low-flush," the letter said) replacing the roofless brick shed half-hidden in tangled briars and a mature holly tree in the back garden. There was also a recent and unattractive coal shed across the courtyard, its cement blocks stained unevenly with wetness. The rain and damp defined the portions of the house by shading their ages variously, and the side that faced the road was darkened by soot and exhaust fumes, the stone foundation covered by dry inland limpets and a deep green moss like patches of felt, the shade of the cushions on the billiard table at The Yew Tree.

"Courtyard," said Munday, kicking open the iron gate. The gate made a grinding sound as Munday walked across the flagstones. A puddle at the entrance was being filled by a gurgling drain-spout. "Double doors," he said, fumbing with the large latchkey. He entered the gritty hall with its ragged rope mat, then the chilly damp kitchen. He taught himself the meanings, bitterly, by sight. Now he knew "snug" meant tiny and "character" inconvenience and "charming" old; the ceiling was low, and though it was unnecessary for him to do so—he was not tall—he stooped, oppressed by the confining room and making his irritation into a posture. He glanced around; he said, "Sunny breakfast room." The house was cold and held a musty stale odor that not even the draft from the open door freshened—an alien smell, not theirs.

Munday came to attention before a still clock on a kitchen shelf which showed the wrong time on a bloodied face. He was afraid and heard his heart and felt it enlarge. He recovered, saw the rust, and feeling foolish went to the sink which was coated in grime. He turned on the faucet; it choked and spat, brown water bubbled out and patterned rivulets into the grime, and then it became colorless and Munday shut it off. What a stubborn place, he thought. He tried the lights; they worked. He opened the oven door, the furnace door, a cupboard. He peeked into a corner room and mumbled, "larder." He sniffed and looked for more.

Emma stood in the doorway, still holding her suitcases. A tractor went by and rattled the windows.

"Hello, what's this," said Munday in his sour voice, "power points."

"Don't," said Emma. "Don't say anything more. Please, Alfred. Or I'll cry—"

Munday was silent; behind him his wife began to sob. She went to the kitchen table and sat down and took a lacy handkerchief from her bag. Munday wanted to touch her hair but he kept himself away and tried to give his feeling for the house a name. He told himself that this house was what he had surrendered Africa for, it was the object of his return home. It made him uneasy—not sad like Emma (if her tears meant that), but restless, exposed like a blunderer to staring cupboards and walls. It was as if someone in all that strangeness knew him and was hunting him.

It was not that the house was cold and unused, nor that it was so different from the agent's description. It was not derelict, and if it had been truly empty he felt he could have possessed it; Munday—again sniffing and moving rapidly from room to room—was anxious for an opposite reason. He sensed, and he was searching for proof, that it held a presence that the apparent emptiness warned him of.

The dampness and that dusty odor lingered as a clammy insinuation in every corner of the house, and while Emma sat at the kitchen table and cried—the door open to the drizzling courtyard completing the picture of abandonment in which she occupied the foreground: the kind of portraiture she admired but could not achieve with her own paint-box—Munday busied himself with a coal hod he found in the shed, split some dry branches for kindling and tried to drive out the dampness with fires at each end of the house. After a smoky uncertain start in the living-room fireplace (the old newspaper smoldered, too damp to flare up), the pile of dry sticks Munday eventually shredded and splintered caught and burned noisily and filled the stone opening with slender flames. He heaped on it pieces of broken coal and short halved logs from a brass-studded keg near the hearth, and he watched the fire until he could smell its heat.

In the firebox of the kitchen stove, a low stout Rayburn of chipped yellow enamel, he laboriously started a fire, following the instructions from a manual provided by the owner and using the fuel specified, anthracite knobs, like smooth black buns. He worked with a poker and tongs and several cubes of white crumbling firelighter. The firelighters flared and roared for minutes, then burned out, leaving red edges on the fuel which quickly cooled to blackness. It took him nearly an hour, but he had a good fire, and after he shut the door to the firebox he opened the vents so wide he could see the flickering light and hear the roar of the flames being sucked around the elbow of the stovepipe, their gasps in the chimney's throat. With the stove alight he boiled a kettle and put hot water bottles in the double bed; he found the electric fires and plugged them in and turned them on high, making them ping like egg-timers. Later, remembering the cost, he adjusted them to warm.

Munday smiled at his fires and rubbed his hands before them. He went outside and was delighted to see smoke billowing from his chimneys—that signal, so poignant and reassuring, of active habitation; like winter breath, swirling from a man's face. Emma cheered up in the warm house. She made tea and swept the floors, she put sheets and towels in the airing cupboards and discovered the view from the bedroom window that gave a glimpse of the sea. Munday joined her at the window; seeing that she had stopped crying he had paused in his brisk movements and shuffled and stooped to reassure her.

He said, "No need to cry."

"It was that carpet in the kitchen," she said. "It looked so worn and horrid. I couldn't help myself. God, whose feet—"

"I'll take it into the shed," said Munday.

"No—your heart. Please."

"It *does* look depressing," he said in the kitchen. What he had taken for a floral pattern were dark tulip-shaped stains and spots like blossoms in the gray tattered nap.

"Let me help you," said Emma.

The husband and wife knelt on the kitchen floor, side by side, and rolled up the carpet. The activity, seemingly so abrupt and insignificant, was important to them as an illustration of their marriage, what was best in it—and what both would remember when the apprehension they felt, the suspicion of the strange place, the fear of an unwelcome surprise which neither wished to call death, was answered by proof, so that in the end only one of them would be able to recall that rainy morning, the rolling carpet, and that movement, bumping forward on their knees.

They carried it to the shed and left it with other discarded things, the garden tools, the summer chairs which all appeared to be broken, a dog's dish, a pitchfork, a scythe, paint cans and enamel basins and two porcelain chamberpots nesting on the worktable. Munday lifted the top one out. It was ornate and had flowers on it, still brightly colored. Its handle was whole.

"I haven't seen one of these in years," he said.

"When I was a girl," Emma said, "I used to stay with my aunt and uncle in Eastbourne—"

Munday listened to the story; she was happy, he laughed appreciatively. She had told him the story before, but this telling of it was hopeful evidence that he had her support, that she was calmed and would share the solitude of the village with him as she did this memory.

With the fires going and the lamps blazing in the windows the house was alive, its personality was established with the heat and light; the dark late-afternoon helped, and the gusts of wind blew gouts of raindrops against the side windows and then seemed to push at the glass with a pressure like spread fingers that strained every inch of it and then released it. The dark and the weather which was growing wild outside and perhaps threatening the slates made the house seem a good shelter: the exaggerated storm outside, the warmth inside, maintained in Munday's imagination the illusion of the place as a refuge. And the husband and wife moved more freely knowing that the room they were about to enter would be warm.

But still the suggestion of a menacing presence, a half-formed fear, like a small creature of liquid, swayed and seemed to yawn in whatever room was adjacent to the one Munday happened to be in. He trusted the room he occupied; he was uncertain about the other rooms and could only verify his safety by entering them. Each time he stretched his arm to switch on a light in a darkened room he dared not step into, he was cautioned by a pain in his heart that was like a brief bright star.

"I must take it easy," he said to his wife. "I think I'm overdoing it."

"You're restless," she said. "Let me make you a drink."

Munday was one of those men who looked at his watch before he had his first drink of the day. His rule on weekdays was no alcohol before sundown, and he was obedient to the rule. It was dark; he said yes; Emma poured the gin out, and only then did Munday look at his watch and see that it was four-fifteen, that sundown was at mid-afternoon and that he would be drunk before dinner.

"Emma, look at the time!"

Emma laughed and handed him his drink. She said, "It looks as if we'll have to adjust our habits. It gets dark so early in winter. I'd forgotten. I must remember to get a bottle of sherry from Mr. Flack."

"Amontillado," said Munday. "That's a good drink for this time of day."

They talked at length about what drinks they would depend on through the winter. Then Munday said, "The freight hasn't come. What do you suppose is keeping them?"

"This isn't a very easy place to find," said Emma. "And there's just that brass knocker out front. I wonder if we can hear it from here?"

They were seated before the living-room fireplace. Munday said, "Is the outside light on? It should be. And if the kitchen's dark they might be put off and go away."

"I'll have a look."

"I'll do it," said Munday, but he didn't rise. Then Emma was out of the room and her opening and shutting the door made a damp breeze from the dark hall settle on Munday's shoulders. He shuddered and leaned towards the fire and warmed himself.

There were his fires, but still dark and cold parts of the house remained. Now they were in a place where doors were always kept shut; a house was not an open sunlit breezy place, but many separate closed rooms, one or two of suffocating smallness, and each with its own smell and temperature and purpose. Already the house had doubtful corners, the alarmingly cluttered box room where they put their empty suitcases, the drafty unlighted stairs with its protruding candle-holders on the walls, and the several doors which swung unaided by a hand and surprised him when their iron latches clanked; the dark back hall where there were so many rubber boots and raincoats and walking sticks—he'd find a light for it, but who did all that clobber belong to? He could not be certain they were alone. The unfamiliarly early darkness made him doubtful, or the old men whose suggestion of ghosts he had mocked, or maybe he was tired. It was not fear but doubt; and he told himself his heart was sick and half-broken. He would not admit superstition—he had seen too much of that. Emma had said he was restless, he was always that in new places. He felt stupid; something he had known since childhood he had now forgotten, and he believed the reminder of this knowledge, something to animate the thought that slumbered on a ledge in his mind—but it lay hidden—was in this house.

Just like the rat. That hurrying rat in the African bungalow, at the Yellow Fever Camp. Seeing it enter the kitchen he had stamped, and the rat had scuttled into the pantry. Munday had yelled for the cook and together they cornered it. But the terrified thing had leaped at his legs, and fear made Munday recoil when he should have kicked out. Then the rat was past him, in the hall, under the bookcase, in the bedroom, the study, cowering and scampering wildly when it was threatened with the cook's broom. Munday was separated from the cook; the rat shot along the passage, skidding on the waxed floor, and into the living room. The cook shrieked, and when Munday entered the room the cook told him the rat had run into the garden. But Munday had not seen it go, and

long after, even on the sunniest day, he could not
make himself believe that the rat had gone as the cook
said. He smelled it—it smelled of sex, musky and
genital—and he heard at the level of the floor the
rat hurrying through the bungalow with a querulous
panic, clawing with its forepaws, rising up and
nibbling with its yellow teeth. He had not told Emma
his fear, but he had often lain awake at night and
listened to the sounds near his bed.

So the sense of a substantial shadow in the house
remained with him, in spite of the fires and the warmth.
He sat massaging his knees like a man who has not
arrived at his destination but is only stopping in a
place too unfamiliar to afford him the rest he expected,
who may get up at any moment and move out. But
he stayed where he was.

The nine crates arrived that evening. The driver,
his eyes bright from driving in the dark, said he had
got lost in the country lanes.

"You should use a map," said Munday.

"I do," said the driver. "You're not on it." The
crates were not large; some were put in the shed un-
opened, the rest in the house. The driver used his
crowbar to open the heavier ones, and when he had
finished Munday saw him to his truck. The man looked
around, like someone caught in a wilderness, and said,
"Now how the hell do I get out of here?"

Munday showed him the way.

In the living room, unwrapping the taped parcels of
artifacts (weapons, tools, and ornaments; but all re-
sembling each other), he constantly heard sounds in
the kitchen. Though he knew Emma was making tea he
stopped what he was doing and wondered if there
were someone with her only he could see. He considered warning her of the danger, but checked himself
and went on unpacking, because if it was a danger it
was one to which he could not assign a name.

"I didn't realize we had collected so much junk,"
said Emma. She entered the living room carrying a
tray and had that erect stateliness of the tray-

bearer. She held a teapot, cups and saucers, a milk jug, a plate of sandwiches, and a small cheese board. She put the tray on a footstool in front of the fire and began preparing the tea things, arranging the plates, pouring the milk.

Munday was handling a short knobbed club. He tested it, wagging it back and forth. He said, "I'd be lost without my collection."

He looked fondly over the objects he had already unwrapped, the neatly labeled knives, the clay pots, the digging sticks, the beaded necklaces. "They've stopped making clubs like this," he said. The old fool in the decayed coat at The Yew Tree, with his treasured clasp knife: had he said that? Something like it. "I feel very lucky to have these things."

"The necklace there," said Emma. "We made ones like that when I was a Girl Guide."

Munday said, "That's the sort of remark—"

"No," she went on, "they don't make clubs like that anymore. They don't have to. Why make a club when you can steal the window bars from an Indian shop and use those to beat—"

"You're being rather a bore," said Munday, still admiring the club. "This was carved from a single piece of wood—a mangrove root."

"Damn, I've forgotten the sugar."

"I'll get it."

Munday rose and went into the dark hall and came face to face with a man in black. His heart wrenched and a searing bulb of pain stung him with fire and threatened to burst through his chest. He stepped back into the lighted living room and said with a stammerer's effort, "Do you always walk into people's houses without knocking?"

The man was calm; there was a smile on his pink face. He said, "Not if I know they're carrying weapons," and he pointed to the club Munday held tightly in his hand.

5

IN THE HALL, that little space, there had been a fusty odor from the net curtains and the window nailed shut and the rising damp that soaked the walls. He had breathed the bad air and it had made him more anxious by gagging him. He was off balance, he felt surrounded by a single man, and he was startled bumping into the man and meeting that broad warm face in his own hall. But Munday could not manage his fear, and what the stranger saw was a very angry man backing into the middle of a great pile of shredded paper and ripped cartons and wrappings and an assortment of thick objects of wood and stone. They were worn and oddly-shaped and scratched with feeble tracings of decoration, crude patterns, spirals, crosses and dots which attracted his eye but were too simple to engage it. Munday held his heavy club half-raised and Emma, behind him, a saucer with an unsteady tea cup rattling on it; she warned him about his heart in a pleading voice, "—Getting upset won't do you any good at all, Alfred."

"I'm terribly sorry," the man said over Munday's stammered complaint, and he smiled at Emma and shrugged as if to indicate that Munday was a slight embarrassment to them both.

"You damn well should be," said Munday. The man in black clutching a wet hat in his hands had surprised him, but it was not what Munday feared or expected, so even the considerable ache of the shock he had just had gave him no relief: now he was no less afraid and he was angered by this false alarm, an interruption of his older fear.

"Bob Crawshaw," the man said and put out his hand. "I'm vicar up at St. Alban's. I was just passing—"

"Will you have some tea, Vicar?" Emma said. She had risen, not as the vicar thought, to offer him the cup, but to be in a position to reach over and steady her husband, who had looked a moment earlier as if he was about to assault the man.

"That would be lovely," said the vicar. He looked rescued. He stepped past Munday and took a long stride over the discarded packing material to accept the cup from Emma. He began stirring the spoon very fast and looking from husband to wife. With the offer of tea, order was established, and holding the cup in his hand the vicar felt he could cope.

"I'm not a well man," said Munday.

"Sorry to hear that," said the vicar.

"And I'm astonished that someone like you . . ." Munday began, his eyes bulging.

"Alfred, the sugar," Emma said firmly. "Please."

Munday left the room.

"I think you gave him a turn," Emma said. "But I really must apologize for him."

"He's quite correct," said the vicar, "and I'm completely in the wrong. I don't blame him a bit. I should know better."

"He can sound awfully offensive—"

"No, no, he's absolutely right," said the vicar, insisting, and dismissing Emma's apology. "But you see I used to visit the previous tenants and I know that knocker on the kitchen door can't be heard from here. It's such a confusing house. So when I saw your living-room light on—"

Munday, looking calmer and not carrying the club, returned to the room with the sugar bowl, and setting the spoon toward the vicar, offered it. He said in a subdued voice, "You gave me a turn."

"Two for me, please. Thanks so much." The vicar

had smiled at Munday's remark, a repetition of his wife's. It was a habit of their marriage; they had reached that point of common agreement where language was shared and experience reported in identical words. Though they were unaware of it, they disputed their similarity using the same idioms, the speech—like a local dialect—that their marriage and their years in the bush had taught them.

"I was just telling Mrs. Munday that I used to visit the previous tenants, and I know that brass knocker on the kitchen door—"

He continued speaking. The information disturbed Munday: he wished he had not heard *previous tenants;* it gave the house the flavorless character of an inn, a shelter where occasional people, birds of passage, came and went, indistinguishable in the brevity of their stay. And the mystery of the house, the ghosts of other occupants, sensations hinted at by the old men at The Yew Tree that Munday had begun to savor, were diminished. Two opposing feelings occurred to him: a curiosity about the fate of the previous tenants, a dread that the vicar might tell him. But especially he disliked being associated with them or any other visitor (the choice of cider had marked him at the pub) and he was disappointed by all the vicar's news—it had the effect of withholding the house from him by making him and his wife temporary guests, and it insulted his arrival home.

Munday leaned against the bookshelves which covered the wall to the right of the chimney. On the facing wall there was a mirror and a color print of the Annigoni portrait of the Queen; he mocked it and remembered the Omukama's portrait that hung in the camp bungalow, the leathery face of the aged king with the blank eyes whom Alec, a tea-planter friend of Munday in Fort Portal, had described as looking like a crapulous gorilla. Munday had made no comment; the African District Commissioner had insisted he hang it, and later he had been invited to the Omukama's palace. ("Palace!" he had whispered to Emma;

it was new, unswept, looked like a supermarket, and it smelled of dogs and cooking bananas.)

Emma said, "But how marvelous!"

Munday tried to read the spines of the books. He saw Walter Scott, *Sketches by Boz,* Hammond Innes and Agatha Christie, a child's history of England, Readers Union in uniform bindings, some thick paperbacks with unfamiliar titles, probably American, Bibles in two sizes, church pamphlets, a school atlas, a row of Penguins, a woman's annual, a guide to wildflowers. He had seen identical libraries in a dozen East African hotels and rest houses. Their condition was identical, too; they were unused, and unused books rotted and stayed moribund in their uniquely vile dust. Beside the shelf there was a patch on the wall, sweating paint, and this rising damp had made a trickle of water on the stone floor.

"—galloped like this through the back pasture there," said the vicar. He put his tea cup down and imitated a horseman, his jowls shaking. His chirpy prattle and exaggerated friendliness was a result of being met by Munday and made uncomfortable by the challenge. Munday was behind him, not saying a word, but he saw how hard the vicar was trying.

The vicar went on to explain the rooms, the experiences of the other tenants with that inefficient knocker, and he finished, "It's a very old place, you know. This room we're in is Seventeenth Century, the back section and kitchen are Eighteenth, and the lavatory—well, that's modern of course!"

Emma laughed, Munday stared—he objected to being told about his house. If it had secrets he wanted them to be his, to discover them for himself. He slid a book out—*What Katy Did*—pushed it back and noticed how low the ceiling was. Small men had built the house, laborers dwarfed by vast clouds and lit by a pearly glow from the sea; he saw them working in the rain, gathering stones in heavy wheelbarrows to claim a corner of the landscape. Then they had gone back to their cottages and seen other people inhabit the house, perhaps people from far away. Munday was not of the village; and Emma, in spite of her sentiment, and the vicar—his accent said it—neither were they. But the vicar was proprietorial; he wouldn't admit what Munday had already reluctantly acknowledged: that they were all trespassers.

"Is it a big parish?" Emma asked.

"Quite," said the vicar. "Marshwood Vale on the west and the Beaminster road on the east. We go straight up to Broadwindsor. I have a church there as well. But don't be misled by the size—attendance is very poor. We're trying to raise money for a new church hall. Hopeless!" he said, and he laughed.

"Maybe God intends that as a sort of—"

"Alfred."

"I say," said the vicar. His eye strayed over the objects on the floor. He knelt and picked up a short knife, the size and shape of a grapefruit knife, with a rusty hammered blade. "That's an interesting little chap," he said. "What does one do with that?"

"Ceremonial knife," said Munday. "Used in puberty rites." His gaze caught the vicar's. He said with a half-smile, "Circumcisions."

The vicar squinted at it, holding it gingerly with his fingertips. He shook his head slowly.

Munday said, "That particular one's seen a lot of service."

"Absolutely fascinating," said the vicar. He stooped and put the small knife on the floor near others that resembled it. He grinned at Emma. The vicar had a threadbare and slightly seedy aspect which made him seem somehow kindly; the seams of his black suit were worn shiny, his trouser cuffs were spattered with mud and his heavy shoes had been polished so often and were so old they were cracked, and scales of leather bristled where they flexed.

"It was a gift from a village headman," said Munday. The vicar nodded at the little knife.

"Alfred gave him a packet of razor blades in return."

"Yes, I gave him my razor blades," said Munday.

"Do Africans shave?" asked the vicar. "I don't think of them as having five-o'clock shadow."

"For circumcisions," said Munday, wondering if the vicar's innocence was a tactful way of allowing his host a chance to say that absurd thing. "He asked for them."

"Of course," said the vicar.

"A pity, really. Soon they'll stop making those knives altogether. They'll lose the skill. Notice how that blade fits into the handle—and those markings. They're not random decorations. Each one has a particular social significance."

"That's progress, isn't it?" said the vicar. "Using your Gillette blades for circumcisions, drinking beer out of old soup tins and whatnot. I suppose they're frightfully keen on evening classes as well?"

Munday thought the vicar might be mocking him. He picked up another object, a fragment of polished wood. A fang of glass—it could have been a spiky shard from a broken bottle—protruded from one end, and this was circled by a fringe of coarse monkey hair.

"And this," said Munday, "this is what the Sebei people use on girls."

He offered it to the vicar, but the vicar put his hands behind his back and peered at the object in a pitying way.

"Girls?" he said, and he winced. "I had no idea—"

"They gash the clitoris," said Munday.

"Goodness."

"Hurts like the devil," said Munday, "but it keeps them out of trouble. Blunts the nerve, you see. Sex isn't much fun after that."

"Alfred, your tea's going cold."

Munday took his cup from the bookshelf and drank with his lips shaped in a little smile; the smile altered, becoming triumphant when he swallowed.

"Last year my wife and I went to Italy," said the vicar. "Such an interesting place. And you get used to the food after a bit. They're not fond of the English, you know—like your Africans, I expect."

"My Africans—"

"The stories are so horrible," said the vicar. "The killings, the tribal wars. It's always in the papers, isn't it. That casual business of taking scalps. I have a friend —we were at Oxford together—he went out there, Ghana, I believe. The stories! Evidently, one of their presidents—this was a few years ago—called himself 'the Redeemer.' Now, I ask you!"

"Kwame Nkrumah," Munday said. "But it doesn't have quite the same meaning in the vernacular."

"Yes," said the vicar. "My friend runs a mission in what sounds the most unbelievable place. He's a delightful man, takes it all in his stride, absolutely devoted to the people. And he's marvelous about mucking in and seeing things get done. Once a year we take up a collection, send him bundles of old clothes, tattered books, and bushels of used postage stamps. I can't imagine what he does with those stamps! I suppose they like the bright colors."

Munday had put his tea down. He said, "My Africans didn't take any scalps."

"Not *white* scalps," said Emma to the vicar.

"Not any," said Munday.

"The vicar—"

"Call me Bob, please."

"Very well, then. Bob was speaking figuratively, I'm sure." She said, "They can be very nasty. They're nasty to Indians and nasty to each other. Alfred says he likes them but sometimes I think he doesn't like them any more than I do, and I don't like them at all. They're cruel and silly and they're so ugly their faces scare you."

"They speak figuratively, too," said Munday. "And there were times when I wouldn't have blamed them a bit for taking the odd missionary scalp."

"He doesn't really mean that," said Emma.

"I'm sure your friend in Ghana is an angel," said Munday. "But missionaries can be so arrogant. So damned righteous and discouraging. I've always felt there's something fundamentally subversive about a mission—the vicarage, the church, vespers, the Land Rover, and those beautiful English children playing croquet on their patch of lawn while the village kids gape at them through the fence."

"That used to happen to my children," said the vicar, "when I had a parish in Gillingham!"

"I should have warned you, vicar," said Emma. "Alfred's an anthropologist."

"So I gathered."

"One never hears a good word about missionaries from them. Alfred won't tell you this but our nearest hospital was run by Catholic priests—White Fathers. That's where our friend here used to go when he was poorly."

"That doctor was about as pious as I am," said Munday. "An Irishman. Dowle. Drank like a fish. Father Tom, they called him. He was a cunning devil, and he had the usual prejudices—a regular old quack. But he was first-class at curing dysentery. 'Bug in your bowel, eh?' he'd say. 'Take some of the muck, then.' And he'd hand me a bottle of gray liquid. Did the trick practically overnight." Munday smiled. "We used to call it Father Tom's Cement."

"Sounds jolly useful."

Munday said, "Dowle sent me home. Said I had a dicky heart."

"Don't start," said Emma.

"I imagine you boiled your water?" said the vicar.

"We boiled our water," said Munday.

"And we had one of these filters," said Emma, outlining the shape of the container with her hands.

The vicar straightened up and jerked his lapels. "I'm going to let you good people have your dinner."

Emma rose from the chair. "Don't rush off," she said. "We've just had tea."

"I'll come again. I'd love to hear all your stories," said the vicar. He turned to Munday and said, "I can't wait for your book."

"Book?"

"The one you mentioned in your letter to *The Times*."

"Oh, that," said Munday.

"I was intrigued by your letter," said the vicar. "Really, it held me."

"Just dashed it off," said Munday. "Wanted to set the record straight. Glad you liked it."

"Yes, I did," said the vicar. "Actually, Mr. Awdry put me on to it. And that's why I sneaked in here tonight. Once a month we have a sort of educational do at the church, a film-show or a talk, refreshments beforehand. It's partly to get people together in some kind of fellowship. We have so many new people in the village, like yourselves. We charge a small admission—that goes toward the new hall and the fuel bill. Last month we had a lecture on Hardy."

"How appropriate!" said Emma.

"Chap came over from Drimpton. He'd actually met Hardy—acted in the stage version of *Tess*, though I'd no idea there was such a play. It was fascinating."

"It *sounds* fascinating," said Emma.

"And you want me to do one of these talks?"

"I was hoping you'd be December. I'd be very pleased if you would. Perhaps talk about some of your experiences. Your travels."

"I never saw it as travel," said Munday. "For me it was residence. Travel bores me—it constipates me. All those bad meals. Surly staff. Strange beds."

"Your residence then," said the vicar. "That would be perfect. Have you any slides or pictures? They'd be most appreciated."

"Very little of it's unpacked, I'm afraid. You understand we've just moved in."

"Absolutely," said the vicar. "We won't make any firm dates. But if you agree in principle I can announce it in the church bulletin."

"Go ahead," said Emma, urging Munday to agree.

"All right," said Munday. It was not what he had planned, the learned society, the paper read to scholars at the Institute of African Studies. It ridiculed that image of himself journeying to London or Oxford to deliver a lecture.

"Thanks very much," said the vicar. "And now I will let you good people have your dinner!"

"I'll see you to your car," said Munday.

"Don't bother," said the vicar. "I know my way out. I've been here dozens of times."

When the vicar's car drove past the window, Munday said, "Dozens of times. That reminds me—"

"You embarrassed me," said Emma. "You were horrid to him. That poor man—he was so uncomfortable."

"It's like a sickroom in a hospital. Hundreds of people have been in it. The vicar knows it well, that room, all the others who've died in your bed. He knows something you don't."

"You've been so morbid lately."

"I have reason to be," said Munday. "Emma, my heart."

"But you go on about it."

"So would you."

"No," she said. "I'd try not to think about it."

"People come here to die," said Munday. "New people in the village. Did you hear him? He means retired people—'like yourselves.' "

"I'll start the dinner."

"Emma—" There was something more Munday wanted to say; he had the will and he opened his mouth, but the words eluded him, the thought had been wiped from his mind. He struggled dumbly with what he recognized as stupidity; his mind wouldn't move. He said, "Nothing. I'll see to this unpacking."

Just before they sat down to eat, Emma said, "Do take that carton of rubbish outside."

"It can wait," said Munday.

"No," said Emma. "I want you to do it now." She opened the door for him, and a damp draft rolled into the kitchen.

"I'd rather not go outside just now."

"For my sake," Emma said in a tremulous voice.

"You're not going to cry," said Munday.

"Alfred, *please*."

"As you wish," he said.

The rain had stopped. He put the carton in the shed and shut the door, and he had just started back to the house when he heard an owl call him. It was a low distinct hoot, in bursts, like a bewildered child mispronouncing a curse in the dark. He went to it, it drew him through the yard. He couldn't see the owl; it stopped; it began again, the clear notes reaching Munday and making him feel as if the hidden bird was speaking directly to his fear.

Munday walked into the road; the hoots ceased. He imagined the plump thing roosting above him in the row of oaks he had seen that morning. He could see their outer branches and the lower part of the trunks illuminated by the light from the windows of the house. A few steps down the road and he was in darkness; he smelled the wet trees and now in the black he heard them dripping—that dripping, it was fast, from many branches, a crackling patter on the dead leaves and on the road, a kind of sprinkling which went on and on, the rapidity insisting he remember. He was afraid; his fear was new, and the fear made his thoughts formal. He thought: There is no jungle as strange as this. He thought: When have I ever been in jungle? He admitted he never had, there was none. He had driven through rain-forest and he had camped in low bush with guides and porters; he had marveled at the pathless forest that stretched behind the Yellow Fever Camp. In the daytime, sun flashed on its wetness; at night it was loud with the scrapings of locusts, but not one low owl and all those quickly dripping trees. There, he had been prepared to endure remoteness, but here he was surprised seeing no human trace, no sign of habitation except lights so distant and small they were like an answer to the mist-shrouded sky with its meager scattering of stars. There was no moon

or wind, only that pattering on the pillows of leaves
and a rich vegetable smell.

He looked back and saw the windows of the cottage,
shining yellow, lighting their own peeling sills and
rhomboids on the road and patches of hedge. He
smelled the acrid coal-smoke but couldn't make out the
chimneys. Apart from the owl squeezing out those
clear hooting notes, and the falling drops from the
tree branches, everything was still—a stillness he was
unused to. He had forgotten that; had it always been
like that? He heard his feet and his sigh, and anxiety
gripped him by the throat. He was aware of having
looked for someone and found no one, only the hiding
dark and the sea-mist at the windows and the stillness,
all suggesting their opposites: the bright clamor of a
surprise, like a phantom huntsman waiting on a horse
in the hills that lay in that blackness, who chose not to
show himself. He had come back for that.

He tried to tell Emma his fear. As he spoke he
felt it all retreating on his tongue.

"Oh, I once heard an owl," she said. She was tasting the soup. "I once heard an owl in London."

6

THERE WAS no relief the next day. They woke to the
muffled pinking of the electric heater, to a motorbike
passing under the window like a dying bee slowly losing
its buzz, and they were in darkness so complete the
bedknobs at their feet were impossible to see. Emma
was up first, as always; she cooked breakfast, which
they ate together, but it was still so dark at the windows they ate hurriedly, as if it were an extra unde-

served meal. Dawn came soundlessly, more quickly than they expected and without warning, suddenly silvering the windows, clarifying and giving shadows to the layered twists in the mass of low clouds and showing the wet road and the shining slates of the shed. Some of the trees were full of trembling leaves, a copper beech near the shed, the laurel at the edge of the courtyard, the holly tree out back. The rest were bare, or nearly so, and leafless their branches seemed especially crooked; but their high trunks were thick with bushy bandages of ivy. Emma saw them and said, "They look as if they're wearing green jerseys."

Far off, mist dimmed the landscape and made the woods in the depressions of the rolling hills into level rows, flat cutouts of trees, one behind the other, lighter and lighter, and at the greatest distance, white on the white horizon. Munday went from window to window, cursing the shadowy rooms and low ceilings; he stoked the fires and chewed the unfamiliar air and he muttered for sun. But it continued overcast, they ate their lunch of beef stew and bread in a flecked twilight that strained their eyes. In this poor light all their clocks seemed wrong—"What's the right time?" Munday asked continually, sighing at Emma's replies— and the lamps of the house burned orange throughout the day.

Unpacking the crates became a strenuous routine, but they welcomed the activity for the fatigue it gave them, and were calm with their regulated days. They noticed how the African artifacts lent their odor to the study, a dusty pungency of tropical grass and leaves, a slight spice of wood, and even a hint of the bitter smell of Africans—the sweat they had left on their tools. It consoled Munday and then it saddened him. He said little to Emma. She was always cooking or sweeping or leaning at the sink. "Playing house again?" he said; she didn't reply. He had never seen her so occupied. The African kitchen had always been the province of the cook. Munday had felt uncomfortable in it; the order of things was the cook's, who stood and worked in his torn laceless sneakers. Emma had left the cook alone. But here, Munday saw, their meals were like a ritual of settlement, a tribal ceremony involving food and certain actions which helped them to possess more and more of the house. Using the kitchen, which was the warmest room, made it their own; and the living room where they read and unpacked was theirs. But the extra bedrooms, the passages, the box room, the chilly stairs—so much of the house did not belong to them.

Then there were no more cases to unpack and their days were empty; Munday was restless and Emma worked with her dishmop and broom. They tried new routines, fumbling like people newly idle, to justify the passing of days. One afternoon, on an impulse, Munday bought a second-hand Mini; it was fire-engine red, and when Munday drove it back to the house to show Emma he said, "I've always wanted a car that color." That night they drove to Lyme Regis, but on the way back Emma said, "You can wash it on Sunday mornings," and Munday lost his temper. For several days they did not use the car. They stayed in, taking longer and longer to prepare the food; they ate it swiftly, in silence, and did the dishes meticulously, putting every plate and fork away. Munday made coffee after lunch and dinner, grinding the beans he bought from Pines, warming the milk, setting out the Demerara sugar. When the weather improved they went for walks, to force exhaustion on themselves and work up an appetite. They went to bed early and always got up in the dark and made breakfast in front of the black windows. But still the house was not theirs and they were like people on vacation, or visitors, or—but only Munday felt this—retired people trying to be busy in a secluded corner of the country. They spoke distractedly, their voices sounding older and fussier, reporting their thoughts and not expecting replies.

"We eat too much," Emma said. And: "I must see about getting some new curtains."

Munday said, "I can't work in this light."

Emma said, "There goes our friend," speaking of a man in gaiters and a tweed cap who always passed the window at noon, walking his dog.

They both said, "Why am I so tired?"

Munday said, "I should do something about that talk at the church."

Emma said, "We must have the vicar back."

They discussed the vicar, and with the perspective of a week, that evening visit which at the time had seemed such an intrusion took on the character of an important event. Believing it might be typical, they prepared themselves for something similar to occur, but nothing did, no one dropped in, and so the vicar's call came to be special, a way of measuring time, four days since the visit, then five and six, like a historical date in a nonliterate culture. They began conversations, "He said—," and didn't need to name him. Munday spoke in a low voice. He believed they had a listener, that third presence whose traces were everywhere but impossible to name. He looked for it and he turned on lights in dark rooms (reaching around the doorway into the darkness for the light switch) expecting to see it seated, perhaps leaning in an accusatory posture, to scare him and make him sorry. He bit his lips with that expectation, and when he was alone he made faces.

"I think I'll do a little work," he said. He didn't say write. He didn't write. He sat in his study, turning over the artifacts and sketching them and feeling a great pressure on the front of his head.

One day, just at sundown, he went for a walk alone. On the way back he stopped in at The Yew Tree and bought the bottle of amontillado. He spent more than he planned because he refused the cheaper South African variety Mr. Flack recommended. The refusal, the mention of South Africa, gave Mr. Flack an opportunity to add more detail to his Capetown story, how he had stayed drunk on brandy for a week and how he had seen (he explained this closely to

Munday) a black woman, "black as Newgy's knocker," with a load of wood on her head walking along a road suckling her child, "as if it was the most natural thing in the world."

While Mr. Flack told the story Munday nodded and watched Mrs. Flack kneeling at the fireplace with a coal hod and crumpled newspapers and bits of wood. Her hands were sooty, her back small and bent; she wore one of her husband's jackets, a long apron, and high rubber boots, and she knelt in a way that allowed her to sit on her heels.

Munday offered to help her—it was one way of silencing Flack—but she said, "No, you'll just get as filthy as me. Look." She showed her black hands and made a horrible comic face, squashing her lips together until her toothless gums met. She said, "There's no proper draft. We're in a perpetual whirlwind."

Hosmer, who was drinking by the window, put his glass down and without a word took the center page from the *Daily Telegraph* on the bar and spread it and held it against the fireplace, blocking the opening. Inside a minute the fire flared at the bottom and soon lighted the back of the newsprint. Munday could see the fire growing through the paper. Then Hosmer took the paper away and folded it and creased it.

"I was going to do that," said Mrs. Flack.

"Was 'ee?" said Hosmer. He laughed and took his seat.

They talked about fires, and Munday found himself adding to the conversation. As soon as he began speaking the others fell silent and became attentive. He said how he had gone into the cold damp house and started his own fires to drive out the chill, and how he had gone outside later to see the smoke curling from the chimneys.

He believed he had awed them, but Hosmer turned to Mr. Flack and, as if continuing a story Munday's arrival had interrupted, said, "She were down by the river with her dogs, lying there on the grass, her legs open like this. That's what Sam said. He walked by and looked up her dress and the dogs barked at him."

"Disgusting," said Mr. Flack.

The doorbell jangled. A man entered, about Munday's own age, dressed in a heavy jacket and corduroy trousers and thick-soled shoes.

"The usual?" said Mr. Flack.

Munday, gathering up his sherry and his change from the bar, said hello.

"What will you have?" the man said to Munday.

Munday was confused. He hesitated, then said, "A half of bitter."

"Have a whisky," said the man. "Give him a whisky, Bill."

"A beer's fine," said Munday, and when he had it in his hand he said, "Cheers."

The man said, "To your very good health," and drank. Then he said, "You all moved in?"

"Just about," said Munday.

"I had a moving job last month," said the man. "Over Shaftesbury way."

"I take it you're in the transport business," said Munday.

"I drive," said the man. He mentioned the name of his employer and said, "He's a good guv'nor."

"When he ain't got a drink in him," said Hosmer. "A tickle of whisky and he's drunk as a hand-cart."

Mr. Flack said, "Guess who Sam saw by the river exposing herself."

But the man was looking at Munday. He said, "You like it here?"

"Very much," said Munday.

"We'll have you and your missus over some time," said the man.

How dare you, Munday thought. He said, "Oh, will you?"

He was furious at the presumption in the driver's vagueness; it was not an invitation, but a pronouncement of a possibility, with the assurance that Munday would come with Emma when the driver bade them.

The driver would never have said that to his employer. He thought: Supper at the driver's cottage, a talk at the church hall; but he hid his anger and said, "Actually, we're pretty busy at the moment seeing old friends." The bottle was under his arm. "And we'll be spending quite a bit of time in London."

There was worse, but not from the driver. Munday had said good night and was at the door. There was a trampling of feet and a young man threw the door open. Munday faced him; he had long hair, red cheeks, and a bushy beard and wore a woolen checkered shirt. The hair and beard gave him the appearance of a Biblical figure. He smiled at Munday and said, "Evening, maister," and looked past him and greeted the others.

"Excuse me," said Munday and moved sideways. But the young man blocked the door.

"You be Doctor Munday?" he asked politely.

"That's right. And I'm on my way home."

"Out in the tractor today," the young man said, still blocking the door, and raising his voice, "and wasn't she making a howling! Pugger, I says, and throws up them flaps on her bonnet. Got my arm inside her and the wind picked up and blowed the bloody flaps down. Here, look."

He rolled up his right sleeve with care and showed Munday a long cut, opened and roughened on his forearm, a rip with the appearance and texture of the burst part of a cooked sausage. It was uncovered and raw and edged with black pepper-flakes of dried blood, and part of it was smeared with bubbly yellow ointment.

He offered the wound to Munday and said, "What have you got for him, Doctor?" Then he cried, "Don't he hurt!"

"I can't help you," said Munday.

"Now hold on there—"

"I'm not that kind of doctor."

"I thought there were only one kind," said the

young man, smiling as Munday pulled at the door-handle.

Munday was nearly out the door; a thought came to him, and he said stiffly to the young man who had started toward the fire and whose back was to him, "No, as a matter of fact, there are as many varieties of doctor as there are varieties of farm laborer—perhaps more. Good night."

He walked angrily away from The Yew Tree, past the pillar box at the cross roads and the lighted telephone booth. The lights in the pub window illuminated the road, but the road curved off to the right and when Munday turned and lost the lights he stumbled, peering into the darkness for the house lights and trying to stay in the center of the road. The perfect darkness clasped his body and slowed him. What he feared most was meeting someone who would startle him, maybe injure him, by slamming against him in the dark. He felt there was someone walking near him, just in front of him, in the dark, and as always the pinching was in his heart, hurting his blood. A car appeared—the mild glow and engine noise, then the blinding lights and the terrifying rush of wind and metal sweeping past him, forcing him to lean against the bank. The car left him dazed in an even more confusing darkness. He plodded on, taking elderly steps, and then he saw the lighted windows of the house and wes guided by them. But he knew he would remember that stretch where the road curved, the lights of The Yew Tree lost at one end, the house lights lost at the other, the elbow in the road, marked by oaks, completely dark. He knew he would always hesitate before walking down it at night, and the experience came to represent so much of his arrival home, the rediscovery of old fears, aimlessness he hadn't bargained for, and a feeling of age and loss he mocked in a way that seemed to make his mockery an expression of greater fear.

"I hate this place," he said, stepping into the kitchen. There was no reply. He called, "Emma?"

"In here." Her voice was weak, but Munday was

reassured by it. She was in the living room, stretched out on a chair, her hand over her eyes. She said, "I don't know what came over me. I had to sit down."

"Have a glass of sherry," said Munday. He peeled the plastic from the bottle top. "I'm going to have one myself and then ring the vicar about that talk."

"Didn't you say Silvano was coming down one weekend from London?"

"Yes," said Munday. "One weekend."

"Give your talk then. You could exhibit him—they might never have seen a real African before."

"I'm not in the mood for that."

"Bad joke, I suppose," said Emma. "I'm feeling awful, I must say."

"But I'll show him around, you bet I will. And the first place I take him will be The Yew Tree. I want to see what these local people have to say for themselves when Silvano walks in. You know how very English he is."

"They'll laugh at him," said Emma. "They'll laugh at you, too. That myth about these African students being frightfully English, with their silly faces and their five-syllable names—as if Englishness were simply a case of smoking a pipe and wearing a suit and subscribing to the *New Statesman* and saying 'bloody.' And taking taxis—they all take taxis. Who pays for it all? English people, of course, to flatter themselves that they're being imitated. I remember Silvano, with that book he used to carry around the village. How he used to struggle so to pronounce the simple English word 'situation.' How did he say it? 'Stoowation,' something like that."

"You're ranting," said Munday. "You always rant when you're under the weather."

"They'll gape at him," said Emma. "Not that I blame them, but they'll make unpleasant remarks."

"You don't want him to come?"

"I'd like to save him the embarrassment. They'll be cruel."

"Let them try," said Munday. He handed Emma

her glass of sherry. "They tried that with me this evening. Bloody cheek." He told Emma about the driver, repeating the man's sentence, "We'll have you and the missus over some time," and it sounded acutely offensive to him now. Then he told her about the farm boy with the injured arm.

"Oh, dear," said Emma.

"Trying to take the piss out of me. They didn't reckon I'd stand up to them," said Munday, and coldly he spoke the reply he felt had withered them all. He said, "I don't give a damn."

But he was angry, remembering; and the little scene in the pub, like the vicars' visit, forty minutes in the ten days they had been there, grew out of proportion and would be turned from an incident into an event, something (he knew this as he described it to Emma with exaggerations and additions) they would never stop discussing. And he wondered if what remained of his life would be these few public moments endlessly rehearsed in private.

"You'd better ring the vicar," said Emma.

"I will when I finish this." Munday was topping up his sherry.

Emma held her glass to her throat. She sat forward and stared at the fire, and the flames lighted her face, the brightness adding years to her age and giving the long wisps of hair which had fallen loose around her ears and neck an unruly look. Munday was alarmed by the intensity of concentration on her flickering face, the deranged hair, and her unusual jumping shadow on the wall behind her. She stayed like this, studying the fire for several minutes, not drinking from the slender glass, not moving, and it took this long for Munday to realize that it was the fire, flaring and changing so, that changed her expression.

To break the silence he said, "I'd better ring the vicar."

She said, "Alfred, I—" She was speaking to the fire. "—I've had an awful fright."

"If it's half as bad as that business in the pub, those impertinent—"

"No," she said. She held herself motionless and spoke in a deadened voice. Still her shadow leaped. "Don't say anything now. But when I finish I want you to tell me it's nothing—my imagination. Please tell me I didn't see it."

"Emma, what are you talking about?"

"I'll tell you, but first I want you to promise me that it's nothing at all."

"Good God—"

"Alfred." Her voice was urgent, and now she turned, putting half her face in shadow; the other half, waxen with terror, still flickered.

"I promise."

"When you went for the walk I thought I'd better take in the washing while it was still light. You know how windy it is, and the sheets were flapping and making that cracking sound. I had an armful of them and the trees were blowing too. I've never heard such noises in England, I never realized—"

"You've never lived in the country before."

"Don't," said Emma. "It wasn't only the wind. I heard someone calling—someone lost. It sounds silly, I know, but I thought it was, well, a woman in a tree. And the sheets were flying up—I couldn't catch them. I dropped some clothespegs. It seems such a small thing, dropping clothespegs, but it worried me horribly because I could see how frightened I was and the things I was doing. I was hurrying, and I knew why: someone was watching me—that voice. It seemed awfully dark where I was, but everywhere else was light, not daylight, but that sort of silver twilight you get here. I heard the back door slam and I thought, Oh God, I'm locked out. I panicked and started to run across the garden and I suppose I was looking for a window to break. That's when I saw her."

"Who, Emma? Where?"

"It was a woman." Emma's voice became very small, and without force the whisper seemed to stay in her mouth. "She was standing in our bedroom, at that upper window. In a blue and gray dress, peering out with such a white face. She wasn't looking at me—she was looking at the wind and the fields, down where you had gone for your walk."

Munday's legs went cold and the backs of his arms prickled. He said, "What woman?"

"I can't go in, I thought. I hadn't picked up all the washing—half of it was still on the line, behind me, making that flapping, like sails lifting and filling with wind. I felt she had caught me there in that wind, and I kept thinking, *It's her house.* I don't know how long it took because the sheets were all twisted and flying at the window. But when I untwisted them I looked up and she was gone. Now tell me."

"Did you recognize her?"

"Alfred!" It was a shriek. Munday recrossed his legs.

"It was nothing—the sheets reflected on the window, your nerves, suggestions—who can say?"

"You don't believe that, do you? You think I really saw something."

"How could you?"

"You're saying it's nothing because I told you to."

"No," said Munday, "that's not it."

Emma was quiet for a moment. Then she said, "You're right. But I wish it *had* been a ghost."

"Don't be silly."

"I do, because if it really was a ghost then I couldn't be blamed for seeing it. Now I feel foolish and crazy. It was nothing—it was me. You know that, don't you?"

"Yes," said Munday. But he was not convinced. He had more questions, but he knew he could not ask them without frightening Emma. And worse, now he could not confide his own fears, those suspicions that had crept upon him in the house and out in the road; those fears that he had hoped to be able to tell her so she could take his hand and smile and hold his head and say, "It's nothing."

It gave him a bad dream, of a tall house on a black landscape where the wind had flattened the meadows and the gates in the hedgerows were broken. He was walking towards the house, slowly in the yielding grass, his feet sinking with each step; and up close he saw it was a stone house, like his own, with a black slate roof, but (and this woke him) it had no doors or windows.

7

IT CAME to him, what she had said on their first day at The Yew Tree; he forgot what preceded it or prompted it, but her words "You know nothing" had swiped at him. And he remembered how he had changed the subject, heading her off with, "What do you mean by saying I'm ridiculous?"

He was not defeated then, he knew how she exaggerated, and he did the same—the precise managing of exaggeration, on which was pinned a timid sincerity, was a convention of their marriage. They didn't say what they meant, but this manner suggested all that was unsaid. It was an English trait which Africa had intensified almost to the point of parody. They had met by chance, and almost resenting the love they called a deep sympathy so as not to feel foolish, they had married late—Munday was forty, Emma two years older (she had money: it had made her shy, nearly kept her single)—so Africa, which Munday studied and Emma endured, was their honeymoon. Their African isolation had thrown them together, like new cellmates who, once solitaries, learn in a confinement where they are robbed of privacy to protect themselves from greater violation. They had come to each other with a single similarity, a perverse kind of courage each saw in the other but not in himself. That, and an irrational thing—though at the time it seemed like conclusive proof of a common vision—their discovery one evening in idle talk of a fascination they shared for that polished Aztec skull of rock crystal in the Ethnography Section of the British Museum. "There's only one thing in the world I care about," Emma had said. Munday had almost scoffed, but when she disclosed it he was won over and from that moment he loved her. They had seen it as schoolchildren and returned to it as adults. It hadn't been moved; it was still in the center of the aisle, in the high glass case, mounted on blue velvet. It was like an image of their common faith, the carved block of crystal in the dustiest room of the museum, the cold beauty of the blue shafts, sparkling behind the square teeth in the density of that death's head. Emma said that she had whispered to it—Munday didn't ask what—and that it was so perfect it made her want to cry. Munday said it was the highest art of an advanced people and he told Emma its cultural origins; but he venerated it no less than she.

Later, married and in Africa, they discovered how opposed they were, but this opposition, their differences with their determined sympathy, gave a soundness to their marriage. Munday had a vulgar streak that Emma's primness sustained and even encouraged. Munday blustered and was rash; in a professional argument with a younger colleague he would tab his finger intimidatingly at the man and say, "I won't wear it." Anyone interested in his work he saw as a poacher. His colleagues said he was impossible and shortly he had no colleagues. He had a reputation for arrogance, and very early in his career he had learned an elderly trick of blustering, pressing his lips together and blowing out his cheeks and prefacing an outrageous remark with something offensive, "Damn it, are you too stupid to see—" Marriage only made his anger blind: he had Emma, and if he went too far he did so because he knew how his wife could draw him back. He might rage, but it was her sensibility that he trusted, not his own. He protested loudly but secretly he believed in her strength, and that belief in her timely sarcasm gave him strength. He relied on her in all ways, to pay for his research when his grant was exhausted, to support his temper and defend his opinions. His science he knew was opinion, full of guesses that made him sound crankish, and she mocked him for it. But just as often and with more sincerity she reassured him. She allowed him to make all the decisions and complained so haplessly her complaints amounted to very little. But this was insignificant to what bound them, for though in conversation he exaggerated his strength and she her weakness, he knew—and the knowledge gnawed at his confidence—how he leaned on her. So many times in those past days he had tried to reveal his fear to her! Emma, gentle, knew at what moment his pride would allow him to be reassured by her. But they had said nothing and now it was too late. She had seen what he loathed and dreaded, she had named his fear, and in that naming, locating the woman at the window, she had dismissed all her strength. Her picture of the fear was his, she had described his mind. Munday was stripped of his defenses; he was alone; there was no one to turn to.

Without knowing it she had defeated him by confirming his fear, and for the first time she was relying on the strength of his doubt, on his assurance that they were quite safe. Munday had repeated what she asked him to, but he had no answer to console her. He had no answer to console himself. He was staggered by the weight of his own and his wife's fears. He worried about himself; poor health was his egotism: he saw himself collapsing, falling forward dead in the darkest room of the black house. That star of pain which had twinkled on and off now burned ceaselessly like a hot knuckle of decay in the pulp of his heart. His sleep was a kind of stumbling at night, going down in a restless doze and then scrambling to consciousness. Usually he lay awake, rigid in his bed, listening to the slow clock and the ping of the electric fire, his eyes wide open, wanting to wake his wife and talk to her. He envied her slumbering there, her body purring with snores, but he could not divulge his worry and he knew that to tell her his fears would be to have her awake beside him, fretting through the night.

One night, early in December, he slid out of bed to go downstairs for some aspirin. He made no sound. At the bedroom door he heard:

"Where are you going?" Her voice was sharp; its alert panic implored him. It was not the monotone of a person just awakened—it had the resigned clarity of his own when he said he'd be right back. He said nothing more; he imagined that their exchange had been overheard, and when he returned to the bed and Emma embraced him, pulling her nightgown to her waist and fingering his inner thigh, he drew away, whispered "No," and immediately looked around half-expecting to see a witness, staring in a blue and gray dress.

In the daytime he was tense with fatigue, and though he did not sleep much in his bed he dozed in his chair, nodded over his food, and sometimes out walking he felt he could not go one step further: he wanted to drop to his knees and fall down in the sunlight on a grassy knoll and sleep and sleep. His mind spun, stampeding his thoughts, and his arms and eyes were heavy and wouldn't work. So the preparation of his lecture took as long as if he was doing a paper for a learned society. He hated every moment of it, making notes, putting his colored slides and tapes in order and labeling the tools and weapons he planned to pass around to the audience.

After lunch, on the day he was due to give his lecture at the church hall, Emma said, "Let's get some fresh air."

It was cold and windy and very bright, typical of the weather in its new phase. There were slivers of ice in the stone birdbath that lay in the shadow of the house. They climbed the bank in the back garden and stood in the humming gorse and broom at the edge of the high meadow. Beneath them was the vast green Vale of Marshwood, sunlit and so deep they could take in most of it at a glance, the several village clusters—each marked by smoking chimneys and a square church steeple topped by a glinting gold weathercock—the dark measured hedgerows, the nibbling sheep like rugs of spring snow on the hillsides, the scattered herds of cows, and here and there small wooded areas, islands anchored in the rolling seas of the meadows. Wide gloomy patches of cloud shadow, the shape and speed of devil-fish, glided across the floor of the valley, rippling over trees, swept up the slope, and passed over the Mundays, blocking the sun and putting a chill on them. They continued to look, not humbled by the size, but triumphant; at their vantage point on its very edge, where it began to roll down, they had an easy mastery of it, like people before a contour map on a table. Each house and barn and church was toy-sized and the whole was marred only by the file of tall gray pylons and their spans of underslung wires across the southern end of the valley. At the sea was a ridge of hills, gold and green downs which opened where the low late-autumn sun dazzled on the water. That was as far as they could see. Closer, just under them, blue smoke swirled over a terrace of thatched cottages; a dog barked, three yaps, and there was a tractor whine, a laborious noise drifting up from where the vehicle was turning, at the border of a brown oval of earth in a large field. Miles away there was a short flash, the sun catching a shiny object; they saw the flash but not the man who held it. Around them were their trees, beech and oak, the ones that moaned at night and sang in the day; their limbs were bare, the leaves that had not been knocked off by the rain had been torn off by the gusts of wind. There was no mistaking them for African trees, which were only bare in swampland; these were stripped, and as tall and dark as a row of black-armed gallows.

This landscape had been subdued by the season and by men; it was settled and ordered, there were signs

of farming to the horizon, and even those far islands
of trees with the graceful shapes seemed deliberately
planned. But it was frozen, the hedgerows broke the
fields, and the green looked infertile, threatening to die
and discolor for the winter. The mystery of the landscape was this apparent order, for which Munday, who
saw signs of habitation but no people apart from the
tractor driver—and he was tiny—could not discern a
purpose. This emptiness seemed unlikely, and it was
unexpected; not an England he had ever known, so
green and new to his eye, it was a rural scene he
had always suspected was spoken about because it
did not exist, a willfully inaccurate nostalgia duplicat-
ing the Bwamba's inability to describe their own
swampy homeland because they did not see it. He
wanted to deny it. But there it was before him, like
an illustration in a child's book of ambiguously menacing rhymes. Emma said, "I told you. It's lovely. I knew
it would be like this—you see?" The colors were right,
the air pure, and the enclosing valley so shaped at
their feet it invited them to wander down to explore
it.

They descended the slope to a hedge fence of
brambles and immediately lost the view. The high
hedge hid coils of rusting barbed wire in long thorny
whips of untrimmed raspberry bushes with some
withered berries still blackening on them. They had
a new view, the rise of Lewesdon Hill, a thickly
wooded portion with its spine sliced by a field, and
beyond it the green fortress of Pilsdon Pen. Munday
helped Emma over a gate that was held fast with
hoops of knotted wire, and they made their way down
the uneven field of tough grass clumps and dried
crinkled cow turds to a muddy section by a stone
watering trough in the corner. The bark had been
chewed from some saplings there. In the mud were
large hoof-prints of cows and small precise ones of
heifers, like two parallel texts of a translated poem.
The cows were grazing in the next field; they raised

their heads and, champing slowly, observed the man and wife.

"God, how healthy they look—what fat beasts! Do you remember—?"

Emma was reminding him of the skinny humped African cattle, switching their crooked tails at the flies on their sores and nosing at the dusty grass. But Munday had looked back at the brow of the hill they had just descended and seen the upper part of the house, and understood the name, the Black House. Stuck in that greenery, surrounded by bare trees and one high holly bush and a dense yew, it seemed a place blighted by age, stained dark like the nightmare house with no windows or doors he had seen in his dream at this exact angle—his dream spectacle of conventional grief had been the creepiest of foreshadowings, and he was glad the house was not his: he could discard it and leave, simply go away. He turned from it, glad to be free of all those rooms, which were colder than the thicket at the edge of the field they were now passing through. The walking tired him, and when he replied to Emma about the cows his throat was dry, his voice strained. He gasped, his breathlessness causing in him a confusing annoyance. He saw thorns and dead berries and what had seemed so green was soiled tussocky grass in a pasture disordered by muddy tracks. He smashed at the hedge with his walking stick.

They were in a field, entirely boxed in by deep, closely woven hedges, with no gate except the one they had entered by. They had to walk back, retracing their steps through the mud, past the cows gaping in the upper pasture, untill they came to tire tracks which led through another gate to a narrow lane. Munday stamped the mud from his boots. Emma said, "Look."

Two boys were coming towards them in the road, laboring up the hill from the direction of the valley. They were in a bend in the road the sun never reached: banks topped with grassy cliffs and scored with rain gullies rose up on either side, and pools of

tracked-over mud had collected where the gullies
met the road. In that damp shadow the boys were two
forlorn figures, stooping with their loads and scuffing
the mud as they went along. Their hair was mussed,
and tufts of it stuck up like owls' horns; they had a
dirty rumpled look, as if they had been sleeping outdoors in a nest of leaves. The taller one, who was
not more than eleven or twelve, had large unlaced
shoes on his sockless feet and wore a man's pinstriped
suit jacket which flopped open to his torn shirt; the
younger one, who was half his size, wore a checked
woolen jacket that was much too small for him, and
red mud-smeared boots. They both wore shrunken
shorts and now Munday saw they were carrying empty
beer bottles in their arms.

"Hello there," said Munday.

The taller one giggled and dropped his eyes, the
other put his head down shyly and both walked a bit
faster. It was their color that appalled Munday; their
pinched faces were that pale luminous white that is
almost blue, and their knees, so absurdly larger than
their skinny legs, were also bluish. They had the round
shoulders and the gait of very old men, and shining
mustaches of snot, and their bottles clinked as they
splashed past, seeming to hurry.

"Terrible," whispered Emma. "The poor things. Did
you see their teeth?"

Munday had not realized how cold it was until he
had seen those ragged boys in shorts. Now he noticed
it was near freezing. He said, "They should be in
school."

"Where do you suppose they're going?"

"Obviously to The Yew Tree, to return those bottles. Get a few pence."

"They must live down there in those cottages," said
Emma, starting down the hill.

They walked around the bend in the road, squelching through the mud, to the row of cottages. What
had looked so charming from behind their house, the
sweep of the valley coming up to meet the thatched

cottages with the smoking chimneys, the quilt of fields, the browsing sheep, now lost all its simplicity. The thatch was torn and partially mended, bristling brooms of new straw stuck out from the eaves, sheets of chicken wire held it together on the roof peak. The wall of the end cottage bulged, seams of cement had burst, and the foundation at one corner had cracked and come loose. The fields were sodden and criss-crossed by deep ruts, the sheep was spattered with mud, and their yellow wool, the texture of elderly hair, was painted with crude red symbols. A dog bounded past the sheep, scattering them, and then ran to the Mundays and barked fiercely, holding itself low on the ground, crouching and inching closer as he snarled.

"There, there." Emma spoke softly to the dog and reached over to stroke its head. It lifted its jaws and snapped at her hand and continued to bark. Emma stepped away, but still murmured her gentle disappointment, hoping to calm the dog.

"No friendlier than anyone else around here," said Munday. He held his walking stick tightly and he noted a spot at the back of the dog's head where he would land the blow.

"Aw, he won't hurt you."

The voice, Hosmer's—they looked up and saw him in the yard, peering at them from under his hat brim—was flat, without encouragement or welcome. He was just above them, leaning on a shovel, in a green jacket with the pockets torn and flapping, wearing high gumboots.

"Likes to play, he does," said Hosmer.

The dog had mounted Emma's leg and left streaked paw prints on the light mac she had bought especially for these walks. She took the dog by its forelegs and pushed at its slavering mouth. She said, "Naughty— stop it!"

"Off 'er!" said Hosmer sharply to the dog. It pulled out of Emma's grasp and bounded a few feet away and yelped and shook itself, turning in circles.

"So this is where you live," said Munday, starting up the bank towards Hosmer. It was the bluff, genial tone he used with Africans in their bush compounds. "Very nice indeed. Your garden?"

"Yes, sir," said Hosmer, straightening on his shovel and speaking with a guarded respect Munday felt might be impossible to penetrate with any friendliness.

"It's a perfect site," said Emma. She brushed at the paw prints with the heel of her hand.

"Mr. Awdry's," said Hosmer. "He owns the lot. We rent her, this end of the cottage. One of Duddle's tenants has the other half."

"But you get the sun," said Emma.

"When she's out," said Hosmer.

"It's a beautiful view."

"That's Shave's Cross," said Hosmer, choosing to indicate a smudge of squares on the landscape, a small cluster of distant gray cottages in the miles and miles of green farmland and trees. It occurred to Munday that a Bwamba might have done the same. Hosmer said, "Over there's Lyme Regis." It was a purpling hill, a promonotory at the horizon.

Munday was looking at the cottages. "I see," he said. "Each of these three buildings is divided in half. That would make five more families living here. Almost a hamlet."

"Four others," said Hosmer. "Last one's standing empty."

"You're a lucky man," said Munday. "There are people in London who'd give anything to have a place like this."

"Would they?" said Hosmer gruffly. "Well, they can stop where they are."

"They're not so bad," Munday joked. "Once you get used to them."

"I don't get used to them," said Hosmer. "Twenty guineas a week they pay—for a cottage! All that whisky, and the things they do. They want us in the council houses. Bloody nuisance, I say. They can bloody stop where they are."

"They put the prices up, that it?" said Munday. He smiled; it was an African remark, made of foreign visitors.

Hosmer said, "And my back."

"Is this all your garden?" asked Emma.

"Yes, ma'm."

"May we look around?"

"Mind the mud," said Hosmer. "Been raining. The cows come through here and churns it up."

"You still have sprouts!" Emma showed Munday the tall plants with the pale green bulbs on their stalks.

"No bloody good to me," said Hosmer. "Growing into flowers and rotting." He turned on his shovel and watched the Mundays stroll to the bottom of the garden, Emma looking at the view, Munday lifting a tangle of vines with his walking stick for a better look at the marrows.

"It's magnificent," said Emma. She faced the sea where the low sun, wreathed in a gray shallow cloud, still shimmered on the water.

Munday headed for the back of the cottages. He heard Hosmer say, "Sorry I can't offer you anything," and Emma reply, "Oh, we were just out for a walk—" In the straw-clumps behind the cottages Munday saw rusting tools, an unused generator black with oil, a gutted motor, and tractor parts, a crankshaft, bolts and wheel-rims and a pile of lumber. He poked at them with his stick. A line of washing, faded overalls, yellow underwear, and blue shirts whitened with bleach stains blew noisily, the arms and legs filling with wind, and the line itself lifted. Munday crossed the humpy ground to the fence at the edge of Hosmer's property to get a better look at the valley, and he was standing trying to memorize the rhythm of the hills, the play of light and shadow, when his thoughts were interrupted by a ribbon of decay leaking past his nose. He sniffed and lost it and then smelled it powerfully, the ribbon growing to a whole rag of stink.

A few feet away, just by a wire fence, was a little platform covered by an old brown piece of canvas. He

saw that Hosmer and Emma were out of sight; he
stepped over to it and lifted one corner with his stick.
He saw white flesh, narrow sinews and the tight bundles of muscle. His first thought was that it was a
human corpse, and that fear of discovering a dead
man lessened the shock of seeing the hairy rug, the
paws, and—lifting the stiff canvas higher—the two dead
dogs, lying side by side on the wooden platform. They
had been killed, and Munday thought flayed (the
word came to him before he actually saw the slashes),
and they lay there on the shelf, speckled by decay,
beside their own folded pelts.

Munday dropped the canvas and hurried to the side
of the cottage, where Hosmer and Emma were still
standing and talking.

"I was just telling your missus," said Hosmer,
squinting. "That end cottage—she's rented."

Walking home Emma said, "Those were his boys.
I asked him. I wish there were something we could
do."

"Bring them to the attention of Oxfam," he said.

"Alfred."

"There's nothing," he said. "He doesn't even want
us around."

"They look so beaten."

"Not beaten," he said. "Detribalized."

"It's so ironic," Emma said, "living in such squalor
with that magnificent view."

Munday said, "Let's keep to the road this time,
shall we?"

And he knew as they talked about the early twilight,
the dusk falling on the hills around them, that he would
say nothing about the dead dogs. That baffling scene
he understood only as an enactment of violence, but
something no usual motive could properly explain or
make less beastly was another secret he would have
to keep from her and bear alone. It was like a hidden
infidelity, a habit of faithlessness he was starting to
learn, suppressing what frightened him so that Emma
would not be alarmed.

8

THEY EXPECTED an unheated church hall, so Munday wore a zippered cardigan under his thick tweed suit, and Emma her wool dress and jacket; she carried her mac carefully folded on the arm because of the paw prints. But it was very warm in the hall, Munday felt the heat as soon as he stepped inside, and he commented on it to the vicar.

"They like it this way," said Crawshaw. He smiled at the seated people as he spoke, and led Munday to the stage. "Pensioners, you see—they really feel the cold. It's why we have these monthly talks. The central heating in here is so expensive. We put some of the proceeds toward the fuel bill. It's oil-fired. One day we'll have a new hall."

Munday said, "If anyone asks me whether it's hot in Africa I'll say, 'No hotter than this room!'" There was also a dusty sweetness in the air, like flower scent but cloying, the odor of talcum, cologne, and bay rum, perfumes of the aged that rubbed against Munday's eyes.

Every seat was taken. Some people turned and stared as Munday and the vicar walked up the center aisle, but he saw most of them from the back, the suspended lamps lighting their white hair and giving it the thin wispiness of little nest-like caps of illuminated cobwebs. The bald spots shone. It might have been a gathering for a church service they were so still, almost prayerful; and that look of piety was somehow intensified by the size of their heads, which were very small and set on disproportionately large shoulders.

65

When Munday reached the front of the hall and mounted the stage he saw the reason for this—they were all dressed for outdoors, each person wore a heavy winter coat. From the front, bundled up in this way, they looked defiant to Munday, annoyed in their cumbersome winter clothes. But there was a general unbuttoning and opening of the coats when they saw Munday and the vicar.

A man on stage was fumbling with a screen, trying to set it up. Crawshaw introduced him to Munday as Chester Lennit.

"Sorry I don't have a free hand," said Lennit, flashing Munday a faintly sheepish smile. "Be through in a minute, though," he said, but as he spoke the tripod collapsed, and the telescoping upright shot down with a great clatter. Heads bobbed in the audience. Lennit pulled it again into position and said, "Bally thing won't hold."

The people in the audience watched with bright eyes.

"Mr. Lennit is in charge of our visual aids," said Crawshaw.

"Not *trained* for it, or anything like that," said Lennit. "I used to be with British Rail, on the accounts side, in London. For years."

"Perhaps I can give you a hand," said Munday.

"No, I've done this lots of times before," said Lennit. He wouldn't let himself be helped. He said, "Very fiddly, these things. You just have to know the right combination." He looped the screen once again onto the upright and nudged the tripod into place with his foot. It crashed again. "Oh, God," he muttered, and his grip on the apparatus became strangulatory.

Crawshaw turned to the audience: "While Mr. Lennit's putting the screen into shape, I'd like to make a few announcements. First, Mrs. Crawshaw asked me to thank all of you who kindly brought fresh flowers for the memorial service last Sunday. Those of you who spent Saturday afternoon polishing the brasses deserve a special vote of thanks. The Christmas supper is scheduled for the twenty-second, and may I just say a word about our charity drive for the less fortunate in Four Ashes? It's not too early to start thinking about setting tins and warm clothes aside—"

Emma, in the front row, was listening to the vicar. Munday tried to catch her eye—he wanted her to wink at him; she turned and smiled slightly and went back to the vicar. She looked calm, but after the walk that evening she had stopped in the courtyard of the house and said, "I don't want to go in." Munday had entered first. He called to her; there was nothing. Behind her now, making her seem almost girlish in her Indian silk scarf, the rows of elderly listeners hunched in their dark coats received the vicar's news without reacting. Then Munday realized that they were not looking at the vicar, but rather at Mr. Lennit who at the back of the stage was stretching the screen into position for the fourth time.

Munday, scowling in the heat, was struck by their certain age, which he took to be around seventy, and by the uniformity of their appearance. They looked so similar, they shared so many features: their faces were small, bony, skull-like, some of the women's faces looked dusted with flour, and yet none gave the impression of being sickly. Their postures were the same; they sat on the folding chairs, their hands clutched in their laps, bent slightly forward, as if straining to hear, or perhaps to get a better view of Mr. Lennit. Many of the men wore lapel pins, some two or three, and the women small corsages, sprigs of winter flowers on their coats. It was a vision for Munday of old age crowded in a hall, like a council convened by the geriatrics in a village convinced of their own doom. There were such villages on remote African hillsides, from which all the young people had fled in a time of famine or drought, leaving the aged ones to resist, huddled in broken huts. Munday had seen them crouched in shadows, facing fields parching in a killing sun.

"—I think," said the vicar, glancing behind him,

"that Mr. Lennit has succeeded in putting up his awfully complicated cinema screen. Before we begin I must ask you to avoid stepping on the cord to the slide projector. We don't want a repetition of the Hardy talk!"

A mirthful hum vibrated in the audience, and chairs clanked as people shifted in their seats.

The vicar said to Munday, "Someone plunged us into darkness that night. Gave some of the good ladies here quite a shock."

Munday nodded and said, "Rather."

"This evening," said the vicar, raising his voice, "we are privileged to have with us a man who has spent a good part of his life in some very sticky places. Africa has always had a strange fascination for the English. We explored its jungles, we fought there—many Englishmen still lie buried there—we colonized and brought light to that dark continent. A few of you here tonight have yourselves been to Africa and can claim some credit for these accomplishments. Today, Her Majesty no longer rules over Africa, and the territories that flew the Union Jack now have their own flags of various colors. From what we read in the papers they seem terribly confusing—"

The introduction went on for several more minutes and continued to embarrass Munday, and when the vicar said, "I give you—Doctor Munday," he stepped forward to the dry clapping and realized how inappropriate the opening remarks he had prepared were, how scholarly and ill-suited to the mood of this provincial place. So he began by saying, "The vicar called it sticky. It's only that in the literal sense, never very dangerous. In fact I should say it's a good deal safer than London!"

They laughed at this, and he went on, encouraged by their amusement, trying to find a way into the talk he had prepared. "They say Africa gets into one's blood. It's probably truer to say it gets under one's skin!" This time he paused for the laughter, but it was slighter than before, and scattered, and he quickly resumed, "Unless you're a chap like me who rather enjoys poking his nose in all sorts of out-of-the-way places. It's a queer kind of community, an African village, but in many ways no different from your own village. The social organization is quite similar, there are meeting places like this church hall, and shops, and village elders to whom, like the vicar here, people look for counsel. So when you think of an African village, don't think of a great mass of gibbering black people with bones in their noses, shaking spears and beating on tom-toms"—here there was some laughter, but Munday pressed on without acknowledging it— "think of yourselves."

And then he said, "You understand in Four Ashes what it's like to be a bit off the map, and tonight I'm going to talk to you about another remote people—"

He sensed a slackening in the audience's attention right away, an adjustment to heaviness in them he tried to shift with his voice; fighting for their eyes made his tone preachy and somewhat strident. Emma had advised him to pick one person and speak to him. He did this: the man was in the third row, and was distinguished by a fine tweed coat, lighter than all the others. Munday continued speaking; the man put his chin in his hand reflectively; his head tilted to the side and the hand seemed to tip the head onto his shoulder. Asleep, he seemed especially aged. Munday searched the hall for another face.

"It's a law of nature," he was saying, "that once a group of people has been cut off from the world they begin to change. Their direction alters—though they have no sense of having turned. They have nothing, no one, to measure themselves by, except a distant feeble memory of the way things were once done. You must bear in mind that certain activities put us in touch with other people—trade, selling our skills and goods, travel, reading, even warfare helps us to come to an understanding of the world outside the village. But where there is little saleable skill, a sub-sistence economy, a reluctance to travel, and where people are entirely self-sufficient, they withdraw to a shadowy interior world. This inspires certain fears —irrational fear, you might say, is a penalty of that isolation. Who can verify it or tell you it doesn't matter? Who can witness this decline? The remote people begin to act in a manner that looks very strange indeed to an outsider. Their sense of time, for example, is slowed down. The sameness of the days makes them easy to forget and so history goes un-witnessed. It's a kind of sleep. There is little innovation because really there is no need for it. What is not understood—and this can be as simple and casual as a tree falling across the road in a storm—is called magic. And this happens in more places than the witch-ridden society of semi-pygmies at the latter end of the world.

"But the most remarkable thing is that a village isolated in this way becomes wholly unaware of its isolation. The village is the world, the people are real, and everything else is mysteriously threatening. So the stranger comes, as I did ten years ago to that remote village, and he is viewed from an alarming perspective. He might be seen as dangerous, or else —it happens—as a kind of savior. He is not a man like them. The Bwamba, who had never seen a white woman before, thought my wife was a man. Ten years ago the Bwamba believed white men were canni-bals, who fed on Africans. It's odd: the only mystery for the stranger is that little clearing in the jungle, which thinks of itself as the only real thing."

He thought the paradox might drag them into mo-tion, but they were unresponsive, sitting at doubtful attention, some in the sleeping postures of broken statuary. Many were still awake—he knew that from their coughing.

"What if it happened," he went on, "that the stranger was himself from a remote village? Suppose the English villager meets the African villager— the isolation they have in common is the very thing that isolates them from each other. There is not a syllable of speech they can share. Common humanity, you might reply; of course, yes, but if each has been marked by his solitude, aren't we then dealing with two separate consciousnesses which have evolved in circumstances so different that nothing at all can be spoken and no judgment can be possible? The English villager might report that what he has seen is strange. What will the African report? The same, of course. Mr. Kurtz said his Africans were brutes; what did those Africans make of Kurtz? What did Schweitzer's patients make of that shambling old man playing his pipe-organ in the jungles of Gabon? Imagine, if you can, the opinions of Livingstone's porters, Burton's guides, Mungo Park's paddlers! Anthropology is man speculating on man, but when the man who is the subject turns around and becomes the speculator, you see how relative the terms 'barbaric' and 'simple' and 'primitive' are.

"And reality, what is reality?" he asked of the dozing people in the hall. "It is a guess, a wish, a clutch of fears, an opinion offered without any hope of proof. One might say that only pain can possibly substantiate it. You see the oddest things, you know, dead things or specters, that can cause you such panic that to dismiss them makes any argument for reality a series of arrogant notions inspired by the sharpest fear."

Emma's eyes were fixed on him. He spoke to her: "We accept what reality is bearable and try to ignore the rest, because we know it would kill us to see it all. I see I've wandered a little from my subject," he said. And he had; the impassive, unresponding audience had caused it. He was talking to himself and to Emma. He said, "In closing, let me say that for a long time I've thought of doing a rather unfashionable book, in which we see anthropologists through the eyes of their subjects. Think about it for a moment. Malinowski as described by the Trobriand islanders, Lévi-Strauss's fastidious Frenchness noted by the Nambikwara Indians in the Mato-Grosso. The headhunter's view of the anthropologist, you might say. It would be interesting to see how we invent one another."

He expected a reaction but got none. There was not a murmur of recognition from the audience. Munday had been talking forcefully in a high-pitched voice, that preaching tone, to stir them. They had not moved. Now he could see that several more had fallen asleep and the rest had a look of nervous fatigue, as if in speaking so loud (he imagined that, being old, many of them were hard of hearing) he had intimidated those he had not put to sleep. He wanted to fly up to the ceiling and look down at those shining bald spots, that white hair, all those small heads.

He described Bwamba music and played his tape, an old Bwamba woman's lament for a husband who died young. He translated the song, which was a description of the man, praising him, likening him to a powerful crested crane. The song was a harsh series of caws, with a sad muttered refrain; it was accompanied by a plunking finger-harp and several gourd horns. Afterwards there was some whispering in the hall.

Munday said, "Now let's look at the people themselves. Mr. Lennit?"

Lennit inserted a box of slides into the projector. He said, "Lights, please," and the hall, in total darkness, began to purr with the murmuring voices of the old people.

Huge trembling fingers appeared on the screen, fretting like swollen spider's legs. There was some laughter. Lennit said, "She's jammed, I think," and the fingers clutched in the empty square of light.

With a resounding clang, a slide of the eastern slopes of the Ruwenzori Mountains appeared on the screen. It had been taken on a clear day, the mountains were emerald, the cloudless sky a bright blue, and in the foreground was a thick grove of banana trees. There were lingering exclamations in the audience, "Oh!" and "Lovely."

"Mountains of the Moon," said Munday. He stood next to the screen, tapping it with a slender stick. "Next slide."

This was of a back road, russet-colored mud cratered with wide pot-holes. "That," said Munday, "is the main road into the mountains." He mused, "I broke any number of springs on that particular stretch."

Succeeding slides took them beyond the mountains to the rain-forest, the bush track through the papyrus swamp, the path at the Yellow Fever Camp, and then they were at the village itself. There was a sequence of village slides: of the huts; of Munday smiling (sunburned, almost unrecognizable in shorts and bush jacket) with the headman; women pounding bananas; small children making playful faces at the camera. The whispers, appreciative of landscape slides, grew flat and noncommittal when Africans were shown. Munday had captions for all the slides: "Women's work is never done," he said of the banana pounding; "Children are the same all over the world, though after I took this picture one little chap said, 'You give me shilling,' " and "Village beauty," he said of a bare-breasted girl taken in close-up: her hair was tightly plaited, she wore a beaded necklace, and her earlobes were rent, pulled into long loops.

The circumcision ceremony, nine slides, plunged the church hall into silence. The men looked wild in headdresses and masks and leggings; the boys' faces were whitened by ashes and their bodies were streaked with yellow and red paint. They held small spears and had feathers in their hair, and they looked very worried. Then they were on their backs and grimacing. "I consider myself rather lucky to have these slides. They only have a male circumcision every fourteen or fifteen years, and fortunately this one coincided with our stay there. As you can see, some are quite advanced in age—there, that one could be twenty-five or so—" Munday blandly explained the procedure, the chanting, the dancing performed to distract the boys from the pain of being cut.

Lennit clicked on, and twice Munday had to say, "Can we have that one back again?"

Casting his shadow on the brown wrinkled pipe of a Bwamba boy's penis being tugged by a decorated hand, Munday said, "Unfortunately, I have no pictures of female circumcision. Sorry about that. The Sebei people practice it—so do the Chiga, and of course the Kikuyu. But they wouldn't allow me to photograph that. Extremely painful. Men aren't allowed to watch. But this reticence is perfectly understandable. We wouldn't be very eager to have an African photograph us on our wedding night—"

A shocked male voice in the audience gasped, "God, don't that look awful!"

The hush in the hall was intense. The slide projector's fan whirred. In the dark village, in that hot church hall, Africa was a bright square of light, pigeons wheeling among huts, a row of dancing men in birds' plumage and shabby leopard skins, foliage so green and wet it looked newly painted, blue curtains of smoke rising from fire pits, dusty feet and legs in every picture, the blur of hands on a drumhead, a wincing white-faced boy. The last slide was of a boy being helped up from the straw circumcision mat. He had turned his face to the camera and wore an expression of utter fear, which was plain even under the ashes of his make-up. Rivulets of sweat streaked his face, his eyes pleaded; he had been forbidden to cry, but there was anguish in his empty hands.

"A few minutes before, he was a boy," said Munday. "Now, he's a warrior. Lights."

The lights went on and the audience blinked, as if they had just emerged from a tunnel, or like mice, suspicious and sniffing and glassy-eyed, awakened by a torch stuck in their cage. Some pressed their eyes or made visors of their hands. But many of them made no move at all, and Munday saw they were asleep.

"I want you to have a look at some of the tools and weapons you saw in those slides," said Munday. "I'll pass them along to you. Take them, feel them—you'll see they're quite strong and well made." He took them, one by one, from a canvas bag at his feet and explained the function of each, making distinctions between the cutter and scraper, the short jabbing spear and the throwing spear, the wrist-knife, the dagger, and the various circumcision knives. He described how the blades were fixed and drew their attention to the markings. When he finished talking about one he handed it to a man on the end of the front row and asked him to pass it around. A man behind that one leaned forward, resting his arms on the chairback and looked over the man's shoulder to marvel at them.

"I've been doing all the talking up to now," said Munday. "While that hardware is making the rounds perhaps you'd like to ask some questions."

Munday gripped the lectern and surveyed the still faces. The steel folding chairs squeaked. He saw the weapons being passed from hand to hand, but there were no hands raised for questions. The people cloaked their shyness in an exaggerated interest in the weapons, handling them, turning them over. Then a man in the third row asked, "Did you ever climb those mountains we saw in the first slide?"

"The Ruwenzoris," said Munday. "Not to the top. I cantered around the slopes quite a bit. The slide you saw of the giant lobelia was taken by Emma here. *She's* the mountain climber."

Heads bobbed, trying to catch a glimpse of Emma.

"A few years ago," said a man in the corner, half rising and clearing his throat, "the wife and I flew out to Majorca for a little holiday, one of those package tours, you know, get a bit of sun. Went out from Luton, everyone saying *Olé!* Well, we arrived and had a wash and a meal at the hotel and then took a stroll down the front, sort of a pier. I can't tell you how hot it was! Temperature must have been in the nineties, and the tarmac was going all soft and sticky—had it all over me plimsolls. I said to the wife, 'I don't know how they do it.' I wasn't good for anything—after an hour I was all played out. The next day it was the same—worse, really, because the food got to us and we were running to the loo every five minutes. That was the first word I learned, *Hombres!*"

There was laughter again—they had laughed when he had said *Olé*—and Munday saw that the audience knew the man as a joker who was seizing an opportunity to perform. Munday said, "I don't see what any of this has to do with—"

"But we took the usual stroll," the man went on, chatting easily, "and I drank gallons of that mineral water. The sun was a penance—couldn't stick it, so I sat in the shade under one of those umbrellas and watched the holiday-makers and the people going about their business. They say Spanish people are lazy and don't want to work, but these blokes were really hard at it. I've been a socialist all my life, and that kind of thing impresses me. I took one aside —I suppose I was getting to be a bit of an anthropologist myself—he was the waiter, and I said to him, 'I don't know how you people do it.' But he just smiled and took my order with the sweat pouring down worse than those African pictures. It's an amazing thing, really, but I got to thinking to myself, do you suppose those people would live in a place like that if they didn't have to? What I mean to say is, they don't have much choice, but if they *did* have a choice don't you think it's a sure five they'd leave a flaming hot place like that Majorca and maybe go somewhere else where they could live a decent life without having to fan themselves with paper plates? That's my question."

Munday, irritated by the question, said curtly, "No," and looked for another questioner. But when the same man began to speak again, he interrupted, adding,

"Those Spaniards would be as uncomfortable in Four Ashes as you were in—where was it, Palma?"

"Playa del Sol," said the man. "Fillet of sole, the wife calls it."

"Wherever," said Munday. "And the same goes for Africans. Their village is the world. Beyond it is *terra incognita*."

A tall man stood up in the center of the hall. He had good posture, a kind of military bearing, and his accent was educated. "Unlike my friend in the corner," he said, "I haven't been to Majorca—fish and chips in Spain is not one of my favorite holidays—"

"I didn't—" the man started to object.

"But I agree with him completely," continued the tall man, his chummy agreement silencing the complaint. "I was a D.C. in Western Uganda—well before your time. Your lantern show took me back a few years! Crumbs! I know the Bwamba. Used to think of them as frightful little persons, always *hiding* from one and sort of grinning out at one from the branches. Reminded me of the Irish a good deal, getting up to all sorts of mischief—made my life a misery, I can tell you. I saw a lot of your chaps, too. And I remember, oh, years ago, one of your anthropologists coming into my office and absolutely pleading with me to get him out of there. Couldn't take another minute of it, he said. Claimed they were robbing him blind, all sorts of things. I took care of him—*buck up,* I said, and one of my chaps saw him to the train."

"Your question, then?" said Munday.

"It's not a question so much as a challenge, actually," said the man, and Munday could tell from the laughter that the audience was on the side of the tall man, who somehow represented their unformed boredom and made their disinterest into outright rejection. Facing the tall man he felt he faced them all.

The man bore down, losing his humorous tone: "You told this gentleman the Africans would be uncomfortable out of their villages. It's the first I've heard of it, and it doesn't square with my experience at all. Africans are perfect little *deserters*."

"I don't agree," said Munday. The faces were on Munday.

"I didn't think you would," said the man. "But do let me finish, won't you?"

"Carry on," said Munday. The faces turned to the man.

"I've never met people so anxious to get away— anywhere—to the towns, another village, wherever they heard there were a few shillings or a few women to be had for the taking. Someone would hint that life was better in Kampala and they'd be off like a shot. And pray tell, who are these Africans one sees collecting tickets on the Underground if not villagers? They come as students—the word 'student' covers a multitude of sins—but they haven't the slightest intention of going back. Your younger African is dying to leave. Get to London, streets paved with gold, what-have-you. It used to amaze me. I mean, I liked Africa infinitely better than they!"

"I daresay," said Munday—the faces turned from the man to him—"the Africa you lived in was not quite the same one they did."

"The very same," said the man, now humorously. The humor was like an affectation of tolerance, putting Munday in the wrong. "Though I must admit *th*ey had all the fun. I was stuck behind a desk with masses of official bumf to deal with. I used to hear them chattering outside the window, laughing and so forth—I suppose they were making plans to leave."

"In my ten years—"

"But it's an odd thing. I still dream about the damn place. I have this dream about once a month, a nightmare in actual fact. I see Fort Portal, that lovely little town, but in my dreams it's full of chemist's shops and petrol stations, and neon lights so bright you can't see the mountains. Well, I won't bore you any further, but you understand I felt I had to speak my mind."

He sat and there was an expectant moment, a rustling preparation, as if the people were gathering their hands to applaud him for scoring against Munday. But it passed, the motion in the hall that was like approval settled into silence.

Munday had seen the hall as full of feeble people, inattentive in their distressed old age, derelict, simply warming themselves and going to sleep in the heat. In those snoozing, uncaring faces he had not identified the tall man who was so unlike them, and he had not guessed that the challenge of the man's authority would stir them. Munday heard his own reply as unsympathetic, even hostile; he felt the man had assumed temporary leadership as a spokesman and turned them against him, and he had become defensive—needless on so insignificant an occasion. But what was maddening was the figure of the man, how, seated, he was no different from any of the old people, and standing so assured.

It happened again: this time it was a woman near the back, who was not old and who might have been pretty, though at that distance it was hard to tell.

"I was fascinated by your talk," she said. "I was thinking it must take an enormous amount of courage to live in the place you described. You were so far away! Didn't it ever get you down or depress you?"

"The lack of privacy of course is a very great nuisance," said Munday. "Sort of goldfish bowl existence. But, no, I didn't get depressed. As I say, village life *can* be taxing, and baffling, but that's as true here as it is in Africa."

"Are you saying the Africans are the same as us?" asked a man down front.

Several replies occurred to Munday. He was going to say, "God forbid!" but that was cruel; and "Yes," but that was untrue. He said, "The issue isn't as black and white as that," and there was some laughter.

"You said in your lecture there were pygmies in

that area," said a man holding his hat at his chest.
"What are they like? Are they as small as people
say?"

"Bigger than your hat. About the size of a nine-
year-old. I say that because nine-year-old Bwamba
kids used to stand on the Fort Portal road and flag
down tourists' cars. They'd claim to be pygmies and
ask to have their pictures taken for a shilling. Tourists didn't know the difference. But it's quite easy
to spot a real pygmy. When you see a tiny girl
with fully developed breasts you know you're looking at a pygmy—that's the litmus test, you might
say—the breasts."

"Do they intermarry with other tribes?"

"The Bwamba take them, usually as second wives.
You can have any pygmy woman for life for just
under ten quid, two hundred shillings. They only
marry in one direction. I mean to say, no pygmy man
would ever marry a Bwamba woman. "Once," Munday went on, "I met a pygmy man whose ambition
it was to marry an American Negro. Some writers
want to be Shakespeare and some of you would like
knighthoods. This pygmy, as I say, wanted to marry
a fully-grown Negro woman. Well, we all have our
dreams."

There were more questions, tentative ones about
sanitation, specific ones about hospitals and food.
Mr. Lennit asked about the railway. "I take it you
believe in ghosts," one man said. Munday said he
believed in the possibility of ghosts: "People I respect have seen them." Then a small precise lady
in a fur-collared coat asked about the heat. Munday
swiftly gave the reply he had practiced, and speaking above the laughter, the vicar said, "I think we'll
close on that note—"

Later, with Lennit assisting him, Munday put the
implements into his canvas sack. Emma was talking
to the vicar, as he helped her on with her coat. She
was explaining the muddy paw prints she had not
been able to wipe off.

Munday said, "Something's missing."

"What is it?" asked Lennit.

"I don't know. But I started out with twenty items, and now I only have nineteen."

"You're sure?"

Munday did not reply; it was a doubting question he hated.

"Here, let me count them," said Lennit.

"I've done that already."

"What seems to be the trouble?" asked Crawshaw.

"Says someone nicked one of his spears," said Lennit, and shrugged.

Now, Munday wanted to kick the old man.

"You're sure?" Crawshaw asked Munday.

Emma saw that Munday was furious. She said, "He always counts them before he passes them round."

"It's a habit I picked up lecturing to African audiences," said Munday, and he snatched at the drawstring of the canvas bag.

9

IT WAS like flight. They caught the 8:20 train to London outside Crewkerne at a narrow Victorian station of soot-blackened stone, with high church windows and a steeply pitched roof. The sharp spires and clock tower were wreathed in morning mist, and there was a similar whiteness, mist and a sprinkling of frost on the grass, in the fields that lay beyond the siding. Standing there, waiting for the train, Munday had feared it might not come to take them away, and he felt gleeful when he saw it rounding the bend, the yellow and blue engine hooting. "You keep these," said Munday, giving Emma the day-return tickets in the empty compartment. She slipped them between the pages of the novel she'd brought, an Agatha Christie from the shelf. Munday had his *Times*; he read the Diary, the letters and glanced at the obituaries and then folded the paper flat and held it in his lap, not reading it, his hands spread over it, as Emma's were on the book that rested on her knees. They faced each other, rocking, only looking out the window when the train slowed down. At Yeovil Junction Emma said, "East Coker is near here. We must drive over some time."

"East Coker?"

"T.S. Eliot."

"Of course," said Munday, but he had no clear idea of what she was talking about.

Breakfast was announced at Sherborne, where a tall severe man whom Munday said must be a classics master stood on the platform with a briefcase and a book in his hand, waiting to board. Emma and Munday left the book and newspaper on their seats to show they were occupied and went into the dining car. Emma had toast and tea, Munday the complete breakfast.

"Why no kippers?" he asked the waiter.

"They do kippers on the busier trains," said the waiter, whose tight jacket was stiff with starch. "Not on this line, though. Not important enough."

Munday felt the waiter was getting at him for riding an unimportant line. He said, "I shall write a letter to *The Times*."..

"They're rationalizing the catering. We don't serve more than a dozen breakfasts in all. After Salisbury it's just coffees. How do you want your eggs?"

When breakfast came Emma said, "He's forgotten my marmalade."

"He hasn't forgotten," said Munday. "Rationalizing the catering." He ate methodically, glancing out the window between swallows. There were cows and sheep in the fields, and still fog and mist in some valleys, and vapor the color of the sky hanging in bare branches. He saw a man emptying a pail in a trough; the man paused and looked up at the passing train. Munday saw him clearly, the large-fingered gloves, the peaked cap, the cutoff boots. He knew the man did not see him; he saw a train, only that, but he was completely exposed. Munday felt guilty, observing him in this way, eating his eggs, and he pitied the man for whom a train was an event to relieve his solitude and make him turn away from his work. Then he disliked the man for his curiosity and saw him as a possible thief.

"It'll be nice to be in London again," said Emma. "I've got so much shopping to do."

"It's a bit raw," said Munday.

Emma looked out the window. She said, "I really don't want to go back."

Munday wondered how he might console her. Nothing came to him. He said, "The day-return fare is damned cheap." Then after a while, "They pinched one of my daggers."

"Depressing people."

"I'm glad you finally agree with me." He thought again of the man in the field. He said, "I'm finished," and pushed his plate aside.

They paid the bill, and the car filled up, but they did not go back to their compartment immediately. They lingered, enjoying the warmth, the breakfast smells of bacon and coffee and the pipe smoke of a man at the next table. The train lurched, gathering speed, cups chinked and the hanging folds of the white tablecloths moved like skirts. Trees and bushy embankments shot past the window. Munday played with the heavy silver. Near Salisbury the landscape opened; it was flatter and the fields they passed seemed to revolve, roughly circular furrows spinning on the skid of the train.

"What about lunch?" asked Munday.

"I'm meeting Margaret at Selfridge's. We'll have

lunch somewhere, then spend the afternoon together shopping."

"I can't imagine her without those sunglasses and sandals."

"And that yellow cotton dress," said Emma.

"What's Jack doing?"

"She says she doesn't hear from him."

"Such a scandal there," Munday said. "All that excitement. Here it seems so ordinary and stupid."

"Will you be seeing Silvano?"

"No time for that. My appointment's at eleven-thirty." He looked at his watch. "I'll just make it. And Alec said he'd be at the Wheatsheaf at one. It'll be good to see him. The last train's just after seven. Why don't we meet at that pub in the station at quarter-to?"

"I wish we didn't have to go back so soon."

At Salisbury they groped their way to their compartment and found four people in it, but the newspaper and book remained on the vacant seats next to the windows. They watched the people on the platform, some mothers with large clean children, an older woman who looked like any of the ones in the church hall at Four Ashes except that she was distinguished by a copy of the orange *Financial Times,* rolled like a truncheon in her string bag. Most were women dressed for restaurant lunches, with the soberly elegant clothes that women wear to impress other women, rather than attract men: large hats, gloves, some with neat, damp corsages; they boarded in groups of three and four. One of these entered the Mundays' compartment; she sat smiling and waving discreetly to a woman squeezing down the passage. She had a copy of the *Telegraph,* which she read in glances, folding it and turning it inside out. The windows steamed up, and this woman perfumed the small space with lavender. Near Woking there was a sign saying STOP COLOURED IMMIGRATION in neat square letters on a brick wall next to the track. A *Daily Express* lay on the single empty seat.

It was retrieved by a thin man in a blue nylon jacket when the train drew in to Waterloo.

In the main hall of the station, dangerous with little yellow vehicles towing baggage carts and vibrating with the ponderous throb of announcements of train times and place names, none of which was distinct, Munday showed Emma the pub he had mentioned, and standing near it he thought he recognized the black man he had addressed in Swahili. They parted on the Bakerloo Line, Emma got off at Oxford Circus, Munday continued to Regent's Park where he walked in a fine drizzle to Harley Street.

The receptionist was prompt; he had introduced himself as Doctor Munday, and though there was another man in the waiting room she said to follow her. She led him down a corridor, past framed eighteenth-century cartoons—one of a toothy man falling violently and spouting a bubble of script caught Munday's eye. The doctor's office resembled a study. There was a wall of leather-bound books, a large dark painting of a highland scene, and heavy green curtains. The desk was wide and held a silver inkstand, and the stethoscope which rested on the blotter was the only indication of the work of the dark-suited man who sat fingering it. He rose as Munday entered; the receptionist introduced them, then went out, shutting the door.

"So you were Dowle's patient," said the doctor, motioning Munday to a chair. "He wrote me about you. How is he?"

"Just the same," said Munday. "Full of bluster, and absolutely punishing himself with whisky. They have a new cook at the mission, a Polish priest named Pekachek—mad about cabbage."

"Dowle and I were at medical school together."

"So he told me," said Munday. "Old Father Tom."

"That what they call him? He was a lad, he was—the last person in the world I'd have thought to go into the priesthood." The doctor winked. "A great one for the ladies, you know. I suppose with these black women he's not in any danger of breaking his vow of chastity."

"Some can be quite lovely."

"You'll have a hard time convincing me of that," said the doctor.

"I don't intend to try," Munday said evenly. He would not be provoked. It was a vulgar subject—and anyway he had never himself made love to an African woman: it would have put his research at risk. But something else prevented him from discussing the matter any further with the doctor. He saw himself repeatedly cast in the role of defender of Africans—with Flack, with the vicar, with the pompous spokesman in the church hall. He defended Africans by inverting the abusive generalities, until he had found himself saying things he didn't mean. What he knew of the real weaknesses of Africans he would withhold from these ignorant sceptics who didn't deserve to know.

"I see the wives of some of these black high commissioners. West African, I should think. Great big bottoms. They never pay their bills, but if I refused to take them on they'd complain to the minister."

"And they'd be quite right to complain," said Munday. He added, "But I agree—they should pay their bills."

"Tell them that," said the doctor, who had become noticeably less friendly. With a hint of impatience he said, "All right, let's have a look at you."

He examined Munday thoroughly, running the cold smooth disc of the stethoscope over his chest and back. Then he wrapped a thick rubber bandage around his bicep and inflated it with a bulb. Munday felt his forearm tingle and his hand go limp. The doctor took that off and asked Munday to squeeze his extended fingers. Munday squeezed.

"Harder," said the doctor.

Munday got a better grip on the doctor's fingers and clutched them tightly until his own fingers turned white.

"Fine," said the doctor. "Dowle said something about a stroke."

"It surprised me," said Munday. "I'd always been fit. It was after a large meal. I felt pretty ropey—had a pain here," he said, touching his chest. "My wife said I had awful color and I was gasping—couldn't get my breath."

"Sounds an awful lot like indigestion," said the doctor with scorn.

Munday winced. "Your friend Dowle called it a seizure."

"Sometimes they happen like that. It's hard to tell. Your blood pressure's a little above normal, and I thought I heard a slight flutter. But that's not so unusual."

"Father Dowle said something about a scar on one's heart."

" 'Knickers,' we used to call him," said the doctor, smiling, and the statement mocked at the mission doctor's diagnosis. He pointed at Munday. "The heart's a tough organ, you know—it's a great pumping device. There might have been a constriction, a kind of blockage. It can kill you by pinching off the blood flow, or the heart itself can repair the damage. It leaves scar tissue, that's all he meant. How do you feel? Any discomfort?"

"I don't sleep well," said Munday. "And lately I've felt pain, a burning sensation. I get short of breath. It seems to come with worry."

"Most ailments do," said the doctor. "But I'll book you for an electrocardiogram just the same."

Munday was going to speak of how Emma confirmed what he had feared in the black house, in that inhospitable village. But the doctor's dismissive manner put him off; at that distance, too, the black house and his fears seemed unreal—only a nearness of the dark corners, the liquid shadows, the rub of that unexampled smell at his nose alarmed him. Not near it, he could doubt it. In London it all seemed absurd, and this consultation seemed unnecessary, like a pain struggled with for days that disappears in a miraculous cure in the doctor's waiting room. His fears were hollow words, neutral and without urgency, simply a memory of terror grown quaint in a distance that allowed him to forget. It was the way he sometimes felt about Africa. Up close, as a resident in the Yellow Fever Camp, it excited so many particular fears and made his mind nimble but now he had trouble seeing it except as a formless dazzle of the exotic. The rest was forgotten; it wasn't lost: it was all, he knew, buried in his mind.

"What exactly do you worry about?"

"My work."

"What *is* your work?"

"At the moment—I'm being frank—nothing. An anthropologist studies people. I have none."

"Then you have nothing to worry about."

"You don't know," said Munday. His memory, his fear was of being hunted down, thrown out of the black house by a gulping phantom.

"Do you get depressed?"

It was that woman's question. Munday could not honestly say no. He said nothing.

"A lot of doctors would fill you up with pills. I'm against that," said the doctor. "Get a lot of fresh air, take exercise. Moderate drinking's all right. Do you smoke?"

"A cigar occasionally."

"You're lucky you can afford them. But watch what you eat. Diet's very important. My receptionist will give you a diet card. You can put your shirt on."

Buttoning his shirt, Munday said, "Father Dowle thought it was serious enough to send me home."

"I'm not saying it's not serious. You've got to take care of yourself. But you're better off here in any case, aren't you?"

"Here?"

"England," said the doctor.

A black house in a remote village, Munday wanted

to say, that's the only England I know now. But he said: "Father Dowle specifically said—"

"God," said the doctor. He walked over to the door and opened it. "I remember once when we were doing a urinalysis. There was a girl in the class—forget her name, not very pretty. Dowle slipped gold filings in her specimen when she wasn't looking, then showed her how to do a gold test on it. She thought he had taken leave of his senses, of course, but when it came out positive she was beside herself. 'Gold in my urine!' she said, and Dowle leaned over and said in a heavy brogue, 'They're laughing, but I'm thinking we should sink a shaft, my dear.' "

"That's ten guineas gone west," said Alec in the Wheatsheaf. He had been waiting at the end of a long bench by the wall, and seeing Munday enter he rose and greeted him loudly in Swahili, the way he always had on the verandah of the Mountains of the Moon Hotel on a Saturday morning. That was Munday's day in Fort Portal and he always spent it with Alec in continuous drinking, watching the road and the progress of the sun, until it was time to drive back to the camp, a long bumpy trip his drunkenness shortened by blurring. At the end of those afternoons, watching the fierce blood-red sunset, crimson chased with yellowing pink on the mountains, Alec used to say, "They're killing each other again in Bwamba."

Alec had managed a tea estate, and Munday in town for the week's supplies looked forward to the older man's company while Emma visited her friends and used the British Council Library. It was some relief from what after a year had become monotony in the village. Alec had sat, often jeering humorously with his cronies, and sometimes with the African girl who lived with him, whose picture appeared on the yellow tea wrapper—in the picture she was holding a similar packet of tea. Munday had never seen Alec in England; today he was alone in the crowded pub, looking burdened by his heavy suit and rather older:

a sunburn had always masked the boozy floridness of his face and without it the patches of bright veins only emphasized his pallor. But his voice was the old familiar trumpet and his shouted Swahili caused several people nearby to turn and listen, and Alec, noticing their curiosity, had continued. Only when Munday was seated beside him did Alec lower his voice and resume in English.

"You reminded me," Munday had said, and he told his story of having spoken Swahili to the porter at Waterloo. What had made him feel ridiculous in Emma's eyes impressed Alec, and Alec said, "So you're still the *bwana mkubwa*. That happened to me once in Marseilles. I opened my mouth to speak French and out came '*Kuja hapa!*' Baffled those frogs, I can tell you."

"My porter was insulted," said Munday.

"Served him right," said Alec. "The striking classes always have it their own way, what? Here, let me get you a drink." Alec pushed his way to the bar and returned with a pint. "A handle, right? I never forget a thing like that." He raised his glass and said, "Confusion to your enemies, death to mine! Alfred, it's like old times." Then Munday said he had just come from Harley Street, and Alec had made the remark about the ten guineas.

"He told me I was perfectly all right," said Munday.

"Maybe you are!"

"Maybe so," said Munday. "But I certainly don't feel it."

"You *are* looking a bit unbuttoned," said Alec. "I'm not surprised. I haven't felt at all well since I stepped off that plane. Not at all."

"Who's running the estate now?"

"My branch manager," said Alec, and he snorted at the contemptuous joke. "I hope it goes bust. They had no right nationalizing me. I was employing four hundred pickers—I've heard they're down to a hundred and fifty now. They haven't a bloody clue. And here I am." Alec looked disgustedly around the pub.

Munday didn't encourage him in his anger. He had
seen Alec aggrieved before, and aggrieved Alec
turned abusive, inviting witnesses to his pain. Munday
respected the vigor of Alec's settler opinions, though
he always steered him away from the talk about Africans, which strained Munday's loyalties. He wished to
keep them separate, the Africans in the village, Alec
and his cronies in Fort Portal. What he admired in
Alec was the knowledge he had—a subtle expression
of his attachment to the country—of the local flora, the
names of wild flowers and trees, the types of grass;
Alec made distinctions about landscape few Africans
made, and he remembered Alec drunk one night outside a bar he called "The Gluepot," stooping to the
sidewalk and plucking a flower and holding the frail
shaking blossom in his large fingers to identify it.
Munday had once considered writing an anthropol-
ogical study of people like Alec, the tribalism of the
post-war settlers, but he felt he might have lost them
as friends if he did that. Then his Saturdays would have
been empty.

"The last time I saw you wearing a suit was at the
Omukama's funeral," said Munday.

"Remember that?" said Alec. "That was a bash! All
those women screeching, those sort of round horns
they were blowing. The High Commissioner was there
—God, he hated me. I got pissed as a newt afterward
with Jack at The Gluepot." Alec shook his head and
smiled.

"Do you ever see him?"

"Jack? Not really. The last I heard he was applying
to London Transport. Imagine Jack driving a bus!"

"He can do better than that, surely," said
Munday, though he saw Jack clearly in the badge and
uniform of a bus driver.

"A foreman on a tea estate? There's nothing for
him here. He'll be bloody lucky to have a job at all."

"Emma's seeing Margaret this afternoon."

"Margaret! Wasn't she a dragon? Always reminded
me of that film actress whose name I can never think

of when I want to. I remember the night she came af- ter Jack. We were drinking late at the hotel—Jack had his African popsie. 'Excuse *me*,' I says and Margaret tore a strip off them both, told Jack she never wanted to see him again. I could hear her all the way out to the garden, swearing like a navvy. I'll never forget that."

"We were at the camp then."

"You missed all the fireworks," said Alec.

"Not exactly. Emma saw Margaret at Allibhai's that Saturday and got a blow by blow description."

"He got the boot, too, Allibhai. I expect I'll be seeing him in Southall one of these days."

"Do you live out that way?"

"Bleeding Ealing—not far off. I hate the place. Ever been there? It's a five-bob ride on the Under- ground, and I'm paying the earth for a one-room flat —that's what they call a bedsitter these days. Aus- tralians upstairs, always stamping on the floor, South Africans, you name it. Beside me there's a family of Maltese—kids all over the place, God only knows where they sleep. It's a right madhouse, toilets flush- ing, water running, radios playing. African bloke lives somewhere in the building. One day I saw him in the hall and says, '*Kitu gani?*' 'I am an engineering stu- dent,' he says and gets all shirty with me. Filthy? You have no idea. Leaves turds the size of conger eels in the pan for the next person to admire. The pubs are a disgrace, all noise and music, television sets, and these horrible little chaps in old clothes with se- quins pasted to their faces—queers, I fancy. Look at that bloke there."

Alec, breathless from his tirade, nodded at a tall young man in a black cape who was standing at the bar with his back to them. He held a glass of red wine in one and and in the other a chain leash. A wolf- hound with damp hair squatted panting beside him, its long tongue drooping and quivering.

"Ever see anything like it?" said Alec.

A woman entered the bar, striding past Munday

and Alec. She wore a bowler hat tipped back on her head, a fox-fur coat, a shirt and tie, striped trousers and black patent leather shoes; a young man, shorter than she, with long hair and a pale face and faded velvet jacket, held her hand. The woman ordered a whisky for herself, a beer for her companion. She talked loudly to the barman while her companion smoked.

"They're all on drugs," said Alec. "It's incredible how this country's gone downhill. Saw a couple of queers the other day having it off in Walpole Park. And the prices! I pay ten quid a week for a room barely big enough to swing a cat in."

"We're not paying a lot," said Munday, "but we're finding the country a bit of a strain. The cold toilet in the rented house. It gets so dark. And those country roads. It's all retired people."

"I keep thinking," said Alec, "there should be a pub somewhere in London where blokes like us from the *bundu* could go and talk over old times. Sort of club."

"Malcolm used to drink at The York Minster."

"Poor Malcolm. They say he looked awful toward the end. Where was that? Nairobi?"

"Mombasa."

"No, I'm sure it was Nairobbery." Alec smiled grimly. "I'd even settle for that."

Munday was jostled by a man with a briefcase. He said, "It's filling up."

"Packed. Where do they all come from?" Alec clamped his lips together. "If this was the hotel they'd all know me, everyone of them. Hi Alec."

"Have you thought of moving out of London? Maybe into the country?"

"I would, but"—Alec leered—"There's no *nyama* there." It was a settler euphemism, the Swahili word for meat, and he made it sound vicious.

"Is there any here?"

"Animals," said Alec. "Read the cards at the news agents! Notting Hill Gate's a good place for them.

'Dancing Lessons,' 'French Lessons,' 'Games Mistress,' and whatnot. Some are quite young, just getting started. I usually ring up 'Dusky Islander Seeks Unusual Position'—I always liked the black ones. They're not a patch on those Toro girls but at my age you can't be choosy. I'm past it—I admit it—but they don't mind." Alec sipped his beer and said, "We didn't know when we were well off. But it's too late for that now. It's all finished. We're stuck here. I suppose we should make the best of it."

Munday objected but said nothing. Alec, fifteen years his senior and with little education, was including him in his declaration of futility. He said, "I've been thinking of perhaps going back."

Alec said, "They'll kill you."

"I doubt it."

"Why don't you then?"

"My heart," said Munday.

"What a shame." Alec sounded as if he meant it.

"Money's a problem, too," said Munday. "I can't get another research grant unless I finish this book."

Alec smiled. "You're a liar," he said. "Emma's got pots of money. We all knew that."

Munday stared at him, but his stare turned sheepish. He said, "And I hated being a white man."

"I thought you rather fancied it."

"That's what I mean," said Munday.

"I never thought much about it myself."

"Maybe that's why you lasted so long."

"Twenty-three years," said Alec, and gulped the last of his beer.

Munday bought the next round of drinks, and when he returned with them Alec was singing softly,

> "Mary had a little lamb,
> It was *mzuri sana;*
> It put its nose up Mary's clothes
> Until she said, *'Hapana.'* "

"Reminiscing again?" said Munday.

"Remember that little road to Bundibugyo, over

the mountains? And the pygmies—what a nuisance they were, little buggers."

"In the Ituri Forest."

"The rain-forest! It was so dark there. The ferns were four feet high. We used to park there, Jack and I, and wait for the tea lorries from the Congo. It was easier for them to sell it on the black market than bring it by road to Leopoldville. They were a rum lot, those Congolese lorry drivers—spoke French worse than me. And that's saying something."

"I didn't realize you were involved in smuggling," said Munday, and he saw Alec brighten and purse his lips with pride.

"I kept quiet about it there—highly illegal, you know," said Alec. He winked. "I'm a smuggler from way back. Where'd you think I got all those crates of Primus Beer? That was a good beer. Not like this stuff—tastes like soap to me."

Alec told a smuggling story: a late night on the Congo border—a poker game in a candle-lit hut in the forest—the drivers showing up drunk with the tea chests and arguing about the price—Alec choosing the biggest African and knocking him to the floor—not a peep from the others—tossing them out "bodily" —and Munday was taken back to the lounge of the Mountains of the Moon Hotel; he was listening to Alec, who would soon start arguing endlessly about the merits of the "head shot" over the "heart shot." He was forgetting the Bwamba village, as far from him then as Four Ashes was now, and cheered by the old man's company and the long whine of the locusts. But he was not so absorbed in the story that he failed to see that what had brought him to London was what had made him look up Alec at the hotel on a Saturday; he saw his motive. The woman in the church hall had asked him how he stood it; he had not mentioned those weekends. He listened to Alec without enthusiasm and saw himself as a small anxious man, and Alec rather foolish, supporting each other. He *was* depressed—that woman's word—

for so much had changed, traveling to London would
be an inconvenient and expensive habit, and really
Four Ashes was farther from any relief than that
little village beyond the mountains.

"We' better eat something or we'll both be under
the table."

Alec had the macaroni and cheese, Munday the
hot-pot—the barman shoveled and clapped the meals
to the plates, cracking the spoon against their edges
to clear it—and both men sat, jammed together on
the wooden bench, balancing their plates on their
knees and raising their forks with great care. Alec
reminisced about the five-bob lunch at the Uganda
hotel, but in each reminder of the place Munday saw
a new aspect of the ritual he had invented for himself there, and he wanted to be away from Alec, to
return to the black house with Emma and verify his
fear. Pehaps he had imagined the panic; much of his
Africa seemed imaginary, and distant and ridiculous.

"I'll tell you who I *did* see," said Alec. "It was over
in Shepherd's Bush. I was waiting for a bus by the
green. Bloke walked by and I thought to myself, I
know *him*. It was Mills."

"Ah, Mills," said Munday. But he was thinking of
Alec, in the grayness of Shepherd's Bush, waiting for
a bus—the tea planter with four hundred pickers,
who had employed a driver, when few did, for his new
Peugeot sedan.

"The television man," said Alec. "Education for
the masses."

"I remember Mills."

"He remembered you," said Alec. "We had a
natter, he said to drop in sometime. I said fine, but I
doubt that I will. I never liked him. I liked *her*,
though."

"So did I."

"I should say you did!" Alec gave Munday a nudge.
He narrowed his eyes and said, "He never knew, did
he?"

"I hope not. It doesn't matter. It wasn't what you'd

call an affair. But she meant a lot to me. I wondered what happened to her."

"Like everyone else," said Alec. "They're all here, bleeding to death."

"Did he say he lived in Shepherd's Bush?"

"No, I think he said Battersea. He works in Shepherd's Bush—that's where the studios are. You thinking of paying him a visit?"

"Not him," said Munday. "But I'd like to see Claudia."

"Drinking still makes me randy, too," said Alec, and he laughed.

"I had thought I might go over to the British Museum. And I was planning to leave a message for a Bwamba chap in Mecklenburg Square. I don't know," said Munday, pausing. "If Claudia's home—"

"They're in the book, and the phone's over there," said Alec. "Give her a ring. I'll get the next round." He stood up and gave Munday's shoulder a friendly push. "Get *on* with it."

When Munday came back to the bench, Alec said, "I watched you phoning. It remended me of that night at the hotel—remember?—when Emma was in Kampala and old Mills on safari. 'Who's he ringing?' I wondered—you were so damned secretive! And then I saw your car parked in the Mills's driveway that Sunday morning."

"She's home," said Munday. "She invited me over for tea."

"Are you going?"

"I'd like to see her again."

"I remember that night so well."

"That was the first time," said Munday. "There weren't many others."

"Mind what you do." There was pleasure in Alec's face. "It's like old times," he said. "Wish I had Rosie here."

"I won't do much," said Munday. "She said her daughter's due home from school—little Alice."

"Jesus, now I remember the story. She saw you in

bed with the old lady and said, 'You're not my daddy!' "

"Where are you off to?" asked Munday quickly.

"Notting Hill Gate for me. Dusky Islander, I expect," said Alec jauntily. "Some bitch in white garters in an unmade bed in a basement flat to insult my body—you should try it sometime, Alfred old man." He sighed. "Then I'll go back to my room in the monkey house and watch television. That's all I do. I'm getting more like them every day."

"I'd better be off," said Munday.

"How are things up-country?" Alec was stabbing his umbrella into the carpet. "Emma her old sketching self?"

"She's fine, sends you her regards," said Munday, but he thought, *up-country*: it was the way Alec had always referred to the Yellow Fever Camp on a Saturday night. But this time they would part in a cold London drizzle, Alec to his bedsitter, Munday to Four Ashes.

Outside the pub Alec held his collar together at his throat and looked at the street and the dripping brown sky. He said, "This fucking city, and none of them know it."

"You should come down and see us some time," said Munday.

"No fear," said Alec. "But give Emma my love—I still have her picture of my estate. The pluckers. The gum trees. That hill."

"She'll be pleased."

Alec leaned closer, breathing beer; he said with feeling, "Tea's a lovely crop, Alfred."

The walked in different directions, but met again by accident a few minutes later near the Leicester Square tube station. Alec was walking up Charing Cross Road. He smiled at Munday and called out, *"Kwaheri!"*—and people turned—and then stooping in the rain and still gripping his collar he continued on his way, trudging into the raincoated crowd of shoppers.

Munday walked by the house several times, preparing himself to meet her by calling up her face and rehearsing a conversation. He almost went away. His interest in seeing her, encouraged by Alec, had dwindled as soon as Alec had left him; now it had nearly vanished and there was moving him only a youthful muscle of curiosity. In the taxi he had felt a jumping in his stomach, that pleasurable tightness that precedes sex, but he had stopped the taxi on the other side of Chelsea Bridge so that he could cut across the park, and the pleasure left him. He saw two black boys, running through the trees, chasing each other with broom handles, skidding over a landscape where they didn't belong. Their flapping clothes annoyed him. His feet were wet. He resented his fatigue; the speed of the taxi, the noise and fumes of the city had tired him, he was unused to those assaults on his senses, and already he felt that the trip to London was wasted. His mid-afternoon hangover drugged him like a bad meal. He wanted to lie down somewhere warm and sleep.

It had not been hard for him to find the house. It was prominent, announcing its color in a long terrace of bay-windowed three-story brick houses on a road just off the south side of the park. The road stretched to a lighted corner, where more blacks, whose idleness he instantly resented, lingered under a street lamp. The conversion of the Mills's house reproached the other gloomy house fronts. The brick had been painted white, there was a yellow window box, and the door was bright yellow; the iron gate was new and so was the brass knocker and the mat on the top step. In the little plot in front there was a square of clipped grass and a small bare tree: on one limb a florist's tag spun.

He tapped the knocker and waited. He was trembling; his heart worked in troubled thumps—he always heard it when he was nervous, and hearing it increased his nervousness.

The door opened on a woman's thin face. "Yes?"

"Is Mrs. Mills at home?" Munday spoke sharply to the stranger.

The question bewildered the woman. She said, "What is it you want?" And then she smiled and said, "Alfred?" and flung open the door.

"Claudia," he said in a weak expression of surprise. He did not dare to look closer. He almost said, *Is that you?*

He could not hide his embarrassment, his kiss was ungainly, he bumped her chin. He wanted to stare at her, to compare her with his memory, she was so thin and sallow, and her hair was brown. It had been blond. He was disappointed—in her, in himself; was deeply ashamed, a shame so keen he heard himself saying, "I'm sorry—" Then he was moving into the lounge and talking, apologizing for being early, explaining the train he had to catch, complimenting her on the decoration, the bookshelves, the chrome and marble coffee table. She was naming stores, Liberty, Heals, Habitat, as he named objects of furniture. He avoided her eyes and now he was talking about the carpet—it was orange—but his eyes were fixed on the narrow bones showing in her feet. He wished he had not come; he wanted to go.

"And a color television," he was saying. It was on, a large screen swimming with yellow and blue, and the deep orange face of a talking man. He felt obliged, having made the comment, to watch it. The man was talking very slowly, as if to a child, and tearing a newspaper into strips.

"Not ours," said Claudia. "It's on loan. The BBC gives them to all their senior staff."

"I've never seen one before," said Munday, and at a loss for words he went on watching the program. Now a small-breasted girl was singing a nursery rhyme in a halting way and waltzing foolishly with a stuffed bear.

"Do sit down, Alfred." Claudia picked up a glass. "Are you sure you want tea or would you like something stronger? I've been drinking gin ever since you rang—for courage!"

"Tea's fine," said Munday. He sat in a chair which had a spoon-shaped seat. He swiveled awkwardly.

"I was so surprised to hear from you."

"Really? I thought you might have seen my letter to *The Times*."

"We get the *Guardian*," said Claudia. "Not that I ever read it. That Northern Ireland business is so awful. Have you been back long?"

"A little over a month—we're in the country. Dorset."

"Dorset's lovely," said Claudia. "I can't remember the last time I saw you. Was it—?"

"Years ago. That party," said Munday. "At Margaret's."

"Poor Margaret."

"Jack's driving a bus."

"He deserves to," said Claudia, pouring herself another gin. "They ruined my theory, you know, breaking up like that in Africa. That ludicrous court case."

"What theory is this? You never told me."

"About divorces. As an anthropologist you might be interested," said Claudia. She sipped her gin. "Not very complicated. It's just that everyone says that marriages go to pieces in the tropics. That's a myth. Why should they break up there? There's no housework to do, the kids are off your hands, no worries. It's like a holiday. I don't know where these writers get the idea it's such a great strain on a marriage—that scene at the club where the outraged husband throws his drink into the lover's face and says, 'You've been seeing my wife.' That sort of rubbish."

"I've seen it happen, but not in those precise words."

"It never happens! No one cares. Do you remember when we did those Maugham plays? 'Sybil, have you betrayed me?' and all that?"

"The Uganda Players," said Munday.

"What a farce," said Claudia. "And that pansy di-

rector—I forget his name. Those plays made me laugh.
I don't know why I joined that silly drama group.
Emma wasn't in it, was she?"

"She had her painting to occupy her," said Munday.
"And we were at the camp."

"You lived so damned far from town," said Claudia.
She smiled. "I'll bet she's not doing any painting
here."

"How do you know?"

"I know. She's doing housework, going to the laun-
derette, shopping, cooking. What a bore. I know—
that's what *I* do. That's my theory—marriages don't
break up when people go to the tropics, they break up
here, when they get back. There's a name for it."
Claudia snapped her fingers.

"Culture shock," said Munday.

"Right, right—culture shock. There's none of it in
Africa, but there's masses here."

"I suppose I'm having a bit of it myself," said
Munday. It slipped out, and he was angry with himself for having revealed it: she might ask why. But
she hadn't heard, she was still talking.

"I'm not saying that Martin and I are thinking
of separating. We're muddling along well enough. But
it's tough sometimes. You'll see. You haven't been in
England for a long time, Alfred. Marriage is hard
here."

"It's hard everywhere, let's face it."

"No, not in Africa—it's easy there," she said.
"Everything is easy there, isn't it?"

"Is it?"

"You know it is!" she said. "But here—it's part of
my theory—every married couple is on the verge of
divorce."

"You don't say." He could see she was drunk; he
wanted to calm her, and leave.

"You see, marriage is grounds for divorce," she
said. "Marriage as we know it. Young people don't
even think about it any more."

"So the younger sociologists say," said Munday.

"But marriage has never been sacred among the Bwamba. They're always swapping partners. I worked it out once—the divorce rate among the Bwamba is twenty times that of the English. As for adultery—they simply choose a woman and stick a spear in the dirt in front of her hut to show she's occupied. The husband won't interrupt."

"Did you bring your spear with you today?" She laughed coarsely.

Munday said, "I've got a train to catch."

"You and your Africans," she said. "Didn't you get sick of them? *I'm* sick of them. I'm not a racist, I'm just sick of them—seeing them, hearing about them. They're always on television, and Battersea's full of them. Why don't people ever talk about the Chinese? There are more Chinese than there are Africans, and there's more to talk about." Claudia had finished her drink. She licked the lemon peel and said, "The Head Prefect at Alice's school is an African. That's why they made him Head Prefect."

"He's actually a West Indian," said Alice, entering the room with a tray. She looked at Munday and said hello with a coolness that seemed so calculated he could not reply immediately. He thought: *She knows me.*

"Just put it down there," said Claudia.

"You're a big girl now," said Munday at last.

"Sixteen," said Claudia. "Though she thinks she's a few years older."

"Mummy, please."

"She hates me," said Claudia. "It's a phase."

Alice was attractive; she wore denim slacks that fit her high buttocks tightly, and her hair was long, in a single rope of braid, with the blondness that had gone out of her mother's. She poured the tea and brought Munday his cup and a plate with a slice of fruitcake on it. Munday smiled, but she did not respond. She maintained that sceptical, knowing look, which was an adult frown of accusation, worn deliberately, Munday guessed, for her mother's former lover. It put Munday on his guard, but disturbed him, because it rubbed at the memory of his lust. All the old forgotten feeling he had had for the mother, who inspired nothing in him but a vague pity and shame for the woe in her eyes, came awake in the presence of the pretty daughter, for whom he felt a twinge of desire. And that awakening was enough of a reminder of his lust for the mother to make him uneasy.

He said, "I have to be at Waterloo—"

The phone rang in another part of the house.

"Excuse me," said Claudia, and went to answer it.

Alice was seated cross-legged on the floor, her hand lightly resting on her crotch. "Where's your hat?" she asked. "You used to have a funny hat."

"I still have it somewhere," said Munday. "You *do* have a good memory."

"I remember you," she said. Her stare was as solemn as any adult's.

Munday looked away. He had seen the same face at the bedroom door. He said, "How do you like living in London?"

Alice said, "Mummy fucks my friends."

Munday was shocked by the simple way she said the brutal sentence, but managed to say, "Oh? And do you disapprove of that?"

"It embarrasses me," said Alice, as simply as before.

"Yes, I suppose it does," said Munday. "But don't be too hard on her. I mean, don't judge her too harshly. Maybe you'll see when you're her age that there's not that much love around. And it can be a frightening thing—" He stopped, at the girl's stare, her look of total innocence; he felt he could only disappoint her if he went on.

She lifted the plate. "Would you like another piece of fruitcake?"

"I'm fine," said Munday. But he was shaken, his mouth was dry. He took a sip of tea and said, "I must go—I'll have to find a taxi."

"I'm sure mummy would love to take you to the station."

"That won't be necessary," said Munday.

"I'll just have half," said Alice, reaching for the cake. "I shouldn't—I'm supposed to be dieting." She broke a piece and ate it, taking large girlish chews. "Because I'm on the pill."

"Then you *are* a big girl," said Munday, and now he saw her as only insolent, made so by the mother.

"Mummy doesn't think so."

"That was Martin," said Claudia, entering the room. "He's going to be late." And as if she had guessed at the conversation that had been going on, intuited it from the silent man and girl, she said accusingly, "What have you been talking about behind my back?"

"Doctor Munday was telling me about his African tribes," said Alice, gathering the plates.

"That's right," said Munday, astonished at the girl's invention. In that girl was a woman, but a corrupt one.

"You're not going?" Claudia said, seeing Munday stand.

"I'll miss my train if I don't hurry," said Munday. He kissed Claudia at the door; she held on and made him promise to come again. She pressed against him, and he was nearly aroused, because he was looking past her at the girl with the tray on one arm walking through the room on long dancer's legs, showing her tight buttocks as she picked up an ashtray, straightened a lampshade.

"You haven't forgotten," said Claudia, feeling him harden. He pulled her head to his shoulder and watched Alice slowly leaving the room, tossing the loose rope of her hair. Then he said, "No."

Waiting with Emma at the platform gate in Waterloo Station, Munday heard "Hello there," and felt a tug on his sleeve.

He turned and greeted the stranger in a polite way, and then he remembered the face and said nothing more. It was the tall man from the lecture who had contradicted him.

"You're Munday," said the man. "I thought I recognized you. Up for the day?"

"Yes."

"Shambles, isn't it?" They were in a crowd, pressing toward a gate, where a conductor stood clipping tickets.

Inside the gate the man said, "We've got to be up front—Crewkerne's got a rather short platform."

"I know," said Munday. "We've been this way before."

"Will you join me?" The man was smiling at Emma.

"That would be nice," said Emma.

"We haven't been introduced," said the man. "My name's Awdry."

He shook Munday's hand and they made their way up the platform and boarded the train. Awdry slid open the door of a first-class compartment. He said, "This one looks as good as any."

"I'm afraid we're in second," said Munday, relieved that he would not have to endure the man's company for three hours, and embarrassed at having to admit he had a cheaper ticket.

"Oh, what a shame," said Awdry. "You're way down there." He pointed down the passage with his umbrella.

"Perhaps we'll see you in the village," said Emma.

"I hope so," said Awdry. "I've got a crow to pluck with your husband." He turned to Munday and said genially, "Your letter—'confused observations of a generation of misfit District Commissioners'—all that." He laughed. "I was livid when I read it, but I think I can discuss it sensibly now."

"That's good to hear," said Munday.

"I'll be in touch with you—you're up at the Black House still, I take it? Say, you'd better get a move on or you won't find a seat!"

They didn't find a seat. The train was filled with returning commuters, who had taken all the seats while they had been standing talking to Awdry. Munday and Emma stood in a drafty passage outside a second-class compartment as far as Basingstoke. Inside the overbright compartment they drowsily read the evening papers, which were full of news of an impending miners' strike; and when, at Salisbury, the compartment emptied, and they were alone, Emma spoke of Margaret: she was doing part-time secretarial work, she was seeing a man, she had put on weight.

"Alec is at the end of his tether," said Munday. He made no mention of Claudia, but heard repeatedly Alice's cheerless phrase about her mother, and saw the young girl in the room, dancing past him as he embraced Claudia.

"What did the doctor have to say?"

"Him? He examined me, said to take it easy," said Munday. "He was a bit of a fool. Kept going on about Father Dowle."

Emma put the paper down and opened her novel to the first page. She flexed the book and began to read.

Munday said, "He told me my heart's in a rather dicky state. That scar business. Blood pressure's way up."

Emma looked at him closely, "Did he say it was serious?"

"I'm not well, Emma," Munday said. "Not well at all."

From the lighted carriage the night was black, but at Crewkerne they saw the full moon, and across the road from the black house, in the moonlight, a field of sleeping cows.

10

But even then, returning after a tiring day in London, their eyes heavy, their feet burning, hungry and yet unable to eat, they saw the house as no more familiar to them than it had been on that first day. Munday kicked open the gate with a clang; now he was sure of his feelings. It was in darkness, his England, all he could lay claim to; it was—everyone said it and he agreed—the Black House. The day in London taught him that he could not live there, cast up like the others whose only friends were those who had been similarly reduced in size by their years in Africa. He had expected more, but he had stayed away too long: no one was waiting for him. He was resigned to the Black House. He went inside. The stove had gone out, the rooms were cold, the dampness had crept back leaving on the crumble of its streaks a smell of mold. It was too late to make a fire, and without hot water for the bottles they slept between cold sheets.

They were not less afraid of the house, and they were conscious of an awful demeaning failure. They continued in the house hopelessly, habituated to their fears, with the sense that each room held the traces of a person who had left moments before—the suggestion of moving cones of air, the dying vibrancy of a word just whispered. The haunting left them with the uncertain mood of a sickness, but haunting was not the word they used; it was not a physical fear of attack—an amorphous jelly ghost rushing at them with cold arms—but rather a sense, numbing their minds, that they had put an intruder to flight and were witnessing the last vagrant clues of its presence. Emma believed she had seen a woman at the window, and so Munday had begun to see something feminine in those traces. The woman, ghostly inhabitant of the house, was like an aspect of his heart, and his ache told him that she shared much of what he himself feared. He was linked to her, more than to Emma, and when, entering the house after the day in London, Emma said, "Someone's been here," he did not dispute it, it was what he felt, and he knew what Emma never would: that it was a trespasser surprised, someone like him, restless, perhaps sick and very lonely, imploring him to believe so that he might see her.

But he saw her only in his dreams, which were half of Africa, green walls of bamboo pipes with feathery branches on mountain roads, banana groves hanging thickly with clusters of fruit, heavy red blossoms, and of the warning motion of blacks in high elephant grass; the heat that rose from the slippery decaying earth, and blue four-inch dragonflies in the papyrus swamps where hairy plants choked the waterways and odd huge birds suddenly took flight, beating the air with clumsily hinged wings; but he belonged there, he had his own canoe and two solemn black paddlers with saw-toothed daggers at their waists. In some of the dreams he was swimming and speechless, and plunged in smothering foliage towards a girl-woman with the softest thighs, who showed him the flesh in her mouth as red as the blossoms. The dreams aroused him and denied him rest. He had one the night of his return from London.

The confusion over the charwoman followed a few days later.

Useless in his study, brooding among his notes and weapons—he bitterly resented the theft of the dagger—Munday saw Emma's housekeeping as a possible source of her unhappiness. She was sad, and busy, and her work reproached his inactivity. What she did was drudgery, and the cleaning and cooking left her exhausted. There was much more to do, strenuous chores like washing the spattered windows, beating the rugs, cleaning the oven. Munday did not want to do them himself, so he could not insist that Emma do them. They remained neglected. Claudia's comment ("She's doing housework") had made Munday see Emma at the sink, heaving the coal scuttle, riddling the fire in the Rayburn; he watched her examining her reddened hands or pushing a wisp of hair out of her eyes; he noticed that she borrowed books from the Bridport library and returned them unread.

Once, looking through the back pages of *The Times,* Munday said, "There's a job going in Algiers. Looks interesting. But the salary's quoted in *dinars.*"

Emma sighed. "What about your book?"

"I could work on it in the mornings," he said. "Do a little teaching in the afternoons."

"You could do that here." She was polishing the brass fire tongs; she didn't look up.

He said, "I think we need someone around to help you out."

"You don't think I'm capable of doing the housework?"

"I hate to see you looking so tired at the end of the day," he said. Emma went on polishing. He said, "I'll bet there are lots of people in the village who'd be glad of a chance to earn a few pounds."

The advertisement in the Bridport paper, a weekly, appeared that Friday. They had a dozen phone calls, most of them preceded by rapid pips, inquiring whether child-minding or cooking was involved. Emma explained the duties and invited all the callers for interviews. But only three women came. The first was old and inquisitive and said she had enjoyed Munday's talk at the church hall. She was not so much interested in the job, she said, as eager to meet someone who'd seen a bit of the world. She warned Emma to be careful whom she hired for the job; there were so many layabouts in the village and they were so undependable. She told a story about one: Munday had heard it before, told by one of Alec's cronies of a Bwamba herdsman he had employed. She said the only way to get things done was to do them yourself. She had learned that in Bromley, which was her home until her husband had retired. Before she left she sold Emma a raffle ticket for the Christmas Draw.

The next woman, Mrs. Branch, was young. She came with her sister-in-law who, confusingly, did most of the talking, asked all the questions and stated the fee; it became clear to Munday after some while that it was not she who was applying for the job, but the big worried girl with her, who sat twisting her handbag in her lap and looking anxiously around the kitchen. They left abruptly, and from the window Munday saw them walking down the road, deep in conversation.

It was dark when Mrs. Seaton came. Munday was at The Yew Tree, borrowing a hoe-shaped poker for cleaning the soot and dust from the Rayburn. Emma told him what had happened. She had been taken by surprise; there was no warning, no sound of a bus or car. The brass knocker sounded and Mrs. Seaton was at the door, shaking the wet from her umbrella. In spite of her mysterious arrival she was business-like and looked capable. She accepted the cup of tea the others had refused and she said she had done similar work for the summer people. It was she who raised the subject of money. And she was candid: her husband was out of work, he was on the dole, they were having trouble making ends meet.

"We'll be in touch with you," Emma had said, and the woman left as she had come, stepping into the darkness and the sea-mist that glowed in a drifting nimbus around the ouside lamp.

"She sounds just the ticket," said Munday, and the next day, which was sunny and cold, the kind of bright cloudless day that seemed to follow a dreary wet one, they walked the half mile into the village to find her and tell her she could begin work immediately.

Bowood House, like The Yew Tree, was not in the village of Four Ashes; with some other cottages —The Thistles, Rose Dene, Ladysmith, and Aleppo —it comprised a nameless hamlet on the village's fringe. Four Ashes (one of the original trees still stood) had some local fame as a place of great charm, but the charm was all on the main road, Hogshill Street: in the market cross and the several antique shops with plates and prints in the windows; in the chemist's, White's, where in his first week Munday had bought a bottle of Friar's Balsam for his cold; in Watkins' Bakery, the two tea shops, the sweet shops, all severely old-fashioned; in Pines ("High-Class Groceries & Quality Vegetables") which displayed in a glass case whole wheels of cheeses, and sold Stilton in stone jars, unusual spices, and freshly ground coffee; in Lloyd's of Four Ashes, the men's outfitter: and in the hotel, The White Hart, a former coaching inn, which retained the look of another century in its heavily rendered and whitewashed front, its archway and courtyard and mullioned windows. The church, St. Alban's, on the crest of Hogshill Street, had a Norman font and some thirteenth-century stonework, and a vast yew tree in the cemetery which spread itself over the deeply pitted gravestones.

But Mrs. Seaton's house was at the back of the village, in an unexpectedly crowded settlement of new and old terrace houses and cottages—the old ones leaning into the narrow street. There was a tiny pub, with a swinging sign, "The Eight Bells," on one corner, and a low block of new council flats stood at the end of the street, a dead end, next to a coal yard.

"I had no idea the village was this big," Emma said. She saw another street, packed with houses, running off Mrs. Seaton's, and like Mrs. Seaton's hidden from the main road.

"Funny little place," said Munday. He knocked on the scarred door.

A boy of about ten opened the door. He wore an undershirt and pajama bottoms. He stared at Munday.

"Hello," said Munday. "We're looking for Mrs. Seaton."

The boy shook his head. "Not here," he said softly, and started to close the door.

"Hold on," said Munday. "When will she be back?"

"She don't live here."

"Where *does* she live?"

Again the boy shook his head.

"What's your name?" Munday asked.

"Peter Tuck."

"Is your mother at home?"

The boy nodded, jerking his head forward.

"Tell her I'd like to have a word with her."

The boy shut the door.

Munday whispered to Emma, "I think he's a bit simple."

The door opened. A middle-aged woman stood there with a baby on her hip. The woman's fatigue looked like suspicion. The baby plucked at a button on her dress.

"Mrs. Tuck?"

"Yes." She lifted the child and held it tightly to her shoulder, shielding herself with it.

"We're looking for a Mrs. Seaton," Munday said. "We were told she was at this address, and—"

"Over there," said the woman. She pointed across the street at a house with a green door.

"Thanks very much," said Munday. "We must have misheard the number."

"Welcome," said the woman, and shut the door.

Munday was knocking on the green door when Emma said, "I didn't mishear the number—she wrote it down. Look." The penciled address was distinct on the scrap of paper.

An old lady answered the door. "What do you want?" she asked.

Munday told her.

"I'm Mrs. Seaton," said the woman. She wore a frayed sweater—it was buttoned to her neck—and she carried a large wooden spoon.

"Perhaps a relative of yours," said Munday. "Your son's wife? You're not the woman we're looking for."

"My children are dead. There's only Sam."

Munday laughed, but without pleasure. He said, "This is all very confusing."

The woman looked closely at Munday. She said, "Are you from the Water Board?"

"No," said Munday. He explained his errand and showed the woman the scrap of paper with the address written on it.

She said, "That's over there."

"They sent us over here."

"I'm sorry," said the woman. There was a cry from within the cottage, an old man's voice cracking with impatience. The woman said to Munday, "Sam."

"Is there any other family by the name of Seaton in the village?"

"Used to be. This was years ago. But they went to Australia." The woman was closing the door. "Bye now—mind how you go."

Munday said, "Are we losing our minds?"

Emma closed her eyes.

"Looks like we're stuck with that Mrs. Branch," he said.

Emma called her by her first name, Pauline; Munday called her "Branch," and sometimes "Mrs. B." She began work the week before Christmas, and her first chores were those hard ones, the neglected windows, the rugs that had lain unbeaten for over a month, the jumble of boots and walking sticks in the back passage that needed sorting out. Mrs. Branch had been nervous in the interview; occupied with housework she was calm, single-minded, but apt to overdo things. She washed the windows in the shed and she beat the hall carpet so hard she broke the rope on which it was suspended. Munday took an interest in her and watched her closely, but his unfriendly humor only bewildered her.

He saw that she carried envelopes of artificial sweetener in her handbag, for the tea she drank in the middle of the morning. She explained that she was dieting.

"Then you won't want a lunch hour, will you," said Munday, masking his irony with briskness.

"Sir?" Mrs Branch was uncertain. She gave Emma a slow puzzled look.

"Don't pay any attention to him," said Emma. "He's joking."

"I was wondering," said Mrs. Branch, and seemed glad to return to scraping soot from the stovepipe.

She had a full round face and grew hot when she worked, and heavy arms, and when she sat she pushed her hands together, hugging herself with her elbows to hide her bulk. She wore high leather boots with her plain clothes, and eye make-up—green lids and black streaks on her plucked eyebrows. She said she was twenty-three, but she had the careworn movements and sighing obedience of a woman twice that age. After a day or two Munday knew her habits. She was noisy, and appeared bewildered when Munday called attention to her noise. She banged pots and slammed doors and dragged chairs back and forth on the hard kitchen floor. She walked through the house setting her feet down as if she were dropping bricks. Munday detested her boots and told Emma that she knew how to go up the wooden stairs on her heels. He said angrily, "Listen to her!" She played the radio and murmured to the music, and when she was vacuuming she turned the radio louder so that she could hear it over the racket of her cleaning. Munday, calling out *"Branch!"* put a stop to the radio, and he urged her to be quieter. She said,

"Yes, Doctor" in the broad accent that Munday associated with ridicule.

But she was useful, she was of the village, a local. She brought them news; of deaths and accidents, of animals she had seen flattened on the road on her way to work. She was their only link with the village, so after the first few days Munday approached her with inquiries, about his stolen dagger and the mysterious Mrs. Seaton—but she said she couldn't help him. She was cheerful and came each morning with a weather report; her predictions were usually accurate. Apart from her talk of the weather she said very little.

Munday refused to eat with her, but he still attempted to engage her in conversation. She let it drop that she had been born in Toller Porcorum. Munday said, "Tell me a little bit about it." It was from Mrs. Branch that Munday learned the pronunciation of local place-names, Beaminster, Puncknowle, and Eype. And Munday often found himself (holding up a pair of secateurs or an axe from the shed) asking, "What do you call this?" Like the Africans whom he had also questioned in this way, she was at first suspicious of his interest in details of puzzling insignificance.

He asked her how she heated her cottage and was not satisfied until she described every stage of the procedure; why did she butter the end of the bread loaf before she sliced it? How had she met her husband? How long had they courted? Why had they moved to Four Ashes? He led up to intimate questions by telling her of Bwamba customs. "In Africa, he said, "if a pregnant girl marries a man who is not the father of her child she has the option of strangling it at birth."

"Well, I wouldn't know about that," she said, but talked more easily of childbirth then. She had two children, she said, and would bring them around one day for Munday to see.

"That won't be necessary," said Munday. He went

on to tell her of the Bwamba marriage ritual, the groom's brothers joyously pissing on a stool, the groom placing his hands in it and then the naked bride sitting on his hands; the consummation that was virtually rape, and the brothers' freedom in sharing the wife later. Simply, he described the patrilineal society. Mrs. Branch was outraged, but talked about her own marriage. Munday established contact with her, and though his questions were intimate his manner was academic, and he maintained an interviewer's distance. He saw that she enjoyed being questioned about herself; she was discovering with curious surprise that her life, seemingly so dull, was worthy of attention and even important to this stranger.

"We call that a rake," she said one day in answer to a question of Munday's. He threw the tool aside and went into the house.

On her fourth day she arrived early, before eight, in the morning darkness that was like night. Coming down to breakfast Munday saw her seated at the kitchen table, tapping a small envelope of sweetener into her coffee.

"Morning, Branch," he said, but nothing more. He had no conversation at breakfast—breakfast being for him not so much a meal as a way of preparing himself for surroundings his sleepless nights seemed to rearrange: breakfast was over when he was calm. He was slightly antagonized by the girl seated at his table while he was standing. He would not join her. He decided to stall for time by reading the paper. But it was not on the table and not outside the door.

"They haven't brought my *Times*," he said.

"I put it on the chair," said Emma, who was at the Rayburn, frying Munday's egg.

"Oh, here it is, Doctor," said Mrs. Branch. "I were sitting on it." She handed it to him with an apology.

Munday tossed it on the sideboard. The paper was crushed, rounded to a template the shape of her bottom. He could not read it; he could not bear to put his fingers on it or have it near his food. He went

into the living room and sat brooding until he heard
the bangings and clatter that told him Mrs. Branch
had begun her work.

While she worked, padding busily from room to
room on the stocking feet Munday demanded of her,
Munday sat at his desk in the study. Mrs. Branch had
restored a superficial order to the house and Munday
felt some of his solitude return. The balance was Mrs.
Branch's, for it was a house that needed a servant
and Munday had come to depend on houseboys; the
house was too large to be run by a man and wife; a
marriage could not fill it or make it work. Mrs.
Branch did more than clean; she aided the marriage,
she justified the size of the house—without her he
sometimes felt the house would have been insupportable. Emma's cleaning had made him guilty,
Mrs. Branch's efforts gave him freedom—the attraction of any good servant—and allowed him time
to think. Soon, without using his notes he started to
write—an introductory paragraph, a page of description, then several. It was the way he imagined it would
be, working by a country window, writing in long-
hand, the fan-heater whirring at his feet, his privacy
secured by watchful women.

But it was a false start. He had groped in his
mind for that distant landscape and tried to be faithful to the memory he had kept of those people who
lived in the steamy exposed swamps beyond the
mountains, in huts they knocked down regularly every
two years. Talking with Alec in the Wheatsheaf, he
had seen them clearly and remembered so much. He
wrote eagerly, his writing flowed; but the eagerness
and the speed was deceptive. He reread his pages
and the words capsized his heart, for in every word
he wrote were the dripping oaks, the gorse and
broom around the Black House in Four Ashes, the
mood of that particular day when they had been
trapped in the cow pasture and seen in the fading
light those pathetic boys carrying empty bottles, and
later his sight of the two dead dogs under the canvas.

He crumpled the pages and began again to describe Africa; but he described an English day, withered leaves, the pale winter sun. Fear.

This new place, a looming vision, drove out all the others—the African scenes which his familiarity only blurred—and it even banished all his earlier memories of England, everything except childhood fear and childhood loneliness. At his desk he saw a young boy with inky slender fingers reading Malinowski in a South London library and guiltily looking up from time to time at men holding newspapers fixed to bamboo rods who he believed could read his deepest thoughts and who despised his ambition. The image of that frightened boy stayed in his mind, and it was as if in the forty years that lay between that afternoon and this, nothing had happened. The years had passed but every detail of experience was lost to him. And he was sorry, because the boy in the library who had imagined himself in a canoe in the western Pacific, and living among naked savages, and famous for it, could not know that the years would fall away and not even all the intervening failure was preparation enough for a return to this room and more fears and a sadder image of himself.

He was distressed to see Emma repeating his disappointment in her painting. She worked from sketches she had made in the back garden. Her colors floated; the pictures were indistinct, a child's primitive vision of earth and sky. Attempting to paint over her mistakes she made the mistakes stand out or else muddied them with greater error. Munday could see that outwardly the Black House resembled the African bungalow: Emma was painting, the servant was cleaning, he was going through his notes. They had never spoken about it, but what had sustained them in Africa was the thought that if they failed there they could always return home. Now they were home, there was nowhere else to go and it seemed there was nothing more for him.

His sense of the fugitive woman in the house grew

fainter with Mrs. Branch's cleanings. He had both regretted and longed for that third presence; he had anticipated the event of her appearing, revealing herself to him and uncovering his memory. He yearned for a great passion, a great idea, a future to complete and release him. He sat in his study, simulating work, to prepare himself for inspiration, believing that his memory was like a dark room which the eye of his imagination would accustom itself to. He labored without motion or progress. He heard sounds and looked up to see the awkward girl at the study door. In irritation he said, "Yes, Branch, what is it?"

"We call this the shortest day of the year," she said. And softly: "I thought you might want to know."

"Thank you," he said.

On Christmas they heard church bells ringing on all sides, in villages sunken from view; huntsmen passed the house, and children in new boots. They exchanged presents, a tie, a scarf, and new diaries for the coming year. There were distant horns, the hunt swarmed in the back pasture and the foxhounds yapped through the afternoon. They talked of going out for a walk, but it was cold; they stayed indoors and between them finished the bottle of amontillado.

11

"AWDRY," said Munday, putting the receiver into its cradle. "He's invited us over to his New Year's Eve thrash."

Emma removed her reading glasses before she spoke. She said, "Tomorrow?"

"Someone must have backed out."

"Still, it might be fun. I hope I can find something to wear."

But Munday was saying to Mrs. Branch, "What do you know about Mr. Awdry?"

Mrs. Branch smiled and paused, and for a few moments she nodded, considering slowly what she would say. It was a habit of response she had picked up since Munday had begun questioning her, and Munday felt that her delay, miming reflection, was a purposeless show of self-importance he had encouraged in her. She said, "They say that in the manor they had these painters doing pictures on the ceiling—lying on their backs they was." She shook her head at the madness of it. "Keeps his dishes locked up in a safe, and he's got this little gold bell on the table, very expensive, that he rings when he calls the cook—that's Mrs. Hosmer. He gave her twenty pounds at Christmas. He's posh, is Mr. Awdry, but they say he's ever so kind."

"I'm sure," said Munday. He doubted that, and the late invitation annoyed him; but he was glad to have it.

Lewesdon Manor was at the end of a long gravel drive lined with boxwood hedges whose fullness and size told the age of the house. In its facade of warm floodlit stone, made mild by the lights, were twelve bright windows—there were candles in the upper ones—and through one of the ground floor windows they could see some people standing before a fire flickering in a hearth. Large, open, and well lighted, it was a house which welcomed with its warmth and its close arched doorway, female with wisteria which, even leafless, retained a look of complicated clinging elegance.

"So glad you could make it," said Awdry, and he introduced the Mundays to Mrs. Awdry, who had just entered the high-ceilinged hall in a dress of green watered silk; she was also wearing a frilly white apron

—"I'm helping out in the kitchen," she explained. "We've got flu."

"We haven't had it, thank goodness," said Emma.

"It's worse than malaria," said Mr. Awdry. "And I know, because I've had malaria!"

"It sucks one so," said Mrs. Awdry.

"I once had cerebral malaria," said Munday.

"I knew a chap who died from a bout of that," said Mr. Awdry.

"It's usually fatal," said Munday. "A mission doctor prayed for me. Fortunately he also had the foresight to treat me with chloroquine."

Mr. Awdry said "We've got lots to talk about" to Munday, and Mrs. Awdry took Emma aside and explained how at a country auction they had picked up the Jacobean church pew Emma was admiring, which served as a bench in the hall. Then Mrs. Awdry excused herself saying, "I must see to the turkey."

Standing near the fire in the living room were the vicar and Mrs. Crawshaw, and two young couples who were introduced as the Stricks and the Motherwells.

"This is Doctor Munday, the writer," said Awdry.

Munday tried to correct him.

Anne Motherwell said, "We're talking about children."

"My favorite subject," said Munday.

"How many do you have?" asked Janet Strick.

"None that I know of," said Munday, "which means I can be perfectly objective."

"Punch?" asked Awdry.

"Lovely," said Emma.

"Whisky for me," said Munday. "No ice, a little water."

"Won't be a moment," said Mr. Awdry and went for the drinks.

"We're all having the punch," said Janet Strick to Munday, as Emma drifted over to the vicar and his wife.

Munday made a face. "But one never knows what they put in punch, does one?"

"Mr. Awdry's punch is quite famous," said Janet eagerly. "He makes it with the local cider and some secret ingredients."

"You see what I mean?" said Munday. But his attempt at humor failed. Though his intentions were friendly his irony was always too peevish to seem like anything but aggression. The woman frowned and took a step back.

"Tell Doctor Munday what you just told us," said Peter Mothewell.

Janet laughed. "Well, only that"—and here her husband began to snicker—"my Rachel's nappy smells like mangoes."

"Incredible," said Peter Motherwell. He was beaming; the vicar's eyes darted, making his smile one of dismay.

"It *does*," Janet protested. "When she makes a poo. There's something about it."

"I should say," said Munday, "you're a lot luckier than most young mothers. Your child must have phenomenal bowels."

"Used to have a delicious mango tree in my garden," said Mr. Awdry, approaching with the drinks. He gave Emma and Munday their glasses and said, "They were like this." He measured with his hands. "Cook used to steal them."

"Cooks are very good at that sort of thing," said Emma.

"Mine wore pink dancing pumps," said Awdry. "Except when he climbed the mango tree. They were my daughter's. She threw them in the dustbin and the next thing we knew he was wearing them. Hate to think what he would have done if she'd thrown away her gym slip. Odd fish that cook."

"Obviously keen on dancing attendance," said Munday.

"Yes," said Awdry coolly, but the others laughed.

"I'd love to be in a place where mangoes grew," said Anne Motherwell. "So would I," said her husband.

"Africa," said Awdry. "Doctor Munday and I were both there." He turned to Munday and said, "I always say it's as if we'd gone to the same school."

"But sent down in different years," said Munday.

"We enjoyed your talk at the church hall," said Peter to Munday.

"Were you there?" asked Munday.

"All of us were," said Peter, surprising Munday: why had he only seen those aged people? He wondered if his failing eyes had obstinately sought those failures to address. He didn't like to be reminded of details he had missed, for he was certain there must be more.

"We were fascinated," said Michael Strick, drawing close to his wife and adding, "Weren't we? Janet and I have been reading some anthropology lately—*The Naked Ape.* So we were especially interested."

"You should write something like that," said Janet. "You could make a fortune."

"Color supplement stuff," said Munday, "written for the credulous semi-educated. And in any case I already have a fortune—my wife is quite wealthy. So you see the whole enterprise would be rather pointless."

"Have you read Lévi-Strauss?" asked Peter.

Munday turned to Awdry and said, "People I meet are always recommending books to me. Why is that? Very curious." Now he spoke directly to Peter: "I haven't opened an anthropology book since I was an undergraduate. It's not necessary—not when one has a people to study. Books aren't much use in the field—even Malinowski agreed with me on that. He was a character. 'Alfred,' he said to me once, 'I can swear in seven languages.' So, honestly, I haven't read Lévi-Strauss," he went on, "but on the other hand I'm fairly sure Lévi-Strauss has read *me.*"

"Caroline Summers said your lecture was the best one she's heard," said Janet.

"She's smashing," said Anne.

"She's coming tonight," said Awdry. "Late as usual." He smiled "Dear Caroline."

"She's so funny," said Anne. "She showed up at the Hunt Ball in a beautiful dress and gloves, very elegant! But she was wearing—wait for it!—*orthopedic shoes*. Did we laugh!"

"Caused quite a commotion," said Awdry. "Some of the lady members went a bit glassy-eyed."

"I didn't know you were at the Hunt Ball," said Janet, coldly.

"Peter had tickets," said Anne. "It seemed a shame to waste them."

"I think hunting is ridiculous and cruel," said Janet.

"Now Janet," said the vicar, "everyone has a right—"

"Princess Anne hunts," said Peter.

"She's a horse," said Michael. "She doesn't count."

"All we did was dance," said Anne to Munday.

"Do you hunt, Doctor Munday?" asked Michael.

"I don't," said Munday. "But if I did I'd look a bit silly admitting it after what your wife has just said."

"Are you happy now?" said Michael to Janet. He was exasperated, but she showed no contrition.

"Of course I feel sorry for the poor fox," said Anne.

Munday said, "Anyone who's been to Africa knows how a fox feels."

"But I love to watch the huntsmen gathering on a hill, all the horses stamping—the steam shooting out of their nostrils. And the other chaps scattering and blowing their horns, and the hounds sniffing everywhere. It's a beautiful sight." She looked at Janet. "I don't care what anyone says."

"Something very military about it," said Awdry, "and at the same time very colorful. Takes a lot of courage really."

"Courage?" Janet Strick snorted and crossed her

arms. "It's just torture, and it chills me to the bone. I stand in my kitchen and hear the horns and the hounds baying and I think of that helpless animal. They tear it to pieces. I can't understand why people do it."

"Thrill of the chase," said Awdry. "The village people love it."

"They love it," said Janet disgustedly to Munday —but they were all speaking to Munday, appealing, looking to him for approval, as if he were judging them. "The local people don't know any better. They chase around on foot while the wealthy ones are on horseback. It's a class thing in actual fact."

"Hunting," said Munday, and everyone listened, "is the perfect expression of the English tribal character. Formal murder, a lot of ceremony, a little blood, the classes together, the aristocrats in the saddle, the poorer on foot, the middle classes gaping from their gardens. It's how all our best wars have been fought. You can be sure that when someone is dealt with that way the English mean business."

"What Janet really objects to is the blooding," said Michael.

"God," said Janet, "they take the fox's brush, dripping with blood, and they wipe it—"

"Yes, yes," said Munday, who had just thought of a Bwamba custom which was an appropriate comparison, one of the puberty rites.

But Awdry interrupted. "They rarely sight a fox— that should give you some consolation, surely? Though on Christmas day," he said, turning to Munday, "we saw one up by the Black House. We lost him behind the mill at Stoke Abbot."

"I'm glad," said Janet.

"Earth-stoppers didn't do their job properly," said Awdry.

"They be drinking," said Peter Motherwell, trying to imitate a local accent; but it was not a good imitation, he was embarrassed, there was a guilty hesitance in his delivery—he blushed—and after he finished by saying, "Oy zeed 'em over yere at The Yew Tree," there was a silence, the vicar expressed frank disapproval and several of the women glanced nervously in the direction of the door.

Breaking the silence, in what was clearly intended to help out her husband by diverting attention away from his gaffe, Anne said, "I wonder what's happened to Caroline."

"And Jerry's coming as well," said Awdry. "I suggest we all have another drink while we wait. Help yourselves to the punch."

"Maybe they're coming together," said Michael confidentially to Anne.

"I don't believe all those things they say about Caroline," Anne said. "Do you?"

"Yes," said Michael, and smiled, but became serious again when he saw that the rest were listening.

"How long have you lived here?" Emma was asking the Motherwells.

"Two years," said Peter. "The Stricks have been here five—they're old-timers!"

"We're starting our seventh year," said the vicar proudly. He smiled at his wife. But she looked apprehensive, as if she were being called upon to speak.

Munday made himself a drink and then wandered to a side table where he had spotted an African carving. He picked it up and turned it over and weighed it in his hand.

"Kamba," he said.

"I know," said Awdry, who had followed him to the table. "I'm told they're becoming quite valuable."

"Nowadays they make them in a factory in Nairobi," said Munday. "To sell to tourists. Horrible shiny things."

"I'll show you some more," said Awdry, and led Munday to the library. "Here, these are rather fun." On a table, covered by a kaross of tawny sewn deerskins, there were rows of small carved figures and African clay pipes and bracelets of silver. On the bookshelves there were more carved things, many with woodworm; several Munday recognized as the work of his people. On another table there was a collection of snuffboxes, some silver and brass and others of plugged bamboo. A water-buck's head stared serenely from under long lashes on the wall between two windows, and over the fireplace was the dark brutish head of a buffalo.

"Head shot?" asked Munday.

"Heart," said Awdry, "but he kept coming. Then I winged him. It took three shots to bring him down. My gun bearer bolted."

"That shows he had some common sense."

On other sections of the walls there were hide shields and crossed spears, and ebony masks grinning under mops of straw hair, with grotesque mouths, like simplified masks of comedy and tragedy superimposed.

"I suppose you recognize this," said Awdry. He showed Munday a soapstone carving of a woman with exaggerated breasts and a pot belly.

"Fertility figure," said Munday. "Probably Luo, from the look of it, and,"—he held the piece and glanced at Awdry—"without question, a fake."

There were daggers mounted on a varnished board, rusty-bladed knives with beaded handles, and some Masai broadswords in neatly stitched leather sheaths. Munday looked for his stolen dagger, but saw none that resembled it.

"Didn't you say in your lecture how African tools look so much like weapons?"

"They do the work of both," said Munday. "That *panga*," he said, pointing at a foot-long machete. "It's used for clearing land, but a Bwamba would say—"

There was a loud rapping in the front hall.

"That must be one of the guests," said Awdry. "Excuse me."

Munday quickly searched the room for his dagger; he looked on the top shelves and opened a Zanzibari chest. He could not find it, but he was convinced that

Awdry had it, and he considered stealing one of
Awdry's own daggers. They were an inconvenient
size. He slipped one of the silver snuffboxes into his
pocket and took up his drink and started out of the
room. But the theft made him self-conscious. He
looked back and saw the high active fire in the hearth
as having a life of its own, making a sound like
ridicule—intimidating, accusing. He turned to go,
but the fire crackling in the empty library remained,
a witness to his theft, a crazy threatening presence.
Munday returned to the table and put the snuffbox
back.

In the living room he headed for Emma, who
was talking to Peter Motherwell. But Awdry called to
him, "I want you to meet an admirer of yours."

It was the new guest, Caroline Summers. She was
Munday's own height, but gave the impression of
being taller. She wore a long blue sleeveless dress of a
silky material which clung and emphasized her shape.
Her neckline was cut low, revealing part of the
rounded undersides of her breasts; a small blue
jewel on a chain rested at an angle just between her
breasts which, unsupported, sloped against the soft
cloth that draped them. Though she stood still and
held a wine glass without drinking from it, Munday
found himself staring at the slight movements in the
cords of her neck and throat and the thin poised bones
of her hands. He felt he could read those bones and
the shadows on the planes of her face.

"I'm delighted to meet you," she said, and took the
wine glass in two hands. Munday saw the jewel right
itself between her breasts.

"We've just been discussing your lecture," said
Janet Strick.

"No complaints, I hope," said Munday. Outlined
in the long blue cloth was her leg, from hip to ankle;
its unadorned completeness more than its shape
attracted him.

"Only praise," said Caroline.

Drawn to her he avoided her eyes, and having ex-

amined her he looked closely at the others, Motherwell
with his pipe, Awdry's Foreign Office tie and suede
shoes, Strick's flowered shirt and tie in matching
material, and next to him Janet Strick in her short
skirt. Janet was pretty, her skin was young, she had a
smooth face, a large head and a good fleshy figure.
Her hair was long; Caroline's was short, and yet there
was something luxurious about Caroline, the message
on her mouth, the angle of her chin, the bones lifting
at the base of the neck, the distinct edges of her
hips and the thrust her dress hugged. She was not
thin, but her short hair and the proportions of her
features made her appear so, the way she stood—her
weight on one leg—the length of her fingers which
circled the glass. From the moment he saw her he
wanted to be near her, to touch her; he felt a mingled
desire and respect, the same helpless yearning he
had experienced watching Alice crouch in her denim
jeans. But he saw in Caroline a power that could be
terrible, not the youthful pleasingness of Alice, but
the sensual wisdom of a woman who knows that she
is within a few years of losing her beauty. Though
she had a veneer of glamour, what cowed him was
the destroying bloom he saw in her bones. She could
hold him and crack him.

She said, "I imagined you'd be very severe and
scientific."

"Perhaps I am."

"No, you're not."

"My Africans used to do imitations of me, behind
my back. They thought I was a bit of a taskmaster."

"Did that upset you?"

"They can be tricky little bastards."

Then she did something that aroused Munday; she
closed her eyes and smiled and rocked her head back
on her long neck.

"I agree," Awdry said, and he began to tell a story
of African treachery.

In an effort to conceal his submissive interest in
Caroline, Munday pretended to listen to the story

(it concerned an African's clumsy forgery of a local chief's official papers), for he sensed the interest was obvious on his face. But attempting to suppress it he felt it more deeply, as he had with Alice. He remembered that he had fled the daughter, not the mother, and he saw himself as a weak man, incomplete, who had denied himself passion, though he had seen it enacted close to him, while he had stayed on its periphery, observing, sometimes mocking, never venturing nearer. He saw that his severity was fear, and what virtue he had always claimed for himself was cowardice.

"What happened to the African?" Caroline was saying.

"Him? Oh, we let him go," said Awdry. "The Crown had a case against him, but we weren't sure how it would go down locally. He was in the wrong, of course—everyone knew that. As it turned out, he would have been safer with us."

"Safer?" Caroline became interested. "But you said he was free."

"He got a dose of village justice," said Awdry. He winked at Munday. Munday shrugged.

"That sounds ominous," said Caroline.

"It was quite a field-day," said Awdry. "Mob of people pounced on him, sank their teeth into him and spat out the pieces. Everyone was laughing—Africans find torture frightfully amusing. When the poor chap died they assumed he must have been guilty."

"I never believe a word you say," said Caroline. "They can't be as bloodthirsty as that."

"Doctor Munday will vouch for me," said Awdry.

"Two points," said Munday in his tutorial manner. "One, there's usually some kind of deliberation before a man is found guilty. And, two, where property is involved the punishment is fairly harsh." He went on, though in doing so he felt an awkward sense of betraying people he knew for people who were only interested in discrediting Africans. It was the penalty of his long residence among Africans, he believed: his knowledge of them only seemed to incriminate them. But he was anxious to hold Caroline's attention. He said, "I remember an African who got a five-inch nail hammered into his skull. He had killed his wife at a beer party. I've heard of others who've had their feet chopped off—and they still use the ant-hill in some parts of Uganda. A Chiga girl who commits incest is thrown over a cliff by her father—"

"Why that's *savage*," said Caroline, her eyes flashing.

"Perhaps no worse than our own death penalty," said Munday. "The gallows, what-have-you."

"You're way out of date," said Awdry. He was laughing.

"Capital punishment's been abolished," said Caroline.

"I had no idea," said Munday.

"Bloody silly, if you ask me," said Awdry. "But there it is. Ah, here comes Jerry. We can eat."

Jerry, the last guest to arrive, was out of breath, apologizing for being late as he handed his coat to Awdry. On the way over, he said, he had stopped to have a look at his cows and had found one which hadn't been milked. The milking had delayed him.

"Jerry's the only one who really belongs here," said Caroline. "The rest of us are all foreigners."

"The native among the expatriates," muttered Munday.

"I was born up the road," he said to Munday. "Broadwindsor way."

He was young, with a frank sunburned face, and square shoulders that had stretched his fashionable suit-jacket out of shape. Though his movements were shy—he glanced continually at his hands and heavy shoes—he had a clipped way of speaking, the local accent Peter Motherwell had tried to imitate (Jerry was saying, with the guileless scorn of a Bwamba, why his wife had had to stay at home). Now Munday understood the embarrassment of Peter's mimicry. It was that of the settler joke, told when the houseboy was in the kitchen.

"Doctor Munday. Jerry Duddle," said Caroline. "Doctor Munday's been telling us the most horrible stories."

"Pleased to meet you," said Jerry.

Munday was about to ask him about his farm when Janet came over and asked, "Jerry, do you have any views on hunting?"

"I don't hunt much myself," said Jerry. "Don't have time for it—too busy with the farm. I do a little fishing."

"But, don't you agree that hunting's cruel?" Janet had stepped in front of Munday and was facing Jerry.

"Cruel? In what way?"

"It's bloody."

"Bloody expensive," said Jerry. "Those floats set you back a few quid."

Janet raised her eyes to the ceiling and said, "I suppose I'm alone in thinking it should be banned."

Jerry said, "I always say if people can afford to do something, and they enjoy doing it, who am I to tell them they're wrong?"

"That's our boy," said Awdry; and Peter said, "Hear, hear!" Awdry crossed the room to show Anne Motherwell and Michael Strick and the vicar's wife a framed photograph on the wall, a group of Africans on the bank of a flood-swollen river, near which a Land Rover was parked. Awdry said, "Five minutes after that picture was taken, this old man was drowned trying to ford the river."

Munday was on his way over to see the photograph of the doomed man. He noticed Emma near the fire, her hands clasped on a drink. She was alone.

"Are you all right?"

"I thought I was going to faint," Emma said. "I think I startled that young man."

Munday wondered which young man she was talking about. He looked around the room and then said, "Seems they've abolished capital punishment. I had no idea. That Summers woman was telling me."

"*I* could have told you that," said Emma.

"What's wrong?" said Munday. "You seem cross."

"I'm not well," said Emma. "And I don't like that woman."

"Why? You don't even know her."

"I know her," said Emma. "She wants you."

"Don't be silly." Munday saw Caroline seated on the arm of a chair.

"I can tell—a woman can always tell. She's making a play for you."

Munday said, "You've had too much to drink."

"This is tap water," said Emma. "That young man fetched it. I thought I was going to faint."

But Munday was staring at Caroline. He said, "How do you know she's making a play for me? I didn't say two words to her."

"Something in her face—the way she was standing," said Emma. "She stares at you."

"Is *that* all!"

"And she hates me," said Emma. "That's the proof."

"You're imagining things," said Munday.

"When I saw her come in tonight," said Emma in a low voice, "I thought I recognized her. I was going to go over and introduce myself. But something stopped me. I took a good look at her and she glared at me in a most hateful way. And then I knew." Emma turned to face Munday. She said, "Alfred, that's the *woman*."

"Which woman?" he asked. But he knew.

Emma pressed a handkerchief to her mouth. Her eyes were large with fright and she seemed to be on the verge of tears. The anger which had masked her fear had left her, and now she looked extremely tired and rather small and defeated.

Taking Emma by the arm Munday started towards the dining room, and though he was at some distance, nearly two long rooms away, he saw Caroline clearly in the candlelight where the other guests were shadowy; she stared, searching him with her very white face, no stranger now, but so intimate she understood his longing. She had seen his conversation with Emma, and without hearing, she knew every word they had said.

12

"Is THIS HOT or cold?" Anne Motherwell's spoon was poised over the soup.

"It's vichyssoisse," said Mrs. Awdry. "I hope you like it."

"That's means cold," said the vicar.

"There's always a first time," said Jerry. Saying this he engaged the attention of the table. Everyone watched for his reaction while he took a spoonful. He smiled and swallowed. He said in a surprised voice, "Potatoes," then, "but very tasty," and the rest began to eat.

"Did anyone here go over to that meeting in Bridport to protest the oil-drilling?" asked Janet Strick.

"We were there," said Peter. "It was very encouraging to see all those concerned people."

"What exactly are they concerned about?" asked Munday.

"Marauders," said Anne.

"They're planning to turn the countryside here into an industrial wasteland," said Michael. "There's a scheme afoot to drill for oil in Powerstock."

"It's got everyone up in arms," said Awdry.

"Not everyone," said Janet. "It looks as if they might go through with it."

The vicar cleared his throat. He said, "Some years

ago—this was before my time—they said they were going to put huge pylons through Marshwood Vale. There were protest meetings and so forth, petitions and letters to the paper. Some people were quite vocal." He smiled. "And then of course they put the pylons up."

"That's always the way," said Mrs. Awdry.

"I've seen them from the back of my house," said Munday.

"Sorry about that," said Awdry.

"It's a rotten shame," said Janet. "Why should the government designate this as an area of outstanding natural beauty one year and then put up oil rigs the next? I can't fathom it."

"They need oil," said Jerry.

"There's plenty of oil in the Middle East and America," said Janet.

"I mean in Britain," said Jerry.

"I see we're divided on the oil question," said Munday. He smiled at Caroline.

"What about the North Sea?" said Anne. "There's masses there."

"There's none here," said Janet.

"They say there might be," said the vicar.

"There is," said Jerry. "It's here, all right. I've seen it running out of the ground over in Hooke—natural seepages."

"I suppose you don't care a damn whether they drill or not," said Janet to Jerry.

Peter spoke to Munday. "It's quite a problem," he said. "People coming down here and spoiling the view."

"People come down here and do all kinds of things," said Jerry quietly. "I know you folks like the country-side and walks and that. So do I. But these hikers treat my property as if they owned it, break down the fences, leave the gates open for the cows to wander about in the road. I wanted to put up a cow-pen and they refused me planning permission, said I'd spoil the view." He laughed. "Never heard that one before."

He had not taken another spoonful of his soup; he continued to talk, toying with his spoon, while the others ate. "There's not a lot of money around here. If finding oil means money and jobs then I'm sorry but I'm for it one hundred percent."

"It's pollution," said Anne.

Jerry laughed again. "The farmers over in Powerstock make fifty thousand pounds from a few acres of pastures and you call it pollution!"

"I didn't chuck a good job in London to come down here and stare at an oil-rig," said Peter. "No thanks. I'll go somewhere else if they start that sort of thing down here. I've had all I wanted of smoky chimneys and factory noise."

"I saw the drilling rig, Mr. Awdry," said Jerry. "She looks like a Christmas tree."

"You don't say," said Awdry.

"With fairy lights," said Jerry.

"What business are you in?" Munday asked Peter.

"I'm in the building trade," he said.

"What about planning permission?"

"It doesn't affect me."

"Peter does up houses," said Anne. "And very nicely, too. But I'm biased."

"Clever chap," said Awdry. "He gets a condemned building at auction for a few hundred pounds, fixes it up with a council grant and sells it for ten thousand."

"Not *quite* as simple and profitable as that," said Peter to Munday. "But you get the idea."

"Barn of character," said Michael.

"Ah," said the vicar, pressing his hands together and looking up.

Mrs. Awdry was carrying the turkey in on a platter. She was followed by a woman in a white bib apron who had a tray of steaming dishes of vegetables. Awdry carved while his wife and the servant collected the soup plates.

Jerry said, "All this talking—I haven't had time to finish my soup." He took a spoonful and held it in his mouth.

"Don't eat it if you don't like it," said Mrs. Awdry.

"It's just that I've never had it cold before," he said, surrendering his plate. "I say, that's a fair-sized bird."

"A sixteen pounder," said Awdry, still carving thin slices from the breast. "Now please tell me whether you'd like light meat or dark. Doctor Munday, I know you'll want dark—all those years in the African bush."

Munday was angered by the laughter Awdry's arch comment caused, and he said sternly, "Light for me, if you don't mind."

The ticking of the mantelpiece clock became audible, timing the silence; Munday relished the pause.

Then Anne Motherwell said, "I saw a rat today."

"Oh, good girl," said Caroline.

"Was it a very big rat?" asked Janet.

"Average size I suppose," said Anne. "I'd never seen one before."

"I hate rats," said Emma. It was the first thing she had spoken and everyone waited for her to say more. She put her head down and stared at the plate that had been handed to her.

"There is something sexual about rats," said Caroline. "I think I know why."

"Do tell us," said Michael.

"Perhap when you're a bit older," said Caroline.

"We had one at the camp," said Munday. "Right inside the bungalow."

Emma said, "We never did!" and Munday realized that what he had just said so easily to all those people, he had never told Emma. He was going to reply, but Jerry had already started.

"Used to be a lot of rats around here," he said, passing a plate heaped with turkey. "Why, I seen more rats in one little place than you see now in five acres. Caught thirty of the buggers one night."

"I've been ratting myself many times," said Awdry.

"Not enough of them for that now," said Jerry. "After the rabbits went down with myxomatosis, the weasels and foxes had nothing to eat, so they started feeding on the rats."

"I was six or seven," said Awdry, "and I was going for a walk with my father. He was a great walker—five miles before breakfast—he gave me my first walking stick. We were on a country lane in South Worcestershire and suddenly he put his hand on my shoulder and said, 'Wait!' I looked up and couldn't believe my eyes. The road was absolutely black with rats, jostling this way and that. 'Don't you move,' he said. 'They're migrating.'"

"That thatcher from Filford," said Jerry. "He was coming up the road one night and a whole mob of rats was crossing the road. Maybe migrating, like Mr. Awdry says. Knocked him down and the bike too!"

"Scrumpy knocked him down more likely," said Awdry.

"I remember him," said Mrs. Awdry. "He's dead now. He thatched for us over at the cottages—up on the ladder with a keg of cider around his neck. Queer old fellow."

"You must find all of this fascinating," said Caroline to Munday.

"I do," said Munday. "Very much so."

"Doctor Munday is studying us," said Anne.

"Not exactly," said Munday. "Though I think someone ought to."

"It must be very exciting to come back to England after all these years."

"Exciting?" said Munday.

"Seeing all the changes."

"The changes I saw weren't in England," said Munday, "though it's true I'm still baffled by the new money, and sick of these television programs perpetually discussing things and ending the show when someone loses his temper. And football results. And God, these color supplements—we never got them in Africa—too heavy to airfreight."

"We decorated our loo with color supplements," said Anne.

"They represent everything I loathe about this country," said Munday. "Everything they stand for, I despise. Isn't that right, Emma?"

"What's that?" Emma stared vacantly at Munday.

"Are you all right, my dear?" asked Awdry.

"I'm afraid I'm not feeling terribly well," said Emma.

"All this talk about rats," said Mrs. Awdry. "I'm not surprised."

"Would you mind if I went into the living room and sat down?" said Emma.

"Please do," said Mr. Awdry. "Can I get you anything?"

"No, no," said Emma. "Don't get up." She rose and went out of the room before anyone could help her.

"Has this happened before?" asked Awdry.

"I think we should call a doctor," said Janet. "She looks very pale."

"Hadn't you better go and see if there's anything she needs?" said Mrs. Awdry to Munday.

Munday, the only one at the table still eating, gestured with his knife and fork. "Please eat," he said, chewing. "She'll be fine."

"I'm worried about her," said Anne.

"Good God," said Munday, "you talk as if she's fading away! Emma has survived Africa, and I assure you she'll survive Four Ashes. She's really very fit." But the large paneled room and the hushed listeners gave his overloud denying voice a ring of falsity.

Caroline said, "I'm sure Doctor Munday is right."

So they resumed, but Emma's absence made the rest of the meal somber. Anxious, they ate quickly and to the scrape of the knives and forks on the plates they addressed each other inconsequentially, with a whispered respect. From time to time Awdry said, "More wine?" but only Munday accepted it, as if the others thought it unseemly to drink with Emma unwell in the next room. Munday went on eating, but his appetite left him. The rest made a show of dining. The strain was evident. Emma's absence, so sudden, was an intensification of her presence, which was felt more strongly two rooms away than it had been when she was seated with them at the table. Her chair was empty, she was missing, and their excessively tactful avoidance of commenting on this was like a continual mention of her.

After the dessert of strawberries and clotted cream, which they ate as solemnly as mourners—not cheered by the vicar's wife saying too clearly "These are awfully good," inspiring several uncertain responses which diminished down the table, from "Yes, they are" to a grunt of agreement from Jerry Duddle—Mrs. Awdry pressed his napkin to his mouth, scraped his chair backward, and said, "Shall we have our coffee in the lounge?"

Emma sat on the sofa with a brave half-smile of pain on her face. There was a copy of *The Field* on her lap; her hands were on the cover, smoothing it. She looked up slowly as the guests entered the room, and Munday at the head of the procession said brusquely, as he might have to a student with a medical excuse, "How are you feeling now?"

She shook her head. "I think you'd better take me home."

"Emma, do you really—"

"Have an early night," said Awdry. "Do you a world of good."

"I'm very sorry," said Emma. "I feel I've spoiled your lovely party."

"Don't be silly," said Mrs. Awdry. "I only wish there was something we could do."

"You've been most kind," said Emma. "Perhaps Alfred could drop me and then come back."

"Not if you're sick," said Munday.

"Do what you think best," said Awdry, and he helped Emma on with her coat as Janet Strick, squinting in sisterly commiseration, said, "I know just how you feel."

Driving back in the car Emma was silent. Munday

said, "There were no paintings on the library ceiling. Branch had that all wrong. Typical! And I saw the gold bell on the table. It was brass." He pulled up at the Black House and said, "Do you want me to stay?"

"Not if you don't want to."

"So you're leaving it up to me."

"You'd only be keeping me company," said Emma. "I think I'll go straight to bed."

"Awdry's right. It'll do you good."

Emma opened the car door and said, "Isn't it odd. For the first time in ages I'm not afraid to go into this house. I know it's perfectly empty and secure. She's not here—she's there."

"Don't talk such nonsense," Munday said.

"I thought I was going mad that day in the garden —imagining things," said Emma. "Now I know I'm perfectly sane. I *did* see her."

Emma's voice was assured, but in the car's overhead light, a yellow lozenge of plastic, the illness dimming her face made her look complacent. Munday could raise little sympathy for her. Her insisting on being taken home was devious, a withdrawal from the challenge she saw in Caroline. He was ashamed of her. She had no life but his life, no friends aside from those he had made. She had pretended her sickness to chasten him, but her apologies only made him embarrassed for her. She was a part of him, but the weakest part, and he saw that without her he might have succeeded. There was still time for him; she had little claim upon him. Her weakness obliged him to be attentive, but he understood: what she feared he desired, and what had confused him before was that her fear had obsessed her in the same way as his desire. But she had deprived him of his pleasure. It had always been that way, from their first day at the Yellow Fever Camp, when the heat and the musky smells had possessed him physically, and the lushness had made him gasp even after the people themselves had lost all interest—to their arrival at the Black House, where she had been the first to name what they had both seen. She had called it fear, and so he had. But it was not fear at all.

She said, "I know you want to go back."

"Would you rather I stayed?"

"I'm fine now," she said. "I'm safe. Please go."

Emma pressed his hand and got out of the car, and Munday felt that she understood how, in leaving her in the last hour of the year, the parting was crucial; and in saying what she did, she had to accept a share of the responsibility for his going. That touched him, and driving back to the party he felt a tenderness for Emma that he had never known before, as if she was his sad jilted sister, whom he might console but never rescue from her disappointment.

He returned to what seemed a different party. The guests' mood had changed—the men were talking loudly, some angrily, and he heard bursts of bitter laughter. He saw Caroline but she was the only one who did not look up at him when he entered the room. "Ah, he's come back," one of the younger men said. The men were seated, hunched forward on the edge of their chairs with brandy snifters. They went on competing with successive interruptions. The women, holding coffee cups, were in more relaxed attitudes, watching closely but offering little to the discussion. Munday saw it as the conventional after-dinner posture of men and their wives, arranged like contestants and spectators. He heard, "—trouble is, we're too nice to the Irish."

"Help yourself to a drink," said Awdry, who was nearest the fireplace. He lit and relit his pipe, and puffing, used the burnt match to make his point. He concluded his argument by tossing the match into the fire.

Munday's glass of port had the texture of silk. And he had taken one of Awdry's cigars; he stood magisterially, just behind the sofa, sucking at the cigar and turning it in his mouth. He heard Anne say to Caroline, "—told me the thing about people nowadays is they never *touch* each other. Here we are in a permissive age and we don't even touch! Well, I told him I agreed with him and that it was really very sad—and I thought so, too. It *is* terrible, I suppose. But I couldn't help feeling he was saying that because he wanted to touch *me*."

He turned to the men's argument and tried to follow it. Michael Strick was saying, "I know one thing, the Russians wouldn't handle it this way." He nodded and sipped at his brandy. "They'd go in there with tanks—that's the way to do it."

"I'll tell you how they could have done this and saved themselves a lot of trouble," said Jerry. "Internment was a mistake. They know who they want. They have a list of known IRA men. It's simple. You just wake 'em up at night and bash 'em. By that I mean, kill 'em."

"It may come to that yet," said Awdry, and flipped a dead match into the fire.

"But that's cold-blooded murder," said Anne, who was clearly shocked. Now she sat forward. She looked to the others for a reaction.

"What is it when they kill one of our young men?" said Michael. "That's murder too."

"Jerry said we should shoot them in their beds," said Janet. "Do you agree with that?"

"Please," said the vicar. "You're upsetting my wife."

"I'm sorry," said Michael, shaking his head, "but I've got no time for the Irish."

Caroline looked from one face to another. She said, "I think it's disgraceful the way you're talking."

Janet turned to Munday. "I suppose you were following this Northern Ireland business when you were in Africa."

"Not really," said Munday. "But I wouldn't be foolish enough to take sides, as some of you are doing, when every side is so barbarous."

"What *would* you do?" asked Anne.

"Disarm them, isolate them, and leave them to themselves," said Munday. "Just as I would any min-

ority tribe that became dangerous. I certainly wouldn't
expect to convert them."

"I know what *I'd* do with them," said Michael.

"They need you to say that," said Munday, aiming
his cigar at the young man. "They need that con-
tempt—it justifies them, and the British army legit-
imizes their quarrel. They want attention—you see,
I believe they like being photographed throwing stones
and marching and holding press conferences. They're
performing and they need witnesses badly, because
without witnesses you have no spectacle."

"What you're actually saying, Munday, is that if
we ignore them they'll stop their fighting," said Awdry.

"They'd go on fighting in a small way, as they've
always done," said Munday. "They wouldn't do much
damage. What none of you seems to realize is that
they enjoy it. This squabbling has a social value for
them—it gives purpose and shape to their lives. Murder is traditional in a culture of violence, which theirs
certainly is. And I suppose you could say head-
hunting is an aspect of their religion. Religion makes
more warriors than politics—God's a great recruit-
ing officer." He paused and drew on his cigar. "But
as I say, I don't know very much about it."

"It doesn't sound that way," said Awdry.

"You should talk to Emma," said Munday. "She's
well up on it."

"Oh?" Anne inquired. "And does she have a personal interest in it?"

"Well, she has family there, you see," said Munday,
and he smoked and watched their faces register shame,
the ungainly muteness that had fallen like a curse
on Alec's cronies when in full cry against Africans
they remembered his mistress was black. Before they
could become conciliatory, Munday said, "It will be
midnight soon."

The guests looked sheepishly at their watches.

"Has everyone got a drink?" asked Awdry.

The empty glasses were filled. They sat in silence,
waiting for the hour to strike. Just before midnight,

Anne said, "I loathe New Year's Eve. You look over the past year and you can't remember a blessed thing that matters."

Awdry rose, and with his back to the fire he said, "I'm not going to bore you with a speech. I just want to say how pleased I am that you're here tonight, and may I wish you all a happy and prosperous New Year." He lowered his head and began to sing "Auld Lang Syne." The others stood up and joined in the song. When it was over Awdry said, "Listen."

Church bells were pealing at the windows, faintly, but the unusual sounds at that hour of the night captured their attention; the muted clangs had no rhythm, they continuously rose and fell, in an irregular tolling, one tone drowning another. Awdry walked through the guests to the front door and threw it open. The bells were louder now and resonant, pealing at various distances in the darkness, their clappers striking like hammers against an anvil.

"I can hear St. Alban's," said the vicar. "And there, that tinkling, that's All Saints."

They rang and rang in different voices, dismay, joy, male and female, coming together and then chiming separately, descending and growing more rapid, and after a few moments competing, like bell buoys in a storm on a dangerous shore, signaling alarm with despairing insistence.

"It's a beautiful sound," said Caroline.

Munday walked away from the others, into the drive, then onto the lawn behind the boxwood hedge. The night was cold, but the chill, after that hot brightly-lit room, composed him. The guests' voices echoed, traveling to him from the very end of the garden where there was only darkness. Gray and black tissues of clouds hung in the sky above the high branches of bare trees, which stood out clearly. Here and there in the tangle of trees he saw the dark slanting shapes of firs. He walked to a white fountain which materialized in the garden as he studied the darkness. He touched the cold marble. Details came slowly to his eye, nest-clusters in some trees and others heavily bundled with ivy, the bulges reaching to the upper branches; he saw nothing hostile in these densely wrapped trees. As he watched, the church bells diminished in volume and number, and those that remained were like lonely voices sounding distantly in different parts of a nearly deserted land, calling out to all those still trees. Then they ceased altogether. But the silence and the darkness he had imagined hunting him at the Black House no longer frightened him. He welcomed and celebrated it as more subtle than jungle. There was no terror in the dark garden, only an inviting shadow, the vague unfinished shapes of hedge, the suggestions of pathways in the blur of lawn, and the dark so dark it had motion.

"In the summer this garden is full of flowers." Caroline's voice was just behind him. But he did not turn.

"I prefer it this way," said Munday. "The dark. Look, that shroud or hood there. In the daylight it's probably something terribly ordinary."

"You must be very lonely to say that."

"No," he said, "I just like things that can't be photographed."

"That's an odd statement from a scientist."

"I'm not a scientist," he said. He turned to her and said, "Why did you ask me at the lecture if I ever got depressed?"

She said, "Why did you remember that?" She was beside him now, and she spoke again with a suddenness that jerked at his heart, "Do you know Pilsdon Pen?"

"That hill outside Broadwindsor?"

"Right," she said. "It's not far from here. It's a sharp left, just as you enter the square. The road to Birdsmoor Gate goes around the hill, but quite high. It's a beauty spot, so there's a small parking lot for the view."

"I've driven past it," said Munday.

Caroline glanced behind her and then at Munday, and he saw her teeth when she said quickly, "Meet me there in half an hour."

She left him and walked towards the doorway where the others were still standing under the bright carriage-lamp. He heard her call out in a new voice, "Doctor Munday's been showing me the Dog Star!"

So all the moves were hers; but it excited him to hear her conceal them—that disguise was proof of her sincerity. Munday looked at his watch and then followed her across the vapor that lay on the grass.

13

IT WAS a high windy spot, on the crest of a hill, with room for a dozen cars, and it was empty. Though Caroline had left the party before he did, and Munday was delayed for what seemed to him a long while at the door by Awdry urging him to explain what he meant by his letter to *The Times* (Awdry knew the letter by heart and kept repeating, "But why *misfits?*"), she was not at the parking lot when he arrived. A light rain began to fall, making a pattering like sand grains on the car roof; the sound of the rain isolated him and made him think she wouldn't show up.

Past the gorse bushes, shaking stiffly at the front of the car, was the valley, some lighted windows which were only pinpricks, and a glow at the horizon, the yellow flare of Bridport. He saw through the dribbling side window an arrow-shaped sign lettered *To Trail*. He sat in the car with his gloves on wondering if he was being made a fool of: he was not used to acting with such haste. He knew the risk, but it would be far worse if she didn't meet him. The wind sucked at the windows—he wanted relief. But the moments of his suspense, instead of provoking in him calm, only recalled similar suspense in Africa, Claudia's eye orbiting his unease, her saying in a tone her clumsiness vulgarized into a threat, "Why don't you ever come over and see me when you're in town?" The first night at her house while he was talking she had got up from the sofa and left the room, just like that, and called to him. He found her naked, smoking in bed: "Are you very shocked?"

"I think it's ill-advised to smoke in bed."

Later, she had wanted to know what African girls were like in bed. Munday said, "Fairly straightforward, one would guess—I don't really know. I've never had one."

She said, "You're lying. Martin's always screwing them."

"I'm not Martin, thank God."

"Are you trying to get at me?"

He had made love to Claudia on three occasions; the first time it was her desire, the second his curiosity, the third time routine—the unchanged circumstances of time and place made it so—and that last time was disappointing for both of them, though only she said it. Those nights returned to him now with horrible clarity: how she had stubbed out her cigarette and then rolled onto her back and lifted and spread her legs, holding her buttocks up with the hands, waiting with a kind of anonymous patience for him to enter her. And he had thought: it was this that troubled women most, it gave them fear, the position that made them most vulnerable, the lifted cunt opened and exposed like a smarting valve the slightest force could injure. Pity killed his desire, but he knew that any hesitation on his part would have ridiculed her surrender. "No, don't stop," she had said when he finished, and she had reached down and held him inside her and chafed his penis against her with her hand, finally dropping it and crying out—the cry that reached Alice. "Never mind her," Claudia had said, but she had changed the bottom sheet so the houseboy wouldn't see the stain. The next time she didn't stub out her cigarette, but rested it in the ashtray next to the bed, as if she would return to it shortly. It was a rebuke Munday turned into a challenge, and he had made love to her until the cigarette had burned to ashes.

Ten minutes passed like this. The rain was hitting the car with force now. He was sure Caroline wasn't coming, and he prepared to leave, but slowly, hoping that in his delay she would appear. The road was dark, there was only the rain and wind; his face was against the glass and he was peering down the road when the offside door opened. Caroline got in—the overhead light had gone on and off, but he saw only her hands and a wet unfamiliar coat.

"I thought you weren't coming," he said.

"I'm glad you waited," she said. "I was parking my car."

"It's windy up here."

She did not reply to that. She said, "Back up and drive a little further on. But don't go too fast or you'll miss the turning."

He reversed and started slowly down the road, commenting on the rain and the fogged windows. But she said nothing, and it seemed wonderful to him that so little had been spoken and yet they knew so much: they carried directions within them, the wordless sex-wish beneath fixed circuits of hinting talk. Caroline leaned forward and wiped at the window. She said, "There, turn left."

Munday swung the wheel and they descended a steep curving lane, wetter than the other road had been, and in parts awash with streams of water spilling from the bank, and rivulets that drained from the road they had left. This water coursed over stones by the roadside and cleaned them bone-white, and the falling rain gave motion to the loose briars that hung in bunches at the top of the partially eroded banks.

The storm was more intense in this valley, which seemed at times a flooding cavern riotous with wind.

They traveled on the lane for some minutes, came to a junction and, at Caroline's word, turned again into a straighter lane; narrowing, the lane led downward. Their slow speed made it hard for Munday to judge how far they had gone; he knew they were in Marshwood Vale, but he had lost his bearings—they might be going in circles, they might easily have been in Bwamba, at night on the forest road in a cold April downpour. It was an unusual feeling, for the size of the lanes and their continuous winding, promising arrival at every curve, suggested to Munday progress through the layout of a gigantic game, crisscrossed with routes. They were players, bluffing their way along, and there was a hopeless comedy in making so many turns. The lanes were walled with earthen banks, from which in places clods had fallen and broken in the road, and just a car's width, the lane passages were deep square grooves cut in the valley slope. The car splashed round another bend, the engine surging and Caroline spoke up: "Look, a badger."

The creature was caught in the headlights, amid shooting white flecks of rain. Munday slowed the car. The pinched black and white head faced them, the bright eyes flashed, and then it was off, bounding away from the car. Munday picked up speed but stayed well behind the animal, and as if being chased, it leaped onto the bank, sniffing for refuge. Then it blundered down and scrambled to the opposite bank, keeping ahead of the car. Munday continued on, fascinated by the sleek dark thing darting from bank to bank, nosing for a burrow and finally shooting straight along the roadside for some distance, pursued by the moving lights, running in a low glide, its head down, its damp tail switching.

"He's scared, poor thing," said Caroline. "Your lights are blinding him."

Munday flicked off the headlights and stopped the

car. They were in complete darkness: the rain was loud, drumming on the roof. Munday said, "We'll give him a chance," and pulled off one glove and reached for Caroline's thigh. He fumbled under her coat and felt her dress, warmed by her leg, and then a pouch of softness he pushed with his excited hand. She parted her legs and helped with her hips, and his hand found the satin-covered jowls of her cunt. At once he was aroused; and the dark, the rain, the road, the badger in flight only provoked a greater fury in him. But she said gently, "No," and she stretched out her arm, reached forward, not so much directing him as seeming to grasp for something that remained invisible to him.

Munday turned on the headlights and the badger's lighted eyes appeared up the road, beyond her hand. The badger had stopped when they had, and for the moment after the lights were switched on it held its look of curiosity on its striped face. It began again to run, and after twenty feet frisked wildly at the bank.

Caroline said, "They kill them."

As she spoke the badger flung itself up the wet gleaming bank and slid into an opening at the top, disappearing through a tangle of brambles.

She said, "They eat their haunches."

Concentrating on the badger's flight and distracted by his touching Caroline (it seemed a swift and crazy memory already—had he done it?—he wore only his left glove), Munday had not noticed that the car was climbing. He crossed a stone bridge; he changed gears and the car labored up a grade. They made their way upward now, along a curving lane, the rain falling in bright beaded screens, slanting against their headlights, passed into the road.

"Don't tell me you *walked* all this way."

"I'm not taking you to my house," she said.

The sentence captivated him and made that circuitous passage through the wet lanes of the valley an extraordinary event: he was lost, she was showing him the way, directing him through a landscape she knew. The route was hers, a surprise, the suspense her doing; he was in her hands.

The road widened and led to another, even wider; there was a cottage, its front door flush with the roadside, and further on a new turning, The Yew Tree's hanging sign with its motto on a painted pennant, *Be Bold—Be Wyse*, the lighted telephone booth, the pillar box, the long row of massive oaks, the bend in the road where he had once panicked— now he drove slowly—the telephone pole, and at last a thick rose-bush beating against a fence. Munday parked. He said, "No—not here."

"Yes," she said.

"We can't," he said. "Emma, she's—"

"She's asleep," said Caroline. "It's late." She spoke with a persuasive kindness; but Munday was pleading.

"No, she never sleeps. She's wakeful." Munday leaned towards Caroline. "She's not well. You don't know."

Beyond the rain-marked window of the car he saw the side wall of the Black House, the irregular contours of the broken dripping stone. It was as if he were facing his own guilt. He heard the wind blowing at the wall, and sounds he knew well, that tearing of wind on the dead grass, its purr on the swaying overhead wires, the tree limbs knocking, the grinding gate Emma had left open when he had dropped her earlier. But it was the familiarity of the sounds, not their strangeness that frightened him.

"Please," he said.

"Go in and see," she said, not budging. The calmness in her voice overcame him.

"Wait here," he said. He got out of the car and hurried into the house, crossed through the kitchen and went upstairs, testing the carpet as he climbed. He listened briefly at the head of the stairs and then he proceeded along the hall to the bedroom. The door was ajar; he eased it open a few more inches and heard the wind-blown rain sifting against the window glass. He saw a heap of bedclothes and Emma's hair spread on the pillow—sleeping, she always looked like a casualty. For seconds he mistook his own breathing for hers, then he closed his eyes and concentrated and heard her breathing with heavy slowness, like someone inflating a balloon. He whispered, "Emma," but the rhythm of her breathing went on uninterrupted. Again he whispered her name, louder, almost as if he wanted her to wake up and in waking prevent him from going any further with Caroline in the house: *"Emma."*

But she did not wake; the sounds grew snorelike, resigned, and her deep sleep was like desertion. He was trapped between two women conspiring in the dark for him to take all the blame. He felt for the latch and took the key from inside. He shut the bedroom door and locked it.

He found Caroline in the living room. There were tall green candles burning in the wall holders over the mantelpiece. Caroline was kneeling in front of the fireplace, blowing at the remains of a fire, a few enbers on which she had placed a mound of woodshavings.

"Where did those candles come from?" asked Munday.

She continued to blow softly at the sparks. Then she said, "I found them in the back hall cupboard."

"I had no idea there were candles in it."

"Pass me some of that wood," she said.

Munday took some small split branches from the keg and placed them on the hearthstone. He stepped away and watched her coax the fire with her breath; her face was set against a small circle of sparks. She knelt and peered as if at a reflection she was attempting to kiss, for her lips, as she blew, were that shape.

"I didn't see the light go on," said Munday. "I would have seen that back hall light from the upstairs bedroom."

"I didn't need the light," she said. "Ah, it's caught." The shavings burst into flames and lighted her face. She piled on more shavings and bits of stringy bark and then wood-chips and the split branches Munday had set before her.

"We have firelighters," Munday said. "They'd have it going in seconds."

"I prefer to do it this way," she said, and pushed a dry stick, white as flesh, into the flames.

Munday said, "It's wrong—us here."

Caroline fed the fire. It crackled, louder than her voice as she whispered, "Don't you see? This is the only place it's right."

"She's sleeping," said Munday, after a moment.

"Ah," said Caroline, and smiled, but Munday was not sure whether she was smiling at what he had just said or at the fire, which she stacked with larger pieces of split wood. It was roaring in the chimney now, and the air moved in the room, larger and much brighter with the tall candles and the sticks alight.

"We'll wake her," Munday said in a voice so small it was as if he had spoken something pointless to himself. He looked at Caroline; she was barefoot, she still crouched, her buttocks on her heels; she was naked under her dress, and her breasts swung as she worked with the fire.

"Then don't talk," she said. He was fascinated by the way she attended to the fire. It reddened her skin, and standing above her and a little to the side he could see through the sleeveless opening in her dress and the long open collar, the snout of one breast with its firelit foraging nipple. For the first time since he had entered the room she moved her shoulders and looked up at him. "Why are you wearing that coat?"

She lunged for it and snatched the edge of it and drew him down beside her, making him drop to his knees. Wriggling, she shook out of the top of her dress and pushed it down her arms and worked it to her waist with her thumbs. She left it there, bunched under her white stomach that jutted forward as she kneeled. She was half naked, in a sarong. Munday watched her, too startled to move, and he saw in her breasts and belly and navel a body mask, the shape of a face, with nipples for the eyes, the kind Africans sometimes carved for erotic dances. But theirs were ebony and this was white, the stark face of a willing girl-woman, given expression by the moving shadow of the fire, a plea hatching from her eye-sockets beseeching him to kiss. Then he was tasting it; it was caressing his tongue. Caroline had reached for his head, and with one hand behind his neck and the other under her breast, she lifted her breast into his face. Munday nuzzled the tender orbit of the nipple while she held the breast in her fingers, offering it like fruit.

The fire had grown larger and noisier with all the wood alight, and the storm over the chimney created sudden drafts, which washed the flames forward in furious bursts. Caroline toppled him, upsetting a chair, and knelt over him and swung her breasts in his face. They were loose, lengthened to purses, tickling his eyes. He tried to reach them with his mouth as she pushed his coat open and undid his shirt and tie. The motion of their bodies made the candle-flames waver, he saw them dance above the short hair of Caroline's head, and he felt the fire in the hearth heating one side of his face and the side of his leg. He got up on one elbow and struggled out of his coat. Caroline pulled his shirt off and pushed his trousers down, and as she dug for his penis he kicked his shoes off and worked his trousers off his ankles. She cradled his penis in two hands and pressed her face to it, kissing it and finally sheathing it in her mouth. Then she closed her eyes and rolled her head, taking long adoring sucks. Munday lay back and held his breath; he felt the flutter of her rapid tongue, a buzz on the rawness of his groin, the tropical heat of her mouth and pressure so unusual and changing he buried his face in his hands and imagined he was being bitten in two. His legs told him she had detached the lower part of his body from the upper, but it was only in the lower part that blood flowed. He watched her then with amazement, as if she was attending to his live half, that two-legged creature with a rigid beak.

Then she stopped.

"What is it?"

She turned her head and sneezed twice, and wiped her mouth and returned to him.

The ceiling swam with mottled firelight, and Munday caressed Caroline's legs, the backs of her thighs, and pushed the silken folds of her long skirt aside, unveiling the cool yellow-white globes of her buttocks. She straddled him, facing away, butting his chest with her knees as she crossed over, and still moving her head and making devouring gasps on his penis, she settled on him and moved her cunt against his face. Munday held loosely to her skirt and received her with his tongue, lapping the slickness of her vulva's lips. He was drowning, smothering pleasurably in fathoms of swamp, the ferns prickling his chin, his mouth teased by a pouring tide of eels and damp spiney plant-roots. His arms were helpless, his hands light, falling away from flotsam that dissolved in his grasp. Caroline moved slightly, thrusting down, and Munday licked the seam in the groove than ran to where her arse budded. She groaned and pitched forward, her face against the floor. Munday felt her saliva chilling his erect penis. She reached back, instructing him with her hand, flicking at her buttocks and whispering, "Yes, yes." Munday parted her buttocks and licked at the rough pebbles of the bud. He warmed it, and it opened like a flower on his mouth; he darted his tongue into it, deliriously urged by her moanings. His skin burned from the fire, it seared his arms, and the side of Caroline closest to the fire was hot to the touch, hot enough for him to imagine her skin peeling from her flesh. This heat and her muffled sobs drove him on, and he ignored the fracture in his heart and licked at her in a greedy frenzy for her approval, until her sobs turned to soft howls of pleasure.

Finally, he released her and turned her over. But she became active and crouched beside him; she put one arm around his back and bent and took his penis in her mouth. She drew on it and fondled it beneath with her hand. He felt heat mounting in his loins and a tightening in the cords of his groin that made him tremble. He tried to push her head away, but the gesture warned her. She became excited and held him in her mouth with even more determination. Her eyes were wide open; she did not close them until Munday gripped her hair in both his hands, and he heard his own roaring voice reaching him from the flame-lit ceiling as he drained into her skull.

He woke after that; she was above him, still naked, putting a log on the fire, and beyond her on the wall, he saw the dead and disfigured candle stumps, horned, with long strings of stiff wax hanging from the holders. There was a blanket wrapped around him and he felt the fire's warmth on his legs. At the base of the fire was a shimmering bed of hot coals, dark waves of chevrons floating across the purest red.

"They're killing each other again in Belfast," he said.

"What's that?"

He looked at her and yawned. "You'd better wrap up. You'll get a chill. That chair," he said, "it's got to be fixed."

She was still feeding the fire, throwing the last sticks into it. She said, "Ireland is so green."

"But even Africa is green," he said sleepily. "And England, too . . . from here to the farthest . . . end of the world—" He dropped his head and dozed; he was talking in his sleep. The fire lit his dreams, which were of swamp and pathless jungle and a molten sun erupting at dawn and black shaven-headed girls in loincloths tending plants like green fountains. The clumsy winged birds were there, and the papyrus; he recognized them, not from Africa, but from his other dreams. When he woke again he was shivering with cold, the fire was nearly out. The room was reduced to the small patch of flickering carpet before the fireplace, where he lay sprawled. The candleholders were empty, the chair righted, and she was gone.

14

OVER BREAKFAST he almost told Emma what had happened the previous night in the living room. Emma was joylessly buttering toast and talking about her sick feeling, repeating her apology for having left the party early—and, in exaggerating the offense, seeming to cherish the pathetic image of herself as wayward and unreliable: "They must think I'm awful," she said. "Did they seem cross? I wouldn't blame them if they were. It was unforgivable. But really, Alfred, you've no idea how I felt."

And Munday was going to blurt out, "Listen to me! I met Caroline afterward. I took her here and locked you in the bedroom. We were downstairs and we—"

What? His memory stammered at the reply. He had the will to confess but he lacked the words. What he remembered were incomplete and oddly-lit features, like the broken images he had once got after turning over his car on an African road, the wrecked dazzle of his own arms and legs: there was the fire, a tipped-over chair, Caroline naked on all fours, himself contorted on the floor, sucking at her with a kind of insanity. He hadn't the imagination to contain it all; there was no way for him to describe it to Emma without disparaging it, and to hint at it would have made it ridiculous—besides, how could he hint at *that?*—so it could only be concealed, an act with no name. So the world turned, and on its darkened half the bravest made love in the postures of animals; but it was the only real life—the earth's sunset, the

senses' dawn—for which no one had contrived a language. It had taken him this long to discover joy in
the dark and he knew how much he had wasted: that
return journey, to Africa and back, denying what he
could not say. But now the phantom was flesh; he was
possessed; he was complete, and Emma was a stranger
to him.

He was not disgusted by the memory, though he
wondered at his bravado, seeing in sexual surrender
a kind of courage. Emma was saying, "After all the
trouble the Awdrys went to—" He pitied her for
knowing so little and he wished to tell her, so she
could know how far beyond her he had gone, how she
would never again limit his life with her timid
shadow. She rearranged her breakfast, making disorder
on her plate, sliding and cutting the egg, breaking
the toast; but she didn't eat. He saw her dwelling
uneasily here, as she had in Africa, where every day
promised him a sensation of special longing and
she had complained of the heat and flies.

"Do you suppose we'll ever see that woman again?"
Her question was innocent; he listened for suspicion
but heard none.

"Which woman?"

"The glamorous one."

"Oh, is that what glamorous means?" Munday continued eating. "I've often wondered."

"She was trying," Emma said.

"She was a welcome relief from the others," said
Munday. "They were awfully silly—going on about
the Irish."

"I think I was unfair to her. I hope she didn't
notice."

Munday was confounded; he had no reply. Even
the smallest observation mocked what he knew. Her
Caroline was an occasional dread, but his lover was
real.

Emma said, "I thought she wanted me to go."

"I don't understand you."

"You don't know how women look at each other.

They don't have to say a single word—their faces say everything. She frightened me horribly."

"They were all pretty frightening."

"She was different," said Emma. "You're not a fool, Alfred—you must have noticed that."

"And that's why you left the party."

Emma nodded. "I really believed she wanted me to go."

"Do you believe that now?"

"No," said Emma softly. "It was foolish of me."

"You had all their sympathy," said Munday. "They asked about you."

"After you dropped me, I felt so—I don't know —so safe. I made a fire, I'm not sure why—it was a lot of bother. I had a glass of warm milk, and then I went to bed. I was dead to the world—I didn't hear you come in, and usually do." Emma put her hands on the table and sighed. "And I know why I slept so soundly, too."

"Why?"

"Guilt," said Emma. "I felt so guilty."

"Don't say that," said Munday, whispering the consolation. *Guilt!*

"You can't be expected to know," said Emma. "I haven't told you everything."

"There was that woman you saw at the window." His bluff businesslike tone suggested it was preposterous.

"I don't know what I saw," said Emma. "I hate this house."

"You wanted to come here," said Munday. "It was your idea, the country."

"Don't throw it in my face," she said. "Can't we go to London?"

"The next time I need a haircut," he said.

"Alfred, I've had such terrifying dreams," she said. But she said it with great sadness rather than shock.

"Tell me about them."

"No," she said swiftly, and her eyes flashed, "I couldn't do that."

"Sometimes it helps."

"Filth," she said. "You'd think I was raving mad."

"Everyone has unusual dreams."

"Not like this. Never." She pushed her plate aside.

"Probably far worse," he said. He looked at her. "I dream of Africa."

She turned away and said, "I dream of you."

"Then I'm sorry I disturb your sleep." he said.

She looked up at him, and as if she knew how distant he was and was calling to him from the edge of an uncrossable deepness, she said, "Alfred, you do love me, don't you?"

"Very much," he said. In the past he had answered her like a man testing his voice to reassure himself in a strange place, hoping to hear a confident truth in the echo of his words. This time he was lying—it had to be a lie: the truth would kill her—but, because he knew its falseness beforehand, he said the lie with a convincing vigor, and he added, "With all my heart."

He spent the rest of the morning in the living room, with his notebook in his lap, writing little, savoring the memory the room inspired in him. Mrs. Branch had cleaned (he had said to her, "Sorry about all those ashes"); she had started a meager fire of sticks and coal—she imposed her frugality everywhere in the house—and restored the room to its former dustiness. The sleeves of sunlight at the window were alive with swirling dust particles that had been hallowed by Caroline; and the few flat splashes of wax on the mantelshelf, seemingly so unimportant, recalled an important moment. The room was special, it held Caroline's presence, her whispers, the worn carpet bore the imprint of her knees; in Mrs. Branch's little fire was a fleeting odor of Caroline's magnificent blaze, which lingered as well in sooty streaks on the mantletree—that was especially blackened, and looked as if it had contained an explosion.

Not a room, but a setting he understood, that had involved him and given him hope. The Black House was finally his, and it was Caroline's doing: she knew the house, she had directed him there, and Emma sleeping through it upstairs had kept the act from being casual. It was deliberate. He refused to see it as betrayal. It was too bad that in being faithful to himself he had been unfaithful to Emma, but he consoled himself with the secrecy of it. He did not believe he had wronged her—she barely knew him and she could not know more without being hurt. So he was determined to protect her, the more so now because she needed his reassurance. He would never leave her, and he told himself that he had not lied to her: he dearly loved her—but in a way she kept it from completion, for she required his love, and she depended on him, but she gave him little for it. She had little to give; she was stricken with a kind of poverty and would fail without him.

But this poverty in Emma, demanding his attention, had diminished his respect for her, and the boldness he saw in Caroline, the skeletal brightness in her hair and bones, cornered him, challenged his heart and gave him a feeling of triumph. It would be brief—that was the worst of sex; but he was under a sentence of death: he deserved and needed that adventure. It had led him to an understanding of Emma, whose doom was to live famished; it had also turned him to examine his body. He had begun to despise his heart as a failure, but now he valued it and looked at it with wonderment and a renewed affection. It was a narcissism he did not think was possible in a man his age; but then, he was not old. He had had a second chance. He had enjoyed another woman and was not sorry. With luck he would repeat it; it was not unusual, many people did the same.

The work he had set for himself, so long delayed, began to interest him, and during the days that followed he wrote with purpose, giving every word a meticulous dedication—as if he were being admiringly watched—filling his notebook with observations about the Bwamba. He had been returned to himself, and he was amazed at his resolve. He loved the Black House now, and in his study, using his new patience, he was able to recall particular details of Africa he had earlier thought had been lost to him. He recovered them and saw their value, which was his value as an anthropologist. He had regained his will; his new serenity allowed him the perspective to see the stages of his African experience, how he had grown and changed beside the people he had studied, who were themselves changeless. He wrote with surprise and pleasure of how he had gone to that remote place behind the mountains and set up house and endured suspicion and the discomforts of the equatorial climate in order to witness the daily life of a people whose past and present were indistinguishable, who had confided in him their deepest secrets, which were heart-breaking, and who stank of witchcraft. Like them, he had cut himself off—gladly at first, then with misgivings. And though there had been times among them when he had despairingly seen himself as no different from them, existing in the seasonless monotony of swamp and savannah, now on the notebook pages they appeared like little creatures from prehistory, fixed like fossils, with simple habits —using the technology of child campers—and uttering inconsequential threats with a murderous charm. He was so different! The ten years flashed in his mind; he saw the Bwamba from a great height, like a man in a meadow who kicks over a stone and looks down at the mass of wood-lice on the underside scurrying for cover.

He wrote, marveling at how many features of Africa lived within him, appearing at his command from a tangle in a distant precinct of his mind. He made notes on ideas to pursue: on the rarefied atmosphere of isolation and its effect on memory; on the queer crippling delusions he had had to overcome —one had stayed with him for days, a belief that everything that lay outside the camp had been destroyed (it was during the April rains, the road was closed, and it had taken a great effort of will for him to stir outside and find it untrue)—or another, more reasonable fear, that having stayed away so long he had been forgotten by everyone in England who had ever known him.

One day at the end of the first week in January, Munday entered the kitchen for lunch and found a letter propped against his water tumbler. Anxiously he picked it up and turned it over. It had not been opened. Still, his heart raced, as if the simple lifting of the letter had caused him an exertion.

"It came this morning," said Emma, putting a dish on the table. "I didn't want to disturb you." She uncovered the dish. "Do you mind having shepherd's pie again?"

"Not at all," said Munday abstractedly. He slit the envelope and held the letter to the window. It was written in spotty failing ballpoint, large regular script on ruled paper from an airmail pad. But it was not from Caroline. He took the message in at once, *Forgive my delay,* down to the cramped overpracticed signature.

"Surprise, surprise," he said.

"Who's it from?"

"Silvano," said Munday, seating himself at the table and shaking out his napkin. "Seems he's decided to pay us a visit."

"But you invited him," said Emma.

"So he says. I honestly can't remember."

"Weeks ago," said Emma.

Munday folded the frail paper and ran his fingers down the crease. "I wish he'd chosen some other time to write. I'm so busy at the moment." He opened the paper again and said, "Here, listen, 'owing to pressure of work I have neglected to reply.' *Pressure of work!*"

"Are you going to put him off?"

"No, I suppose the only thing to do is get it over with," said Munday. "I'll ask him for next weekend."

"Strange," said Emma. "I didn't think I'd ever

want to see another African again as long as I
lived. But I feel so starved for company here. It's
like being back in the bush—this feeling I'm standing still in a wretched backwater, and everything's
out of reach."

"What an extraordinary thing to say," said Munday.

"You know, what I mean. A dead end. You feel
it too, don't deny it."

"I feel nothing of the kind."

"Then you're lucky," said Emma. "I'm quite looking forward to seeing Silvano. He was a nice boy.
What did you say he's doing in London?"

"What they always do," said Munday. "Economics,
political science, moral philosophy. Should be very
useful when he goes back to the Inturi Forest—they're
crying out for people like that in Bundibugyo." Munday made a scoffing snort, then said, "Ah, shepherd's
pie, my favorite."

"You said you didn't mind."

"But twice in one week, Emma!"

"It was all I had time for," said Emma. "I was doing
housework—Pauline left to go shopping. It's early-
closing today."

"*Ayah*'s down at the *bazaar,* is she?" Munday
helped himself to the shepherd's pie.

"I hope they're not cruel to him."

"Who?"

"Silvano," said Emma. "At the pub, in the village
—these local people. You said you were going to show
him around."

"Did I?" Munday began to eat. "Oh, yes. That's
right."

Later that afternoon, Munday sketched out points
to be made on notions of time. It was something no
anthropologist had dealt with, theories he planned to
develop regarding the uselessness of calendar time in
folk-cultures—or any culture: how arbitrary it was to
count years, one by one, when in reality years were
plastic and indeterminate, often reversible, and to

travel in space in a given direction might mean losing a century. He would examine the traveler's platitude about going back two thousand years. ("These people are living in the stone age," said tourists in Bwamba; they came for the hot springs and the degenerate road-bound pygmies.) It could jar the balance of the mind, this toppling back and forth in time, if you were resident and serious; and the Africans, whose time was circular, moved from century to century in licking a stamp for a bride-price letter, or fixing an axe-head with plastic twine from an Indian shop, or keeping sorcery bones and the clippings of funeral hair in a blue shoulder bag marked BOAC. Munday had experienced the slip of those contrasts. He had shunted from the timeless simplicity of the village, to Fort Portal where the atmosphere was of the 1920s, to Kampala—always ten years behind London—to London itself, which had never ceased to be strange for him. Time was a neglected dimension in the study of man; but it mattered, and one had to consider this in judging people who lived in pockets of inverted time. Munday himself had lurched to the past and back by degrees, blunting his memory in the movement, so his own age was a puzzling figure and all dates seemed wrong. He had seen Africans shattered by the same confusions.

Emma stood at the door. Munday saw her but went on writing. *Time is elastic, binding and releasing the—*

"I've decided to bake a pie," said Emma.

"Good for you," said Munday. He saw her lingering, he tapped with his pen. "I didn't realize apple pies were your strong point."

"They're not. But I know where we can get some apples."

"Splendid." Munday continued to write—to pretend to. He scratched at the paper.

Emma remained in the doorway.

Munday said, "Off you go."

"No," said Emma. "I can't. You have to get them."

"Then let's have the pie tomorrow, shall we?" He

showed her the half-filled notebook page. "I'm rather busy."

"I must have the apples tonight," she said, and she added, "Please help me."

"Can't you see you're interrupting me?"

"Alfred," she pleaded, her voice breaking.

Munday snapped the notebook shut. "This is ridiculous. Apples! Emma, I don't care if we have apples tonight or tomorrow or never. I'm not interested."

"You never help me!" Emma sobbed. "I try and try, and you always—"

"For goodness' sake—"

"You've *got* to go," Emma said, the lucid appeal coming between her sobs.

"Hold on," said Munday. Now, he smiled. "Didn't you tell me today was early-closing? All the shops will be shut. It's gone four."

"It's not a shop," said Emma. "It's that place we went before Christmas—that farm on the back road."

"Hosmer's?"

"Yes. There was a sign on one of those cottages. Someone sells them."

Munday tried to remember. "I didn't see any apples when we were there."

"I tell you I saw the sign," said Emma.

Munday said, "You're making this up."

Emma came forward and howled, "I'm not! I'm not! Help me, Alfred—you must go now."

"Send Branch," he said.

"No—*you!*" She set her face at him.

Munday got up and held her; she was shaking. He said, "Do calm yourself, my darling. If you want me to go, of course—"

"You can walk," she said. The hysteria had wrung her and left her breathless. "It's not far—down the road, past The Yew Tree, that valley road, where it dips. But if you don't hurry"—her voice went small, like a child's disappointed protest—"I won't have my apples."

He thought she might be mad, and he recalled what

she had said at lunchtime, *everything's out of reach*.
He had to reply to her unexpected demand by humor-
ing her. He took the money she offered, a pound note
folded into a neat square, and he kissed her and said,
"I won't be long."

It was dusk, a sea-mist was building in the fields,
veiling the hedgerows, and he walked into the falling
dark on Emma's errand. The Yew Tree was shut; one
upper window was lighted, the rest held oblong frames
of clouds and the last of the sun, breaking through in
dim cones at the sea. Munday turned down the lane
and walked briskly, putting a bird to flight—it beat its
way out of a hedge noisily without showing itself to
him—and then to the row of thatched cottages. He
hadn't seen the barn before, but it was there, a rough
building of flint and white coarsely-shaped stone beyond the mucky rutted barnyard. And a large sign was
nailed to the gatepost on the cottage next to Hosmer's,
APPLES. Several chickens pecked close to the house;
their feathers were muddied on their undersides, but
their presence and their color emphasized that some
daylight still lingered.

Munday rapped on the door and heard his sounds
echo in the house. He peeked through the window. He
saw the kitchen table in the center of the room, cruets,
a newspaper, a jam jar. He rapped again, then gave
up and crossed to the barn, stopping midway to catch
a glimpse of the platform where he had seen those
dead dogs under the canvas. He remembered them
only when he was descending the stone stairs. But they
were behind Hosmer's cottage, those flayed things.

His shoes sucked in the mud as he wrenched the
bar door open. At once he smelled the sour decay of
apples and saw in warped racks huge cider barrels,
rags wound on their wooden bungs, and a cider press,
like an early printing machine, the thick iron screw
and the woodframe black with dampness. The para-
phernalia leaned at him: a wheelless wagon resting on
greasy axles, and hose-pipes and glass jugs and a
pruning hook, and on posts supporting the hayloft,

harnesses, snaffles, and coils of rope. The apple smell was strong and stung his nose, but there was in its richness something of the earth, a live hum that engaged all his senses. In the wagon were bushel baskets of apples. Munday carefully stepped over the jugs and reached for a basket.

His shadow sank in a wider shadow as the interior of the barn grew dark. It was as if the door had been shut on him without a sound.

"Is this what you've come for?"

Munday turned and saw Caroline at the door, blocking what daylight remained; behind her legs a white chicken moved, pecking at mud, bustling in jerks.

"You," he said. She had given him a fright. He left the wagon and clattered past the jugs, upsetting one. He saw she held a full paper bag against her chest.

"I had to see you," she said. "I've missed you."

Munday said, "Oh, my love, my love," and embraced her, kissed her and split the bag of apples. Caroline dropped her arms and released it. The apples tumbled to their shins, fell between them, plopping at their feet, making bumps as they hit and their skin punctured and bruised on the barn floor. Munday stepped on one, skidding on its flesh, and hugged Caroline for balance. The apples rolled in all directions, gulping as they bounced.

15

IT WAS a custom among the Bwamba to let their hair grow after a member of the family had died. During this time of mourning their hair sprouted stiffly in a round bushy shape, like a thick wool helmet pulled over their ears. This hair, with their sparse beards, made their faces look especially gaunt, like the pinched ones of defeated men driven into hiding in deep jungle. After a suitable period, and when the affairs of the deceased were settled—all the debts apportioned—the hair was cut with a certain amount of ceremony.

Silvano's hair was uncut, and Munday was sorry his self-consciousness had prevented him from welcoming the African on the platform. A mourner deserved better than to arrive at a country railway station and to find his own way to the exit. Munday had driven to the station and parked, and he stayed in the car until the other arriving passengers had been met and driven away—visiting friends with expensive luggage; weekending couples; the tall son rather formally introducing the smartly-dressed girl to his parents, pipe-clutching father, beaming mother; the yawning wife meeting her husband in her station wagon, two children in the back seat, kisses all around and the wife sliding over and letting the husband take the wheel. Then Silvano. And Munday was ashamed of himself when he saw the African, smaller than he remembered, and not black but gray—the gloss was gone from his face. He emerged awkwardly from the station exit after the other people, with a large suitcase and the long hair, looking worried and overwhelmed in the English setting.

Seeing Munday get out of the car, Silvano brightened and called out a Bwamba greeting, *"M'okole!"* Munday replied softly, *"Bulunji,"* and was glad there was no one around to hear him. He took the suitcase —it was surprisingly light—and offered his condolences.

"No one is dead," said Silvano. "Everyone very fit —I got a letter just the other day."

"But your hair—"

"Oh, that," said Silvano, and he pushed at it with his hand. "Only the new style. London style, so to say."

"Of course," said Munday. "Very fashionable." He noticed that Silvano was wearing a new pin-striped blue suit, a maroon velvet tie and pink shirt, pointed shoes; Munday had never seen him in anything but gray drill shorts and molded plastic sandals.

In the car, passing through Mosterton, Silvano said, "So—grass on the roofs!" and Muncay explained the thatch. Silvano said, further on, "Very narrow road," and Munday replied, "It's perfectly adequate. By the way, have you had your lunch?"

"Yes, on the train," Silvano said. "Chicken-something."

Munday saw him looking out the car window. They were driving along a stretch of road that ran for about half a mile between some hills and then opened on a prospect of the southeast, an uncluttered sweep of landscape, plowed fields and pastures. It was early afternoon and still sunny; the clouds were beginning to gather, rising against the sun, giving height to the sky and dramatizing the mottled fields. The visibility was good, and for miles Munday could see hills like overturned bowls, and forested hollows and severe hedges dividing the farmland. Past a man plowing, surrounded by flights of wheeling seagulls, layered shadings of green and tweedy winter brown marked the distances.

"Look at that," said Munday. It was a vista of country so open and empty he wanted to stop the car and march directly across it and lose himself in that expanse.

"Cows," said Silvano.

"Where?" asked Munday. Then he saw them, at the roadside, cropping grass.

Silvano settled back in the seat and lit a cigarette. He said, "I didn't know there were so many cows in England."

"They keep them to pay bride-price," said Munday. "I had to give half a dozen to Emma's father when I married her."

"I think you're playing, Doctor Alfred," said Silvano.

"You're too quick for me."

"Postgraduate," said Silvano, and held up his smoking cigarette to examine it.

"Actually, England's still heavily agricultural," said Munday. Silvano remained silent, and Munday felt all his old weariness return in the effort of making conversation with an African, commenting on what was most obvious, spelling out the labored joke. Munday would have preferred to speak in the Bwamba language to mask his insincerity. Somehow, things sounded less trivial spoken in the local dialect. Munday spoke the language well, he used the idioms with ease. He had often said that he knew more about the Bwamba than the Bwamba themselves—it accounted, he thought, for his depressions and their unreasonable cheer.

"Is this your first time out of London?" asked Munday.

"First time," said Silvano. "So much work to do—always writing and more writing."

Munday said, "Pressure of work."

"Yes," said Silvano. He added gravely, "And I have a girl friend."

"Lucky fellow," said Munday.

"Young men need to have girl friends," said Silvano. "Otherwise!" His laughter was full of teeth and greed. Munday knew that Silvano was thirty-five years old; he had a wife who worked in his sizable garden; he supported a pair of aged relatives; he had a bicycle, a short-wave radio, and four children.

"Which reminds me," said Munday. "How's your wife?"

"Quite all right," said Silvano. "Expecting number five." He continued to smoke calmly. They were passing The Rose and Crown in Broadwindsor. Silvano said, "Are the pubs open?"

"They close early around here," said Munday. "Two-thirty."

"We have time for a pint," said Silvano, looking at his watch. Munday saw that it was a new one. "I always have a pint at this time."

"I never do," said Munday.

"There was no beer on the train."

"I really think we should be getting along," said Munday as he accelerated past the pub. "Emma's expecting us. Besides, there's plenty to drink at the Black House."

"The Black House," said Silvano. "Is that a pub?"

"No, no," said Munday, and he realized that he had spoken the name aloud for the first time. It was like an admission of his acceptance—he had said it quite naturally. "That's what the locals call my house, don't ask me why."

"Interesting," said Silvano.

Munday explained the English practice of naming houses, illustrating it with the signboards they passed, until, much to his annoyance, Silvano began to call each one out. Munday hoped he would stop, but he kept it up. "The Thistles," he was saying, "Ladysmith, Aleppo, Bowood House."

"We'll let Emma open the door," said Munday. "She likes the drama."

"Ah, Silvano," said Emma, opening the double doors one at a time. "So good to see you." She had changed into her wool dress and wore a wooden Bwamba brooch, one of the ineptly carved curios they had started to make in the last years of Munday's residence, to sell in the mission craft-shop.

"He's eaten," said Munday. He saw Mrs. Branch lingering at the scullery door, unable to suppress her look of astonishment at the black man chatting in the kitchen. "And this is Mrs. Branch."

She hesitated; in her nervousness she traced a water stain on the wall with her finger. Then she came forward in halting steps, twisting her hands. She said, "Pleased to meet you."

Silvano smiled and put his hand out, but Mrs.

Branch didn't take it. She locked her fingers together
and continued to stare.

"Won't you have a coffee?" asked Emma.

"Doctor promised me a beer," said Silvano. He
laughed, trumpeting his hilarity with a wide-open
mouth.

"So I did," said Munday. "It's too early for me,
but have one yourself."

"Let's go into the other room," said Emma. "Pauline's made a fire. It's lovely and warm."

"I'll fetch his case from the car," said Munday.
"Won't be a minute." He carried the suitcase upstairs
to one of the larger bedrooms (Emma had put flowers
in the vase, and a hot-water bottle and towel on the
bed), and on an impulse he opened it. It was a large
suitcase, heavy cardboard with two leather straps
around its middle, the kind that was sold in Indian
shops in Uganda. But it contained surprisingly few
things—pajamas, a string vest, a sweater, a paperback
with *Nigger* in the title, shaving equipment, several
deodorants in aerosol cans (*Body Mist, Ban,* after-
shave lotion). And a picture in a small metal frame.
It was a slightly blurred photograph of a rather thin
and not young English girl smiling sadly on a bench
in a public park. There were thumbprints on the glass.
Munday's first emotion was embarrassment, then great
rage at the foolishness of carrying such a picture.
But he recognized his anger as unworthy and he returned the picture to the case feeling only pity for
the girl, and pity for Emma, and against his will feeling a bit ridiculous himself, as if the glimpse of another man's desire had devalued and exposed his own.

Emma handed Munday a cup of coffee when he
entered the living room. She said, "Silvano's telling
me about his flat in Earl's Court."

Munday moved in front of the fire, warming his
back. "I thought you had a room at London House."

"Yes," said Silvano. "Then I moved. I'm sharing
with some other chaps—fellow Ugandans."

"I should say you're damned lucky to have a flat,"

said Munday. He said peevishly to Emma, "I think of Alec with his bedsitter in Ealing."

"A flat's more comfortable," said Silvano.

"A flat's more expensive," said Munday. "But, then Alec's not on a government grant. *His* money's frozen in a Uganda bank account."

Silvano had spoken inoffensively; he was eager to please and impress. But Munday felt a growing resentment against the hair, the new watch, the stylish suit —Silvano plucked at the creases in his trousers—the casual mention of the girl friend, the flat. He was a villager who had for years shared a one-room, grass-rooted hut with his large family. He had served as a subject for one of Munday's monographs on Bwamba agriculture—he was typical enough for that: a herd-boy, then a clearer of elephant grass, then a family man, indistinguishable from any of the forest people except that he was less quarrelsome, more intelligent, and didn't drink beer. When Munday first met him, Silvano was convinced that God intended him to be a priest, and it was on the mission's motor-cycle that Silvano went to his extramural classes in Fort Portal. Munday persuaded him against joining the priesthood and, tutoring him privately, got him a place at Makerere. Silvano married; Silvano switched from the School of Agriculture to the English Department; Silvano wrote poems; and on his holidays, when he visited Munday at the Yellow Fever Camp, he had a sharp *muhoro* in the belt of his drill shorts, and he carried, as a proof of his literacy, a geography book with a faded, soiled cover which gave off the hut smell of dirt and wood-smoke.

"I thought we might go out a bit later and drive to Whitchurch Canonicorum," said Emma to Silvano. "There's an English saint buried in the church, and it's a charming village. We could have a cream tea on the way back. You don't want to come all this way and miss a cream tea."

"That sounds super," said Silvano.

"It doesn't go very well over beer," said Munday.
"But I never miss my tea," said Silvano.

"Really."

"I know Alfred wants to take you around the village."

"There's not an awful lot to see," said Munday.
"I'm sure we'd be more comfortable right here."

But the visit was unavoidable. They drove to the village of Whitchurch shortly after, found St. Candida's altar with the three openings, and Munday explained how it was thought that a diseased limb could be cured if it was inserted in one of the holes. Emma was over at the baptismal font. Munday said in a low voice to Silvano, "Or I daresay you could stick your *tumba* in, if circumstances required."

Silvano giggled and said, "That's interesting!"

The coarse joke was for the African, and it made Munday view the next days with dread. In Uganda he had been friendly with Silvano, and Silvano had informed part of his research; the relationship had been an easy one. Munday was grateful for that; he had recommended Silvano for a Commonwealth scholarship. But here, and really from the moment Silvano had said, "Only the new style. London style—," Munday had viewed him as someone of ponderous weight whom he had managed easily enough in Africa but whom he would struggle with in England—like the gliding sea-animal which becomes insupportable out of water. It wasn't Silvano's fault, but Munday saw him posing problems to the smallest venture; he was like an invalid guest whose affliction had to be carefully considered before any move could be made. And even then he would remain helpless; he had to be shown things—this church, that house, that view—and for this Munday was required to carry him. Munday was newly conscious of Silvano's color, and while feeling a prompt sympathy for the African, he knew he might have to defend that color to the villagers. He did not relish the possibility; he wanted to hide him.

More than this (now they had left the churchyard and were driving down a country lane to Shave's Cross), Munday had the separated lover's regret, of spending time and effort with people who knew him as the figure he had been in the past, a personality he had outgrown, but one for which they retained a loyal respect: the regret that he was not with his lover, giving her the attention he felt he was wasting on his wife and that burdensome acquaintance. The duties of sentiment and friendship, accumulated obligations, intruded on this secret life. So he drove and he could smell Caroline on his hands and taste the crush of her mouth and breast on his tongue, as pungent as apples.

"Why don't we give the tea a miss?" said Munday.

"I'd love a cup of tea," said Emma. "I'm sure Silvano wants one, too. Don't be a wet blanket, Alfred. You're brooding so."

Eager to get it over with, he stopped at the first signboard that said *Teas*. It was a small bungalow of cob and hatch, set back from the road on a stony drive. The cob had been whitewashed and showed large smooth patched places; its windows were set deep in the bulging walls, as if retreating into sockets. It had a satisfying shape, as natural as a ground-swell, and a well-tendered look; but dense clouds now filled the late-afternoon sky, and the gray light on the dark grass that surrounded the dwelling gave it a cheerless air. Smoke billowed from the end chimney, and Munday found it hard to see all that streaming smoke and not think that the bungalow was about to go into motion and chug out of the garden like a locomotive.

A middle-aged woman in a blue smock met them at the door and greeted them uncertainly, avoiding Silvano's gaze. She showed them to a parlor jammed with small tables. There was a fire crackling in the grate, and two other customers, a man and woman, seated near it. Munday wanted to leave as soon as he saw them. But the proprietor was seating

Emma, and Silvano had already taken his place at the table—he was toying with a small oil-lamp which was the centerpiece. The couple at the other table did not look up. The man was wearing an overcoat, the woman a hat, and both were buttering toast with raised arms to keep their sleeves out of the tea.

"Not many customers," said Silvano.

The woman in the blue smock frowned at her pad. She poised her pencil stub and said, "Will that be three teas?"

Munday said, "With clotted cream."

"Thank you." She scribbled on the pad, and with deft simultaneous movements of her hands dropped the pad into her apron pocket and pushed the pencil into her hair. She removed the fourth place mat. Emma slipped her coat off; she leaned forward, her arms behind her back, her breasts brushing the table, as she worked her arms out of the sleeves. Munday had always found this one of the most attractive things a woman could do. He saw Silvano staring.

"Believe it or not," said Munday, "this cottage is made out of mud. The walls are about two feet thick, of course, but it's mud sure enough—clay, actually—on a wooden frame. Could be a few hundred years old."

"Mudded walls and grass roof," said Silvano. "Just like Bundibugyo!"

"But not as civilized," said Munday.

"Oh, I think so," said Silvano, seriously.

"Down here for a holiday?" It was the man by the fire who had spoken, and it was some while before Munday realized the man was addressing their table from across the empty room. The man hadn't looked up. His hands were still raised, stropping a sliver of toast with butter.

"You might say that." Munday was gruff; he hated the man's probing question.

"It's not a bad place," said the man. "For a holiday, that is."

"The weather's been splendid lately," said Emma.

"It's holding," said the man. "It's been a mild winter—that's why everyone's down with flu." Now he crunched his toast, and his chewing was like muttering, as if he had more in his mouth that a bite of toast. "It's going to be a terrible summer—it always is after a winter like this." He took another bite of toast and sipped his tea.

His wife spoke up: "We'll pay for these warm days!" She stared at Munday from under her crooked hat.

"Yes, it's not a bad place for a holiday," said the man. "But you don't want to move down here. Take my advice—we've been down here for eighteen months."

"It's a glorious part of the world," said Emma.

"Hear that?" said the man to his wife.

The wife leaned in the direction of the Mundays' table. She said, "The people are so unfriendly around here. We've had them around to tea, but they never invite you back."

"Just go their own way," said the man.

"How awful for you," said Munday.

"I know it *looks* very pretty," said the man. "But I can tell you it's no bed of roses."

"We're from London," said the woman. "Retired."

"Silvano's from London," said Emma.

Silvano smiled and started lighting a cigarette.

"Not from overseas?" asked the man.

"From overseas," said Silvano, puffing on the cigarette. "And also from London, as well."

"I knew you were strangers," said the man. "I can always tell. London?"

"It's rather a long story," said Munday.

The man started to speak, then he fell silent. The door had opened and the woman in the blue smock entered with the tea things. She arranged them on the table, cups, teapot, a china pitcher of hot water, a plate of scones and fruitcake, a dish of dark jam, and a large dish of cream.

"Will that be all?" asked the woman.

"Lovely," said Emma.

The woman scribbled again on her pad, tore off the leaf, and slipped it beside Munday's plate. She left the room. An inner door banged.

"*She's* from London," said the man at the far table. "Barnet. Lost her husband last year. Don't get her started." He was biting his toast between sentences. "Road accident. Ever see such driving? They ran this as a bed and breakfast. Now she can only manage teas. That's why we come here. Give her the business."

The man continued to chatter. Munday decided to ignore him. He split a scone, buttered it, spread it with jam, and topped it with a spoonful of clotted cream. Silvano watched him, following one step behind him in his preparations: Munday was eating his scone as Silvano was spreading the cream.

Emma said, "I'm sure you'll be making new friends."

"Not here," said the man. "I don't want them here, thank you very much."

"It's this retirement," said the woman. "It's all so new to us. We're thinking of buying a spaniel."

The man turned to Emma and said, "The way I see it, you've got to have a reason for getting up in the morning."

Emma said to Silvano, "How do you like your tea?"

"Very good," he said. His lips were flecked with cream.

"Look at him eat!" said the man, nodding at Silvano. "*Chagoola mazooli?*"

"*Mzuri sana,*" said Silvano.

"I was there during the war," said the man.

"I'm about ready to push off," said Munday.

"Wait, Alfred," said Emma. She poured hot water into the teapot.

The man and wife were rising from the table, the man putting on his tweed cap, the woman her coat.

"You've got to have a reason for getting up in the morning," said the man.

"Yes, dear," said the woman.

They approached the Mundays' table. "Nice talking to you," said the man.

"Enjoy your holiday," said the woman.

The man clapped a hand on Silvano's shoulder and said, "Cold enough for you?" He left, snickering.

"Poor old soul," said Emma.

Silvano said, "He seemed jolly friendly."

"A sad case," said Munday. "Now, if you're about through, I think we'd better be going."

"Do let him finish his cup," said Emma.

"I'm finished," said Silvano, and drained it.

"You're the one who's lagging," said Munday to Emma.

It was dark by the time they arrived back at the Black House, and Silvano said, "It never gets this dark in London." Munday went to his study, Emma stayed in the kitchen, and Silvano settled himself in the living room, hunched over and watching "Doctor Who."

At seven o'clock Emma came into the study. She shut the door behind her and said, "Aren't you going to take him out?"

"He's perfectly happy," said Munday. He was taking the measurements of a number of Bwamba axe-heads; they were spread before him on the desk, large and small. He picked up a sharp spiked one and struck the air with it. "I've got my axe-heads, he's got his telly program."

"You're ignoring him."

"You know how I loathe television," said Munday. "Why don't you sit with him?"

"I thought you might take him to the church."

"The church?" Munday put the axe-head down. "Emma, there's nothing on at the church."

"There's a service."

"It's Saturday night. It'll be shut."

"I think you should go down there."

"We've *seen* one church today," said Munday. "We can go tomorrow."

"Not tomorrow," said Emma. *"Tonight.* It's important that you go now."

"Emma, that's insane—"

"Oh, God, I have such a headache," she said, and she groaned, "Why don't you ever listen to me?"

"I'm sorry."

"Alfred, I'm not well."

"I'll tell you what—I'll go down to the church alone, and if there's something going on I'll come back for Silvano. In the meantime, he can watch television."

Emma said, "Hurry."

Munday drove to the village and parked near The White Hart. The stained-glass windows of the church were lighted, and entering by the side door he could see baskets of flowers on the altar and all the lights burning, the flowers and the illumination giving the church interior the illusion of warmth and height. It was his first visit to the church, but there was nothing strange about it; no two African huts were the same to his eye, but all English churches seemed interchangeable, and this one, with its smell of wood and floorwax and brass polish, its sarcophagus with a recumbent marble knight and crouching hound, its dusty corners and wordy memorials—this one was no different from St. Candida's, or the hilltop church in East Coker, St. Michael's, which Emma had enthused over (and made an occasion for urging an Eliot play on Munday; "I can't vouch for his poetry, but I can tell you he's fairly ignorant about Africans," said Munday when he had read it). He browsed among the leaflets in the wooden rack at the door, read one of the memorial stones, and then seated himself in the last pew. Above him the ribbed windows were gleaming black, gem-shaped segments of roughened glass fixed in lead.

A figure suddenly stood up in a front pew, and the pew itself growled. Shawled and seated when he had entered, she had blended with the jumble of still shapes near the carved pulpit—he hadn't seen her. She clacked down the aisle, holding the shawl at her throat, her head down. But Munday recognized her before she had gone three steps, and he started to get up. She passed by him without lifting her eyes.

Munday followed her outside to the churchyard, the cemetery of old graves on the far side of the church. She walked along a gravel path, past illegible headstones—some leaning, some broken or tipped over—past a tall grave-marker with a burst plinth, and through the grass, where snowdrops had started, the tiny white blossoms growing in clusters close to the ground, as if they had been scattered there like handfuls of wool: they were lighted by the reflection of the church windows that fell across them. She sat on a stone bench under a large yew tree, out of the glare of the moon and nearly hidden in the shadows of the thick foliage. Munday sat next to her, and though he did not touch her, he could feel her breathing, that warm pulse in her throat, her skin warming his a foot away.

He kept apart and whispered, "What are you doing to Emma?"

"Nothing."

"You're smiling."

"No." But she was—he could see her mouth.

"What are you telling her?"

"Only that I want you." The purr in her voice gave the words an emphatic nakedness.

He said, "Caroline—"

"Hold my hand," she said. She pulled off one glove and reached over and laid her white hand on his thigh.

He covered her hand with his own and said, "You're a witch."

"I'm not," she said, with a pout of amusement on her mouth. "Anyway, what do you know about witches?"

"A great deal," he said. "You're using her."

"I can only reach you through her."

He mumbled something, not words, the syllables of a sigh.

"What did you say?"

"It doesn't seem fair," he said.

Caroline clutched his hand; Munday could feel her fingers, her nails pricking his palm. She said, "You want me, don't you?"

"Yes."

"Then it's fair." She leaned over and kissed him lightly, but his cheek burned, as if she had scarred him where her lips had brushed his skin.

"I want to make love to you now."

"We can't," she said.

"Please."

"Here?" She laughed. "On this bench? In the church? Or there, behind that grave?"

"Anywhere," he said, and looked hopelessly around the graveyard.

She took his chin and turned his face towards hers. She said, "I believe you would!"

"Hurry," he said. He hugged her and tried to draw her up.

"No," she said. "Never that. Don't hurry me— don't push me into the grass and hike my skirt up, then fumble with me and tell me you have to go when you finish."

"I won't."

"But you will. You have to. It would ruin it."

Munday said nothing; she was right—Emma was waiting.

"There's time," she said. "We'll do it properly— not hurrying and half-naked and looking at your watch. I know you would if I let you, but I won't let you cheat me that way. I want to be naked, on top of you, with a fire going like that first night. God, that was wonderful. You were babbling in some African language."

"Was I? Why didn't you tell me before?"

"I thought you knew," she said. "I thought you were doing it deliberately."

"Perhaps I was," he said.

"Next time I want to make love to *you*. Take you in my mouth and swallow you."

"When?" he whispered.

"Soon," she said. "You'll see."

"I've never known anyone like you."

"But then you've been away, haven't you?"

"For such a long time," he said. "And so far away. You can't imagine."

"I can," she said. "You still taste of Africa."

"I used to hate the thought of coming back," he said. "England—but you're not English."

"I am!"

"No," he said, "not like any woman I've ever known here."

She smiled. "So you've known one somewhere else."

"Africa is full of witches," he said.

"You're mad," she said. "And it's a wonder you love me."

"But that's what I *do* love!"

The lights in the church had gone out while they were speaking, and Munday left her in darkness and stumbled through the graveyard, choosing his way among the stones and snowdrops in the moonlight which lay like water on the ground. For all he had said, he was afraid, but the fear beating in his blood animated him, caused a leaping in his mind that was next to joy. The panic he felt was vivid enough and yet so wild in him it might have been something he had learned eavesdropping on another person's passion—emotion so unusual that it eluded memory and that for him to try to recall it would be to lose it entirely, or perhaps admit that it was too intense to be his. And a further fear, which was like a fear of his own courage, one that he had known in Africa, not of being incapable of understanding the witch-ridden mind in the village paralyzed by myth, but of understanding it too well, generating a sympathy so complete it was the same as agreement; the fear that, in time, only the most savage logic would satisfy him and everything else would seem fraudulent and unlikely. It happened, but briefly, and he had overcome it. Now he was home, freed from them by his heart—the blacks and the jungle they owned were a distant trap. He might have died there!

An eager panic held him. It was that glimpse of himself in the churchyard, trampling the tufts of snowdrops he had tried to avoid, his half-remembered desire that approached and taunted him like a masked dance, and the thought of Caroline's promptings to Emma—the witching appeal to his own body. He refused to doubt that, because simply by believing, he had Caroline to gain. He could only dismiss someone else's ghost. But his own haunting rewarded him with desire and he remained astonished by what he would willingly risk for her.

"I was right, wasn't I?" said Emma.

"Yes," said Munday. "There *was* something. But it's over now."

"You can take him out tomorrow."

"I'm off to bed," he said. "Is he well occupied?"

"He's watching 'Match of the Day.' "

"This way," said Munday, starting off the road near the Black House to a path partially arched with high bushes. It was a narrow path and, barely used, it promised greater narrowness further on.

"Isn't the village on this road?" asked Silvano. He hesitated on the tarmac in his pin-striped suit and winced at the untrodden path.

"We'll go around the back by the path," said Munday. "Much more interesting the country way. I'm sure you get quite enough of paved roads in London."

"I like paved roads," said Silvano.

With Munday in the lead, they walked down the path, bent slightly to prevent bumping the overhanging branches. The path became high grass, then ceased at a sudden coil of brambles. Munday circled it and came to a gate made of rusted pipes. Munday vaulted the gate; Silvano climbed it, straddled it, and swung his legs over, taking care not to soil his suit. But he stumbled and duck-walked to his knees on the other side, and he was brushing them as Munday strode on ahead in his heavy sheepskin coat, the turtleneck sweater Emma had knitted and his already smeared gumboots. Over a small hill, Munday stopped, thwarted by a freshly plowed field. High cracked curls of drying mud were screwed out of long furrows; Munday saw himself tripping and falling. He followed the tractor ruts in the yard-wide fringe of turf at the field's edge, and fifty yards behind him, Silvano swung his arms, walking unsteadily in his pointed shoes.

At the far end of the field Munday found a low opening in the thorny hedge fence. Without waiting for Silvano, he stooped and pushed himself through and then trotted down a long slope, steadying himself with his stick. He was on the level field below, poking at the undergrowth, when Silvano burst through the opening in the thorns and immediately began slapping the hedge's deposits from his jacket. He caught up with Munday. Munday sprinted away.

"Please," said Silvano, calling Munday back. "Just a minute." He squatted on his heels like a Russian dancer, kicking one leg out, then the other, to pull at his ankle socks.

"Pick up some burrs?"

"They are paining me."

"You want to keep to the center of the path," said Munday. "Of course you know you're wearing the wrong sort of socks and shoes. Finished?"

Silvano stood up. He was out of breath from having run down the slope; his spotted eyes bulged, his nostrils were larged flared holes in the squashed snout of his nose, bits of broken leaf and the torn gray veil of a spider's web clung to his hair. The wind turned one of his lapels over and sent his tie flapping over his shoulder. He hunched and jammed his hands into his pockets. A froth of cloud showed over the ridge of the hill, and in the morning light diffused by the cloud

Silvano's face was unevenly brown, bruised with various shades of pigment.

They stood at the head of another path, a trough that might have served as a water course in heavy rains, overgrown at the sides with toppling still-green swatches of grass and widening past a thicket where it was trampled by hoof prints. Munday held his chin thoughtfully. He was a methodical hiker, and country walks, never a relaxation, seemed to bring out a militarist in him, an authoritarian streak: he took charge, read the Ordnance Survey maps, chose the route, gave orders, and was usually critical of any companion's slowness. Something that had maddened him in Africa was that when hiking from place to place with his tape-recorder and haversack of note cards, he had always been led by a small naked man, jinking through the bush, grunting directions. But in the end he had stayed long enough to guide himself—that mastery of the featureless savannah was one of the consolations of his long residence.

He pointed with his walking stick and said, as if to a column of men instead of the single African in his pointed shoes and pin-striped suit, "You see that meadow? I think we'd be advised to skirt round there and head towards the wooded bit. That hill is our objective. You're not tired, are you?"

Silvano shook his head.

"Want my gloves?"

"No, it's okay." Silvano pushed his fists deeper into his pockets.

"Off we go then," said Munday. He hurried down the path, slashing at the grass, tearing out tufts on the ferrule of his walking stick and flinging them into the air. Behind him, Silvano dodged these flying tufts.

"This is where it gets a bit sticky," said Munday. They were at the shore of a large pool of mud. Munday took a long stride into it.

"The cows come here," said Silvano. He was balanced, teetering on a stone which stuck up from the mud and stiffened hoofprints.

"Except that cows don't wear shoes, do they?" said Munday. "Horses, I should say. The hunt most probably." He continued to stride through the mud, his boots squelching, his stick waving for balance.

Silvano contemplated a move. He stepped to another protruding stone and sank it with his weight. That shoe went deep into the mud. He swung his other leg in a new direction, placed his right foot in the mire further along and sucked his left foot out. Seeing that both shoes were irretrievably wet and large with mud he relaxed, shortened his steps and stopped looking for footholds. He splashed through like a horse, throwing his feet anywhere in the mud, which now daubed his trouser bottoms. In the field beyond, his shoes made a squishing sound and he wrung bubbly water from his toes with each step.

They hiked towards the hill as through a series of baffles, Munday moving briskly and staying far ahead, Silvano falling back, stumped by the fences and dense hedges and stopping to pluck at the barbed seeds that bristled on his suit. Again Munday waited for him to catch up. He stood impatiently at the foot of Lewesdon Hill, leaning on his stick, watching Silvano approach.

"I see you've made a meal of it."

Silvano brushed at his suit with muddied hands. The wisp of web had worked itself to the top of Silvano's thick cap of hair where it fluttered like a shredded pennant.

"Pardon?" Silvano's eyes were glazed from the wind that had drawn the scattered cloud mass together, behind which the sun showed like a pale wafer.

"You should have worn your wellingtons," said Munday.

"I don't have any," said Silvano, shaking his head, as if asking for charity.

"No?" Munday gave him a squint of caution. *"Never* come to the English countryside without a good stout pair of wellies."

"I understand," said Silvano. "But my feet are wet."

"Bad luck," Munday sang, "however, there's no

sense turning back now." And jabbing his stick ahead of him he ascended the steep rocky path, climbing into the wind. The clouds moved fast, darkening the wooded slopes, then coming apart as the sun broke through and warmed him. The sun on the dead leaves gave him a whiff of spring. He unbuttoned the sheepskin coat and took a delight in being able to recognize the trees by their bark, by the scattered husks of their nuts, beech and oak, and knobbed stumps with sea-white shells of fungus on their rotted sides. The path became level and on this hillside shelf was a grotto of low firs, contained by their own shade. The recent storms had knocked many over; some showed white flesh where they had broken off and others had taken a whole round platform of roots and earth with them—feathery branches sprouted vertically from those newly-fallen. Munday was reassured by the familiar foliage, the freshness of the moss, the cedar smells. He had not forgotten any names: he saw and remembered the light puffballs.

At the highest and most densely wooded part of the hill was a rock with an elevation marker bolted to it, and a sign-post, paragraphs of small print headed *Bye-Laws*. That was England, whose remotest corners bore reminding traces of others; it was her mystery, these vanished people and their lingering tracks, even here in the Dorset hills. He was no stranger to these woods—the stranger was behind him, somewhere below, kicking at the path.

Silvano was nowhere in sight. Munday found a grassy hummock by a tree and he leaned back and closed his eyes, feeling his face go warm and cold from the sun winking past the sailing cloud mass, the glare of the sun burning on his eyes through the blood-red light of his lids. When he opened his eyes to be dazzled Silvano was standing near him, looking a sorry sight, with his mud-caked shoes and cuffs, and his hair and suit speckled with bits of brown leaf, bruises of earth on his knees, and the knot of his necktie yanked small. But it was not only that his clothes were di-

sheveled, looking as if they hadn't stood up to the
ordeal; there was also his color, and the way he was
panting—he was maroon with exertion.

He was obviously relieved to have finally caught up
with Munday, and he wore a smile of exhaustion and
gratitude.

Munday said, "You look worn out."

Silvano said, "I am!" He dropped beside him and
slapped at the stains on his suit. "You were always
a champion hiker," he said. "This mountain climbing
is too much for me."

"This isn't mountain climbing," said Munday. "Just
working up an appetite for Sunday lunch. Good English habit—Emma's doing a joint."

Silvano with his fellow Ugandans in their Earl's
Court flat (Munday could see the disorder, hear the
radio, smell the stews) knew nothing of that. He didn't
know why they had been hiking or where they had
been. It had only confused him. He had allowed Munday to bully him into a walk: he had followed the
native through an inhospitable landscape and he had
been reminded of his difference, the shallow lungs of
the lowland African. And when he got back to London
or Africa he would try to tell what he had seen, but
description would elude him and he would be left
with chance impressions of discomfort—cold, briars,
spider webs, wet feet; stinging nettles he would report
as ants (the dock leaf a miraculous cure), the pasture
mud as swamp, the woods and windbreaks as forest,
and how he had spoiled his new shoes. Munday wanted
to say, "How do *you* like it?"

But he said, "You can see four counties from here,"
and he stood and named them, indicating them with
his walking stick, and pausing when he saw Pilsdon
Pen and trying to make out the road to Birdsmoor
Gate. He said, "I saw a badger down there one night."

"But we have lions," said Silvano.

"There are no lions in Bwamba!"

"I mean in Africa."

"Shall we move on?" said Munday. "I want to try a

new path. It'll take us down there, through those pines and that farm, and eventually to Stoke Abbot."

"I don't think I can manage," said Silvano.

"I thought we might have a drink in Stoke Abbot," said Munday. "There's a pub there, The New Inn. Lovely place—very good billiard table."

Silvano shook his head. "Maybe we should go home."

"You'll miss the village," said Munday. "Eleventh-century church. Charming cottages. Thatch. Natives. You wanted to see it."

"I don't mind."

"Have it your way." Munday was pleased; he had avoided the inquiring eyes of the villagers, the crowded Sunday morning at the pub when all the local residents drank together, sorted throughout the room according to their class, conversing formally about the weather or the road-work or a fire in a chimney. He had saved himself from that confrontation—the silence upon Silvano's entering, the pause in the skittle game, the awkward stares, the strained resumption of convivial chatter. He led Silvano down the hill, to the road and the Black House.

After lunch, which a power cut delayed (the miner's strike was in full swing), Silvano looked at his watch and said, "What time does the train leave?"

"But I thought you said you were staying till tomorrow," said Emma.

"Classes," said Silvano. "They keep us busy."

"Pressure of work, Emma," said Munday, jumping up. "I'll ring the station." And later, driving Silvano to catch the 5:25 from Crewkerne, he said, "It's been awfully good to see you, Silvano."

"And it was awfully good to see you," said Silvano, the mimicry of Munday's phrase intending politeness but sounding like deliberate sarcasm. "You are just the same as ever, Doctor."

"We muddle along, Emma and I," said Munday.

Silvano stammered, then said, "But she *does* look different."

"Emma? In what way?"

"Thinner, I think," said Silvano.

"She might have lost a few pounds," said Munday. "Change of climate—it's to be expected."

"Not only that," said Silvano. "Also the face is tired and the hands are shaking."

"What you're saying is that you think she's sick."

"I think," said Silvano uncertainly.

"Don't be a fool," said Munday, and he drove faster in annoyance. "She's never felt better in her life. She's home. It's meant a lot to her—to us both—coming back to England. Our life is here. I admit I had some reservations about coming back—it's not easy after so long. But now I see it was what we had to do. I was wrong about Africa, I was wrong about England." He rambled on, as if talking to himself. "You can't stay overseas, miles and miles away in some godforsaken place, and go on denying you have a country and always trying to accommodate yourself, pretending you have a life and friends. Yes, it's depressing. I lost ten years that way. I was a young man when I went out to Africa—I'm not young any more." He gunned the engine and smiled. "But we're back now, and we're jolly glad of it. You can't blame us for that, can you?"

"No," said Silvano.

"And you'll go home, of course?"

"I like London."

"You like London," said Munday. "You have money and a flat—you're luckier than most English people. But what happens when your scholarship runs out and they raise your rent? Have you thought of that?"

"I can teach," said Silvano.

"Rubbish!" said Munday. "*I* can't even get a university job just now, so what chance is there for you?"

"Even bus conductors earn high salaries in England," said Silvano.

"High? What does that mean? Higher than what? Herdboys in Bwamba, coffee-pickers in Toro, Uganda *poets?* You tell me—you're an economist," said Munday. He grumbled, "Bus conductors don't live in Earl's Court."

"I would like to stay," said Silvano in an obstinate whisper.

"Go home," said Munday.

"It's primitive. People starve. You know that."

"No one starves in Bwamba," said Munday. "You put your women to work in the fields. Your wife, Silvano, remember? The system works—inherited land, a little magic, and a bunch of bananas a day."

"I never liked it."

"It's all you have," said Munday. "Read my book."

"I *will* read it," said Silvano. "Where can I buy it?"

Munday didn't reply. He changed gears on a hill and then said, "You have no business here."

"I have friends here," said Silvano, insulted but controlling his anger. "You had friends in Africa."

"I had *subjects,*" said Munday. "Friendship is only possible between equals."

Silvano turned to the side window. He was slumped in the seat, clutching his knees, looking at the fields whipping by. Munday was irritated anew by his hair, its absurd shape parodying mourning, and by his clothes, which Munday saw as pure folly.

Munday parked at the station. He jerked the hand brake. He said, "Don't you dare hurt that girl."

When Silvano boarded the train, the small frivolously dressed black man, pulling his cardboard suitcase through the high metal door of the carriage, Munday felt a pang of sorrow for him, he looked so sad. Munday regretted the conversation in the car—not his ferocity, but his candor. Silvano was behind the window, alone in the compartment, wagging his yellow palm at Munday. Munday waved back, and the train hooted and pulled away. He had said too much—worse, he had simplified. How could he explain that his England was a black house whose rooms and shadows he understood, and a woman—ghostlier than any African—who had bewitched him with passion? He had returned to a house and a woman. But he knew that, as with Alec—that last glimpse of him disappearing into a crowd of London shoppers—Silvano would sink, and nothing that Munday might say could matter, neither consolation nor blame. The truth was simple: he never wanted to see him again.

16

HE HAD WATCHED Silvano go, and it was as if he had rid himself of the continent. He drove home from the station under a sky lighted as subtly as skin, a swell of mild light with a tincture of blood, and raw gold sinews breaking from a sun pulped by clouds. This evening light was too complicated for him to see any drama in it—like the African sunset which altered too fast for him to assign it any metaphor but murder —but the light itself at this hour was his triumph. It was nearly six o'clock, and yet the light continued, thickening and changing, becoming more physical as it dimmed.

He had seen his death in the early darkness of winter, the pale daylight had been for him like a brief waking from sickness. But the seasonal illness was passing; he measured his mood by these lengthening days with a pleasure he had not known in the unvarying equatorial light. The fear had left him: he had overcome it by enduring it, like his heart, which had not pained him for weeks. So he had got well, and he imagined the thick scar on his heart narrowed to a harmless lip of tissue. His health allowed him to ignore his body, the intrusive wrapping of muscle he had felt failing him so keenly, weighing him with a kind of stupidity. Now he fed his mind on sleep, restored himself in the darkened room under the disc of Caroline's face, a fixed image of sensation which, hovering in the room, amounted to a presence almost flesh. He felt her pressure so strongly on him in the Black House he didn't need to ask where she lived, and at times in the living room with Emma, the air before the fire bore his lover's odor so obviously it embarrassed him. It was a haunting that confronted his mind and aroused his body, but it inhibited his conversation with Emma, as Flack's voice had, his mewing mutter against the wall, on their first day at The Yew Tree.

Munday had thought, recovering, that Emma had also recovered. She was, after all, his wife. It had not occurred to him that Emma could be ill if his heart improved, and it was only after Silvano commented on it that he had gone back to the house and seen her unwell. She looked tired, perhaps she was coming down with something; she had that lustreless inattention that precedes real sickness—not sick yet but, abstracted and falling silent, in decline. He was sorry; he was also cross, for what Silvano had said was disrespectful, not necessarily in English terms, but in Bwamba culture which forbade such intimate observations except within a family. Silvano was not part of the family. Munday didn't like his presuming; he objected to an African tribesman telling him his wife had lost weight. He didn't need a stranger to call attention to the hysteria that came over her when he was unresponsive. But he was ashamed that he had been too preoccupied to notice it earlier. He had his own diagnosis: she was taking refuge in illness—refuge from her dread. He laughed at the bitter irony: they had come to the country (she had chosen the place!) for his health, and now it was hers that was shaky.

He was not sure how to deal with it. He was circumspect, then bullying, and finally hearty, offering encouragement, usually at mealtimes, for he was in his study the rest of the time, while she moped, watching Mrs. Branch dust, or sat before the garden window with a sketch pad in her lap.

One evening he said, "Emma, you're not eating."

"I don't have any appetite."

"A good walk would set you up."

"I hate your walks," she said. "You make them such an occasion."

"Why don't you invite Margaret down here one weekend?"

"It's a bother. And there's her job—she's probably not free," said Emma.

"But you never *see* anyone!"

"I see you," she said. "Why do you talk to me as if I'm an invalid?"

"You haven't been looking well lately."

"I'm perfectly all right," she said. But her denial only confirmed that she was sick in a more critical way than if she had agreed with him. She didn't know she was sick—that was worse. She went on, "But I do wish you'd finish your book. Then we could leave this place."

"And go where?" said Munday. "Emma, this is England!"

"It's *not*," she said, and he thought she was going to cry. "It's a miserable house, not like any house I've ever known. Even Silvano said it."

"What did he say?"

" 'Your house frightens me,' " she said. "Those were his exact words."

"Africans scare easily."

"I know what he meant."

"Africans in England seem so pitiful and comic," he said. "Like country cousins."

"You were offhand with him," said Emma. "I've never seen you treat an African that way."

"I couldn't help it. He said he wants to settle in England and become a bus conductor. It's a joke! He likes England, he says, but I took him for a walk around back and he was knocked for six—couldn't take it. Wants to live in London."

"I don't blame him," said Emma. "So do I. I admit it, Alfred, I'm not suited to the country."

He snapped, "That's what you used to say about Africa."

"I can't creep into a corner and thrive."

"Who can?"

"You," she said. "It's in your nature."

"Don't be cryptic, Emma."

"I'm not being cryptic," she said. "I admire it in you. But I still get awfully scared sometimes in this house. We can't all be so self-sufficient."

"You don't know me," he said. "I can't survive alone, and I'm not self-sufficient. Emma, I'm as weak as you!"

"You're not weak at all."

"But I am," he said. "This move was a great strain for me. You seem to forget I have a heart condition."

"I haven't forgotten."

"Why are you looking at me that way?"

"I was thinking of Silvano. You used to be so fond of him in Africa. I can remember you talking to him for hours on end."

"They weren't social occasions," he said. "I made notes on those conversations. And don't worry, he'll get his acknowledgment in the book."

"That weekend opened my eyes. I saw you avoiding him and I thought how much you'd changed." Emma sighed. "He left early, you know. He distinctly said he was going to stay over until Monday. But he wasn't happy here."

"He'll get over it."

"You didn't go out of your way for him."

"Who went out of his way for me in Africa?" said Munday angrily. "Ten years, Emma, ten years!"

"You're not sorry you left Africa, are you?"

"I was at first. It was a blow—well, you know. You were in the room when Dowle told me."

"You cried."

"That was exhaustion," he said. "Not grief, not grief at all. But it seems so foolish now."

"Why foolish?"

"Because we should have come home sooner. Ten years in Africa and I thought I'd be at the top of my profession. But these poaching students who flew out from England on their vacations to do research have already published their books. They have all the jobs, and I'm ten years behind the times."

"You're glad you came home, though?"

"It was the only thing to do."

Emma said slowly, with mingled relief and fatigue, "I was wondering if you'd ever admit that."

"And if my heart holds out I'll finish the book properly."

"Your heart will hold out," she said.

"You seem so sure!"

"I *am* sure. There's not a thing wrong with your heart."

"Emma, you were there when Dowle told me I'd have to leave."

"That dear, dear man," she said.

"A scarred heart. That's what he said. That's why we had to leave."

"That's why we had to leave, Alfred, but the scar wasn't on your heart—it was on mine. And it's still there."

"I don't believe you."

"He knew you'd be impossible if I was the reason for our leaving. You'd never forgive me, you'd always blame me for ruining your research. You can be a frightful bully." She smiled, as if she had at a critical moment discovered a strength she could use for defense. "But now you admit you're glad to be home. You said that, didn't you? So I can tell you the truth."

"There are so many versions of the truth," he said. "Let's hear your smug one."

"I've suffered," she said,

"You deceived me, that's why! He was protecting

you—you and that conniving priest made all this up
so you could leave gracefully!"

"As gracefully as a bad heart allows," she said
quietly. "You see, you're fine. *I'm* the one with the
heart condition."

"You should see a doctor."

"I did, that day in London, after I had lunch with
Margaret. There's nothing to be done. I have pills, I
have a diet. My heart—"

"Why did you keep it from me?"

"I was afraid."

"And that time I fainted? You mean there was
nothing wrong with me?"

"Indigestion."

"That's what that damned specialist said. Dowle
must have told him to humor me." Munday held Emma's hand. He said, "You needn't have been afraid to
tell me. I would have understood."

"It doesn't matter now," said Emma. Her voice had
faded to a whisper.

Munday took her in his arms and said, "I'm sorry.
Poor Emma."

"Having a bad heart's an awful nuisance," she said.

"I know," he said, "I used to have one."

"But I have you," she said.

The trust in her words nearly broke him. It was
more than the news of her heart. He found it incredible
that possessed by Caroline as much as he was, she
could not know it—amazing that after guiding him
to that love she hadn't the slightest inkling of it. He
would have told her then how she was the ghost's
accomplice. But her heart: he could not sacrifice it to
the truth. Emma inhabited the small world of illness
from which he had been released. If he told her,
You've seen the ghost I love, she might die of it—or
she might laugh and say he was mad. But he believed,
and he concealed it because there was no one to tell.

He was sorry for her, but he hated her fretting, the
irritating senility that tension produced in her. Shopping one Saturday for groceries in Yeovil, he and

Emma passed a shop window which had the plainness of a chemist's. A sign caught his eye, *Wonderful Way to Relax*, and he thought of Emma. There were simple surgical goods in the window and medicines of various kinds carrying doctors' testimonies on placards, and soberly wrapped bottles of capsules with photographs demonstrating their effect—handsome men and women splashing vigorously in surf, reassured couples posed embracing. Munday was attracted by the unpretentious display, the clinical austerity of the pale colors. He walked on a bit further and when Emma was occupied he went back to the shop.

Inside it was empty without being bare, a freshly-painted interior with blue curtains on the front window blocking out the street. It had a disinfected air about it that was enhanced by several near display cases. A man rested his arms on one of these cases and read a newspaper with a cup of tea. He did not look up when Munday entered. The man was rather short and old, and on his large studying face were incurious features; his swollen nose and heavy jaw and lips, his fleshy ears and pouched eyes didn't go with the streamlined shop. He might have strayed in to mind the shop for the owner. He was balding, too, and his cardigan was zippered to his neck. He turned a page of the newspaper and as he did so he glanced up at Munday and greeted him, smoothing the page with the flat of his hand.

Munday hesitated. He had seen into the cup of tea at the man's elbow; a skin of wrinkled milk on its surface nauseated him. The cup was cracked, and the sight of this cold tea made Munday doubtful about the shop. The man put the cup to his lips and sipped. Munday wanted to go.

The man said, "Help you?"

"That device in your window," said Munday, straightening his back. "Supposed to relax you. I wonder if I might take a look at it. Could be just the thing for my wife."

The man slid open the back door of the case and

took out a slender blunt object of white molded plastic. It was about eight inches long, the shape of a probe, and had a grooved handgrip.

"That's four pounds, forty pence," said the man, "including batteries."

It was only when Munday had the thing in his hand that he realized its ugly use. He wanted to drop it and hurry out of the shop. He put it down, but he stayed, to avoid looking a fool. He walked away from the man, along the case, and saw the rest, a row of rubber phalluses in different sizes, simulating erections in a villainous ridicule of flesh, with grotesque knobs and warts, like clowns' comic noses. Some had fasteners—belts, elastic straps, buckles, and plungers. There was an appalling rubber torso, inflated like a distended beachball, with a crudely mustached vulva. On a tray there were limp stringy contraceptives, flesh-colored, in amazing variety, tongues of shriveled rubber ringed with fur and feathers, or tentacles or protuberances like clusters of spiders. There were jars of cream, bottles of aphrodisiac capsules, manuals of sex technique with titles promising pleasure, thicker and frankly pornographic books wrapped in cellophane, electric condoms wired to transformers, and more vibrators. It was all displayed as in an ethnography exhibit, the pathetic toys of an especially savage tribe.

Munday started to go.

The man lifted and rattled his newspaper. "We do mail orders," he said. "You want the catalogues?"

Munday turned and said sharply, "No, I do not."

There were men lingering just outside the shop window, hunched expectantly, like the large scavenging marabou storks which had stood bumping shoulders on a particular roadside in Fort Portal every morning watching for the garbage trucks.

Days passed, and Munday waited for Caroline to contact him through Emma—it had become a ritual for him. Sometimes in corners of the Black House where he felt Caroline's presence strongest, near the living-room fireplace, at the store of green candles in the back hall, in the draft at the top of the stairs, he appealed to her and he sensed her moving past him like a vibrant column of warm air. He looked to Emma for Caroline's signal (a watchfulness Emma took for indulgent concern): "Is there anything you'd like me to do, my darling?" But he wasn't summoned.

He worked on his book, but the collection of Bwamba tools had given their peculiar odor to the study and his scribbled pages, and after writing he craved fresh air. In the afternoon he went out, choosing to walk in low sheltered places, hoping that beyond that tree or hedge she would appear to him. He took these walks alone. Emma stayed in the house. There were days when he went out hoping to come back and find it all changed, to return to a simpler, finished place, his book done, Caroline waiting, Emma dead or gone. These solitary walks were a way, he thought, of giving her a chance to die; but when he returned to the house it was always as he left it. Once, he returned to Emma at the door who alarmed him with: "Guess what she said?" Then she reported something Mrs. Branch had said about a tuft of lungwort she had called a primrose. On the way back from his walks he usually stopped at The Yew Tree for a drink. It was a brief drink, never long enough to support a conversation, and so he was surprised one day when Mr. Flack said, "How's your book coming along?"

Munday didn't react. He sipped his half-pint and said, "What book is that?"

"Mr. Awdry said you were writing one," said Flack.

"Mr. Awdry is mistaken."

"He said it wasn't about your cannibals, either."

"No?"

"No sir, he said it's about *us*." Flack challenged Munday with a grin.

Munday said, "Why would anyone want to do a silly thing like that?"

"That's what I asked Mr. Awdry."

"What did he say?"

"Money, he said."

"My wife has plenty of money," said Munday. "She could buy and sell your Mr. Awdry, and don't you forget it."

Flack changed the subject. He spoke about the miners' strike, entering its second month. There were power cuts nearly every day, but there were still regular deliveries of coal to houses; Munday's coal shed was filled to the brim. Munday was not at all inconvenienced by the blackouts; he had learned to read by candlelight and oil lamp at the Yellow Fever Camp, and the Black House was designed to be heated by fireplaces and lighted by candles. The blackouts gave him a great deal of pleasure, but he did not say so.

"You need one of these," said Flack. He showed Munday a dented miner's hat, with a small battery-powered lamp on its visor. Flack put it on his head and switched on the lamp. "I wear it behind the bar during these power cuts."

"Very sensible," said Munday. But Flack looked foolish and comic in his overcoat and miner's hat.

"It's the old people I worry about," said Flack. "A lot of them will die of the cold this winter because of these strikes. But the miners don't care about that. Oh no, not them!"

An old man sat by the fire, holding a glass of beer on his knee. He wore a long greasy coat and Munday remembered him as the man who had shown him his old clasp knife.

Munday asked him, "How are you managing?"

The old man said, "I don't have any electricity."

"None of us has any," said Munday.

"I mean to say, I didn't have any lights in my cottage *before* the strike," said the man. "I've got a paraffin lamp and I cook over coal. If the coal runs out I'll use wood. It's all the same to me."

"That's the idea," said Munday.

The man brightened with the compliment and in a

gesture of friendship he reached into his pocket and asked whether Munday would like to see his pictures of the Armenian massacre in Constantinople.

"I shouldn't have these," he said. He slipped the rubber band over his wrist and shuffled them furtively. Then he licked his thumb and passed them to Munday one at a time. They were brown postcards, thick with handling, of stacked bodies in a plaza and dark soldiers standing at attention with long rifles; corpses dangling straight down on a lengthy gallows beam; a bundle in a gutter that Munday recognized after a moment as a man; and three of them were of fiercely mustached Turks holding swollen severed heads by their hair. The pictures were passed around the bar and discussed.

"They look a right lot of bastards," said Hosmer.

"Never saw that many people on a gallows," said Flack. "Though I've seen one or two in my time. Deserters."

"I can remember," said a very old man, "after a hanging in Dorchester, they used to sell the rope by the inch. This was years ago." He smiled and nodded. "By the inch. I reckon you could make a fortune that way."

"It's about time they started on the Irish," said a stocky and slightly drunk man. Munday knew him. Before Christmas some young schoolchildren climbing in the Cairngorms had got lost in a blizzard. They had made camp, hoping to be rescued, but five had frozen to death. Flack had mentioned it—it had been on the six o'clock news. The stocky man had said, "When I was their age I wasn't in a school. I had to work, help my father with the sheep. No camping trips for me." He was, Munday discovered later with some surprise, a shepherd. Now he said, "That's what they should do, hang 'em."

"They got a few in Londonderry the other day," said Hosmer.

"They should shoot thirteen of the buggers every day," said the shepherd.

The man collected his postcards of the Armenian

massacre, snapped the rubber band around the pack, and said, "Three of them Irish had nail-bombs in their pockets. That's a fact."

"The paras didn't shoot them," Flack said. "They were killed by their own people."

Munday felt they were trying to draw him out. He said nothing, but the subject disturbed him. Even *The Times* had carried a photograph of a girl whose head had been shaved and who had been tied to a pole and tarred and feathered. He had seen victims of African brutality, but this picture of the Irish girl slumped on a pole, with a blackened face and white eyes, had outraged him.

The shepherd was holding forth on the Irish. Munday wanted to interrupt, to lecture them on barbarism. But it was pointless. He listened, as he had so many times on the verandah of the Mountains of the Moon Hotel, when Alec and his cronies spoke about marauding Africans, uprisings, sometimes the Bwamba and their tortures. Munday had not interrupted then; it was idle conversation, horror reduced to small talk, without menace. An atrocity story, offered to the group, was like a ticket of entry, and a challenge or a rebuke was considered to be in poor taste.

"Mow 'em down," said the shepherd. He described how it should be done, how he would do it himself if he had a chance: "Don't think I wouldn't!"

Munday went to the billiard table and pulled out a cue from the rack on the side. Chalking it, he said to the shepherd, "Take a cue."

The shepherd stopped roaring. He smiled at Munday and slipped off his woolen jacket. He said, "If you like."

Flack tossed a coin. Munday called heads and lost.

"You go first, mister," said the shepherd. "Get a tanner from the landlord."

Flack handed Munday a sixpence and leaned on the bar to watch the game. The other drinkers, Hosmer, the very old man, the man with the postcards in the pocket of his long coat, a silent farmboy in boots, drew near, as Munday lined up two balls, red and white, for the break. He aimed carefully and drove his cue ball against the red, sinking it in one of the back holes.

"Red counts double," said the shepherd. "Forty for you."

"Flack can keep score," said Munday.

"Good position," said Hosmer. The white ball had come to rest near the forward spindle which stood in front of the two-hundred-point hole.

Munday took the red ball out of the chute, aimed, and potted both balls, the white in the two hundred, the red in the twenty.

"Two-eighty," said Flack. "Nicely played."

"You played on her before," said the shepherd.

"He never played here," said Hosmer.

"Take your shot," said the shepherd.

"Don't rush me," said Munday. He lined up the balls again and shot; his method ("Munday's One-Two," Alec had called it) was the same, sinking the red, leaving the white at the lip of the forward hole, then sinking them both with the next shot, collecting two hundred and eighty points each time.

"Five-sixty," said Flack.

The old man in the long coat grinned at the score and touched his tongue to his nose.

"Call me when you miss," said the shepherd. He sat down by the wall and chalked his cue while the others watched Munday repeat his shot.

"We should get Doctor Munday on the team," said Flack.

"I'm afraid not," said Munday, and went on setting up the balls, potting them, setting them up again.

There was a *clunk* inside the table.

"Gate's down," said Hosmer. "Everything counts double."

"What's my score?" asked Munday.

"Five thousand and forty," said Flack. "That's a hell of a score."

Munday said to the shepherd, "I'm going to give

you a chance now." He deliberately missed, then stepped aside and said, "Go on."

"You're too good for me," said the shepherd. "I ain't playing."

"It's just a game," said Flack.

"Bit of fun," said Hosmer.

The shepherd glowered at Hosmer. He said, "You play him then!"

"I don't think you'll find anyone around here who'll want to play with you," said Flack.

Munday said, "I don't think there's anyone around here I want to play."

The shepherd came awkwardly up to Munday and said, "Have a drink, mister."

"I must go," said Munday. He replaced his cue and put on his coat.

"He won't drink with me," said the shepherd angrily.

Flack said, "He can't. He's got a house guest, haven't you, Doctor?"

"Excuse me?" Munday was at the door, the men facing him from different parts of the room.

"That nigger-boy," said Flack. "Isn't he still up at your place?"

"I don't know what you're talking about," said Munday, and he bumped out without saying goodbye.

They knew; it was not hard to guess how. He had done his best to hide Silvano, but he could have predicted they would see him. There were few secrets in any village. And yet what Flack had said had given him a jolt, like the rumor of his book *("Not about your cannibals, either . . .")*. Munday was surprised and angry, for what continued to disturb him were the shifting similarities between this village and the one he had left. He had found England in Africa; he had always thought it would be preparation for returning, but he had returned to find Africa in England, not the whole of Africa, but a handful of its oldest follies. In some respects the two places were identical in mood, in the size of their customs. What differences he had found had given him occasions to be complacent. The similarities confused him, they reminded him of how exposed he was: he knew he would never have risked with an African woman what he had risked with Caroline. It was not spoken about—no rumors had reached him—but Munday was not sure this silence meant that no one knew, or that it was common knowledge.

17

THEN THE DAGGER was found. It was the day of a hunt. Munday had seen some huntsmen from the window of his study in the morning, on their way to assemble at The Yew Tree. But not in red—they were dressed in black jackets and black bowler hats and sat very straight in the saddle. They came up from the back pasture, three of them, at a walk, the dark horses snorting, the riders rocking towards him, like outriders at a stately execution. It was an eerie procession, the black-suited figures in that morning mist, but when they came closer Munday saw they were very young girls with tight thighs and small pale faces, black ribbons on their bowlers and their hair tied behind. They held whips lightly across their laps. Then he had gone outside and seen the others, the red coats and top hats, and the floats and trucks drawn up along the road near the pub. There were cars, too, tilted on the grassy verge, the little Austins and Singers of people who had driven up from Bridport and beyond, the retired people and farm laborers for whom the hunt was an event to follow.

At eleven sharp he heard the commotion, the horns,

the hoof-thumps, the yapping hounds, and all day the hunt went back and forth behind the Black House. For periods there was no sound, and Munday waited; then a horn brayed and brought the hunt back, the muffled gallop of the horses and the shouts of the people chasing after. They were circling the house, the pack of hounds driving the fox across Munday's fields. It raised his old fear of being hunted; but recognizing it he saw his distance from it. The sound of the hunt kept him from working. He examined his fear. It was like the memory of a breakdown, which, even after it ceases to disable, can still cause pain in the recollection; not erased but made small, the vision of a frightened man at the periphery of his mind, distress into humiliation, fear into lumpish frailty. Now the horns blared again and the hounds responded with maddened barks. He had been tricked about his heart, but he remembered the fingers of fire in his chest: he had believed himself to be ill as he had believed the shadows in the Black House to be fatal for him. The remembrance of the illness only brought him to self-contempt, and he raged at the disruption of the hunt. Mrs. Branch watched from the kitchen, Emma from an upper window; Munday bore it in his study, pretending to work. In the early evening the noise lessened, but just as Munday returned to his book he heard a car door slam and the bangs of the brass knocker. Then Mrs. Branch at the study door: "There's a man outside says he wants to see you." He went out and saw the dagger. But he didn't touch it, for it was jammed to the metal of its hilt into the throat of a blood-spattered foxhound.

"Is this yours?" the huntsman had asked, opening the lid of the car's trunk. He pointed with a short whip, slapping the thong against the corpse.

"The knife yes," said Munday. "The dog no."

"We want an explanation," said the man.

"So do I," said Munday, bristling at the man's accusation.

"That dog was valuable."

"The dagger's worth something as well," said Munday. "It was stolen from me several months ago."

"Stolen you say?" The man flexed his whip.

"Yes, but how did you know it was mine?"

"I didn't. This happened on your land—in the back. One of our whippers-in found him."

"Bad luck," said Munday. He reached for the dagger, but the man laid his whip on Munday's arm. Munday glared at him.

"Not until we find out who did it," the man said.

"Quite obviously, one of your own people."

"There'll be fingerprints on it."

"Of course. Fingerprints," said Munday with as much sarcasm as he could manage. "I'd forgotten about those."

"We'll get to the bottom of it."

"I hope you do. Mind you, I want that dagger back."

"What a vicious thing."

"Purely ceremonial," said Munday, who saw that the man meant his comment to reflect on him. "It wasn't designed for killing. Africans don't kill animals with knives. They can't get close enough for that."

Emma came out of the house with a sweater over her shoulders. She shivered and tugged the sweater when she saw the dead dog; she said, "Oh, God, the poor thing."

"My best hound," said the man, and he gave it an affectionate pat on its bloody belly. "The rest of the hunt know about it—we're all livid. It's the first time anything like this has happened."

"It's terrible," said Emma.

Munday said, "I agree, but I want you to understand that dagger is extremely important to my research."

My dog, my dagger: the two men bargained, as if haggling over treasures, pricing them with phrases of sentiment, insisting on their value, the dead dog, simple knife.

"Your knife, on your property."

"You don't think Alfred had anything to do with it, do you?"

"I don't know, madam. I'm reporting it to the police, though."

"You do that," said Munday.

"I'm not treating it as an ordinary case of vandalism."

"I shouldn't if I were you," said Munday. "And I suggest you catch the culprit. It's clear he had a grudge against me."

"Really?" The man slapped his whip against his palm.

"One of these rustic psychopaths, trying to discredit me in some fumbling way. It's possible."

"Why would anyone want to do that?" asked the man.

"I haven't the slightest idea."

"There must be a reason."

"Don't look for a reason, look for a man. Munday's law. Now if you're quite through—"

"I was simply asking," said the man. "If there's a reason the police will know what it is before long." He banged the trunk shut, said goodnight to Emma, and drove off.

Emma said, "Why were you so short with him?"

"I didn't like his insinuations," said Munday. "I won't be spoken to like that. Insolence is the one thing I will not stand for. I didn't come here to be treated like a poaching outsider, and if that person comes back I shall refuse to see him. Do you find this amusing?"

"I've heard you say that before."

"Not here."

"No," said Emma. "Not here."

In the house Munday told Mrs. Branch what had happened, and he deputized her: "Keep your eyes skinned and your ear to the ground, and if you hear a word about this you tell me."

The following day at breakfast he looked over his *Times* and said, "Well, what's the news?"

And Mrs. Branch, who in the past had always responded to such a question with gossip, said, "Nothing."

"No one mentioned it?"

"No sir," she said. "Not that I heard."

"I find that very hard to believe, said Munday. "You didn't hear anything about the hunt?"

"Only that they caught a fox out back and blooded one of the girls from Filford way."

Later in the morning there was a phone call from the vicar. He said, "I just rang to find out how you're getting on. We haven't seen much of you. I trust all is well."

Munday said, "I suppose you've heard about the dog that had his throat cut?"

There was a pause. Then the vicar said, "Yes, something of the sort."

"That dagger was stolen in your church hall by one of your Christians," said Munday. "If the police come to me with questions I shall send them along to you. You can confirm my story."

"I didn't realize it was a knife that had been stolen."

"A dagger," said Munday. "Purely ceremonial."

"It's very unfortunate that this happened so close to your house."

"I don't find it unfortunate in the least," said Munday. "It has nothing whatever to do with me. Was there anything else you wanted?"

That was a Friday. No policeman came to investigate, though Mrs. Branch said she saw one on a bicycle pedaling past the house. Munday was being kept in suspense, not only about the dog—which worried him more than he admitted: he didn't like being singled out as a stranger—but also there was Caroline. He had not heard from her for weeks, and he missed her, he required her to console him. Emma tried, but her consolation didn't help, and with the admission of her illness, her bad heart, she had stopped making any show of bravery and she had begun to refuse Munday's suggestions of walks, saying, "No—my heart." He believed her, and yet her words were an accurate parody of his own older expressions of weakness.

But he took his walks still, and walking alone he often had the feeling he was being followed—not at a distance, but someone very close, hovering and breathing at his back. The suspicion that he was being followed was made all the stronger by his inability to see the hoverer; it was like the absence of talk about the dead dog, the silence in which he imagined conspiring whispering villagers. The walks did little to refresh him: he was annoyed, and it continued to anger him that he was annoyed, so there was no relief in thinking about it—it only isolated his anger and made it grow. And he could be alarmed by the sudden flushing of a grouse, or the church clock striking the hour, or the anguish he saw in a muddied pinafore flapping on a low gorse bush.

He had avoided The Yew Tree since the billiard game and that wounding *"nigger-boy,"* but one Sunday several weeks after the discovery of the dagger he stopped in to cash a check. He entered the bar and precipitated a silence so sustained and deliberate among the old men, who sat like jurors, that his voice rattled in the room. And his check was refused.

"I never take checks," said Flack.

"We're a bit short," said Munday. Then he was sorry he had said it: Flack obviously enjoyed refusing his request.

"Try Mr. Awdry," said Flack. "I've been stung too many times by the summer people. Paper-hangers, I call them. I can't help you."

Munday folded the check and put it in his pocket. He was grim, his mouth shut like a savings box, but he smiled as he turned to face the silent, watching men. He said, "Earth-stoppers. What a perfect name."

He left, shutting the door with a force that made the bell jangle in its bracket, and striding quickly away for what he knew would be the last time.

Finally, two days later, he was summoned: that was the word he used when he described it to Emma. He had given up expecting to be contacted, so the phone call at first surprised him, and discovering it was not the police or even the vicar, he was confused. Then he heard and saw. The logic of the man addressing him in a friendly way, using his own and Munday's first name—it was part of the pattern, one of those moments when the English village and its people had an African cast, Munday a stranger in the thick of it, considering his moves, a white man again. The phone call that had seemed so unexpected was inevitable. It fitted. It was from Awdry.

Munday said, "What's on your mind?"

"I wondered if we might get together some time."

"Perhaps later on."

"Thursday's a good day for me."

"I was thinking of April," said Munday. "After Easter."

"Can't I tempt you up here before that?"

"I'm rather busy."

"I understand."

"You should," said Munday. "After all, it was you who told Flack I'm writing a book."

"Mentioned it, did he?"

"Yes, but I set him straight. You see, I'm not writing a book." It was partly true: he hadn't touched the book for days. He thought it might have had something to do with the discovery of the dagger—it was an African occurrence, and when the village most resembled an African one he became incapable of describing his people. It seemed to make what he had already written dull, unoriginal, not news at all.

Awdry said, "I'm afraid I must see you this week. Friday's the only day I have something on."

"What a pity," said Munday. "That's the only day I'm free."

"Then I shall cancel my engagement," said Awdry, swiftly. "Come for a drink—shall we say six-thirty?"

He had no choice. He hung up and said to Emma, "That was Awdry. Seems I'm wanted at the *Boma*."

He drove to the manor with a repeating memory. Once, years before, in Uganda, he had received a note from the District Commissioner, Mudford by name, saying that when he was next in Fort Portal he should look in. Munday did so, more out of curiosity than politeness, and was irritated by an African servant in a red fez and sash and khaki uniform who asked him to wait. The D.C. arrived and gave him sherry, and after some pleasantries took him to the window and warned him that his presence in the village might be interpreted as British cooperation in the Bwamba's piecemeal hostilities against their Hamitic neighbors, the Batoro. He suggested Munday do his research elsewhere. Munday said he would do nothing of the kind.

"The least you can do is put Her Majesty's Government in the picture," Mudford said.

"Her Majesty's Government will have to come and find out for itself," said Munday. "I can't offer you a bed at the Yellow Fever Camp, but I might be able to use my influence with the Bwamba and get you space in a hut."

"I was told you might be difficult," said Mudford.

"If you're foolish enough to come to Bwamba, I'd advise you to take care," said Munday. "My people don't like to be trifled with."

Then he had felt very close to the Bwamba. He was identified with them: Doctor Munday's people— he had liked that. It had always been his ambition for his name to be linked with a people who were thought to be savage as if in describing their lives, giving new definition to their culture, promoting their uniqueness, he was inventing them.

Awdry met Munday at the door, greeted him, and said, "Whisky's your drink, if I remember rightly." He made Munday a drink and when they were seated in the library, amid all those artifacts and mounted heads, he said, "I'll come straight to the point. As you know, one of our foxhounds was brutally attacked near your house."

"I daresay the hound was doing some brutal attacking of its own."

"That's open to dispute," said Awdry. "I didn't call you over to argue the merits of hunting—I already know your views on that subject, and I think any further discussion would be unprofitable."

"Go on," said Munday coldly.

"The dog was killed," said Awdry. "We're very concerned about it—why it happened in that calculated way, with your dagger, near your house."

"You say 'we'?"

"The village," said Awdry.

"Ah, the village."

"This has always been a peaceful village. People mind their own business and life goes on very much as it must have done for generations. The locals are proud, and they find the city ways of outsiders sometimes abrasive. But they're very easy to live with once you get to know them. I count myself lucky to have been accepted by them—they respect me."

"That's another way of saying they keep their distance," said Munday. "But I don't blame you for wanting that."

"I have many dear friends here."

"Then you *are* lucky," said Munday. "I'm still learning the language, as it were. To tell the truth, I'm not sure where I stand."

"I can answer that," said Awdry. "From the first, you were regarded with suspicion—a suspicion your lecture at the church hall did nothing to dispel. Every outsider is suspect here. But if I may say so, the outsider who antagonizes locals is a liability to the rest of us. One is expected to come to terms with the village. This hasn't happened in your case."

"You're absolutely sure."

"It is a fact."

Munday said, "It is a bloody impertinence."

Awdry took a sip of his drink, but his eyes stayed on Munday. He said, "I'm sorry you feel that way."

"Evidently, it's of little account how I feel," said Munday. "A dagger was stolen from me months ago. So one of your proud villagers is a thief. The dagger was not recovered until just the other day. So the police force is not up to scratch either. A dog was killed on my property—that's vandalism as well as trespass. Facts!"

"Perhaps," said Awdry. "But you might say they're open to interpretation."

"My foot," said Munday, losing his temper. "Don't play the D.C. with me. I don't know who you're trying to protect, but I can tell you that unless I get a satisfactory explanation I shall raise a stink."

"I could say the same to you."

"Go ahead!"

"Very well then, who are *you* trying to protect?"

"Not a soul," said Munday. "Emma and I are too busy for intrigues."

"You're busy?"

"Yes, I am."

"And yet you say you're not writing a book?"

"That is no concern of yours."

"This is a tightly-knit community. The people here are naturally interested in what goes on in the village. It's not prying, though it may look that way to a complete stranger—"

"I have lived in villages before," said Munday.

"If a person has a hobby or a sport, it's usual for him to share it. If someone has visitors they're frequently taken to the pub and introduced."

"I have no hobbies," said Munday.

"But you have visitors."

"Visitors?" said Munday. "And how do you know that?"

"Shall I tell you something?" said Awdry. "There is very little about your life in Four Ashes that we don't know."

"That 'we' again."

"Does it alarm you?"

"Not at all," said Munday. "Should it?"

Awdry smiled. "That depends on whether you intend to stay down here for much longer. If you leave, of course it doesn't matter—we'll just write you off as another inexplicable foreigner."

"What if I decide to stay?"

"You'll be most welcome, though I can't help feeling you'd be much happier elsewhere," said Awdry. "If you stay you might have some explaining to do."

"Explaining!" Munday laughed derisively.

"And if I were you I'd watch my step."

Munday stood up and walked to the fireplace; he considered the fire for a moment, then spat into it. "I am here," he said. "I pay my rent and go about my own business. I owe nothing to this village—least of all an explanation. The village owes me privacy. For all practical purposes this is my home, and whether I stay or go is no one's concern but mine."

"You say you've lived in villages before?" Awdry shook his head. "I'm surprised. Astonished. It's not as simple as you say."

"It is that simple," Munday said.

"There are certain courtesies here, a certain standard of behavior—"

"Stop lecturing me."

Awdry rose from his chair, but he didn't follow Munday to the fireplace. He said, "I like your wife."

"I'll tell her you said so."

Awdry caught Munday's eye and addressed it: "I'm equally fond of Caroline." Munday said nothing, and Awdry added, "We all are, no matter what people might say."

"You're not a very subtle man," said Munday.

"I don't want you to misunderstand me," said Awdry, and his voice was somber with caution when he said, "Take care."

"I thought we were discussing a dead dog."

"Perhaps we are," said Awdry. "That African—was he one of your students?"

"I have no students," said Munday. He looked at his watch. "It's time I left."

"Don't you see I'm trying to do you a favor?" Awdry spoke with a kind of bullying sincerity that was the nearest he had come to pleading with Munday.

"Do me another one," said Munday. "Leave me in peace."

"I shall be happy to. I only hope the others do the same."

"What 'others'?" said Munday, reacting as if the mere uttering of the word gave him an unpleasant taste in his mouth.

"I think you know better than I."

"Thank you for the drink." Murray started to go.

"Wait." Awdry went to a table. "Your dagger."

Munday took the dagger. "I thought they needed it for fingerprints."

"There were no fingerprints," said Awdry. "Open verdict."

Munday said, "How very odd that in a village where everyone knows everyone else's business they should not be able to get to the bottom of a simple thing like this. Isn't that a contradiction?"

"Well, as you say, it's an odd village," said Awdry. He walked past Munday to the door and held it open.

"Then we must go," said Emma.

Munday had told her what happened at the manor. But it was an abbreviated version. He said there had been objections in the village to Silvano—"Our fair-minded friends here are beside themselves at the thought of a black man in their midst"—and that he had defended him. Emma was shocked. Munday kicked the logs in the fireplace and showers of sparks dropped from them. He said, "It's just an excuse to run us out of the village."

"We shouldn't stay where we're not wanted," said Emma.

"Because the old fool says so?" Munday poked at the

logs. "I won't let them drive me out of my own house."

"We have no friends here."

"You haven't tried to make any," said Munday. "Give a dinner party."

"The Awdrys won't come."

"There are other people in the village," said Munday. "What about those children we met on New Year's Eve? 'Rachel's nappy smells like mangoes'—her, and the others."

"You don't want them."

"No," said Munday. "But we can get some people down from London. We can put them up. This is a big enough house, Emma."

"Silvano, Alec, Margaret—"

"Use your initiative," he said. "Make an effort!"

"My heart," she said, and he wondered if he had sounded so feeble when he had said it.

"Not them, necessarily. There are lots more people who'd love to come down."

"All those poor souls from Africa—they're the only people we know now."

"This is England." Munday warmed his hands at the fire.

"For us this is an outpost of Africa," she said. "I didn't think it would ever come to this."

"I'm staying," said Munday. "I won't be chased away. I'm not a poacher."

"I wish you hadn't seen Mr. Awdry."

"I'm glad I did."

"You're awful when you're challenged."

"You can go if you want," he said.

"I won't leave without you."

"So we'll both stay," he said.

"And mop the floors."

"What do you mean by that?"

"Mrs. Branch has given notice," she said.

"What reason did she give?"

"She's so hard to understand. That local dialect she uses when she's sulking. She said something about our personalities."

"Bitch," he said.

Emma started to smile. She said, "She must have been talking about yours, because as you've often pointed out, *I* don't have one."

The next evening after his walk he went back to the Black House and saw Emma brighter than she had been for months. She was taking a casserole out of the oven, humming to a song coming over the radio, one that Munday had heard nearly every day since his arrival back in England, "Gypsies, Tramps, and Thieves."

"You're certainly cheerful," said Munday. "Are you feeling better?"

"I've decided to take your advice."

"Oh?"

"You said I never see anyone," said Emma.

Munday switched off the radio. "Have you invited Margaret down?"

"No, not Margaret," said Emma. "That Summers woman rang up while you were out."

"What did she want?" asked Munday, and he turned away from Emma to hide his face.

"Nothing in particular—it was just a friendly call," said Emma. "But I've asked her over to dinner on Friday. So you see I *do* have the occasional inspiration."

18

MUNDAY SAT between his wife and his lover, in the high-backed chair, trying to hide a discomfort that was intermittently woe by concentrating on his meal. His head was down and he was cutting his roast beef into neat cubes. He had said nothing, it was the women who did all the talking, and they spoke across the table with the good humor and husky agreement of strangers eager to know each other better.

"I know exactly what you mean," Caroline said. She was seated sideways on her chair, the elegant listening posture of a woman with long legs.

"And not only that," Emma went on. She was confiding her disappointment with the village, but stressing her hardship in such a genial way she made it a lively story. It was her version of those dark months, a kind of farce: "We were absolutely baffled—well, you can imagine!" In it she maintained the fiction of Munday's bad heart; she was patient, standing by while Munday pored over his notes in his study. Self-important, calling out for coffee, he was too absorbed to notice her. She gave it all the flavor of an adventure, cherishing each mishap with uncritical comedy, in the tone of a head prefect reporting a disastrous outing. Caroline laughed appreciatively and urged her to go on.

Munday did not contradict Emma. He was glad to be relieved of the burden of conversation and he was pleased Caroline was responding with such kindness. He said, "Tell Caroline about the mysterious Mrs. Seaton."

They ate in the kitchen, because Emma's hours of

cooking had made it the warmest room. But they might have been anywhere in the house: there was a rightness in their gathering there, and Munday passed beyond his superficial guilt to the feeling he had experienced on New Year's, when he had made love to Caroline before the gasping fire, while Emma slept on upstairs. He saw that the three of them belonged to the Black House, they were its first tenants, and all those rooms, the low ceilings, the protecting shadows, the unusable and makeshift modernity, the sweating windows in the thick walls made an appropriate shelter for a love that had to be conspiratorial. What else could it be? Love was exclusive, a lucky couple making a meal amid famine. It had to be hidden, dragged into the dark; and the Black House, the object of his return, which was for him the whole of England, as the Bwamba village had been the whole of Africa, was the perfect place for this feast. Dining together, it was as if they had now acknowledged what he had always suspected, the November impression he had called a fear, that it was a house so veiled you imagined a victim in one of its darkened rooms. He had thought it was himself; for a while—but without knowing her name—he believed it was Caroline; now he knew it was Emma.

Emma said, "You don't expect the countryside to be so oppressive." She wrinkled her nose. "Alfred says it's my own fault—he's a great one for holding people responsible. He blamed that poor Mrs. Branch for the noisy tractors that go by the window with the bales of hay. And he's so wrapped up in his work. It was the same in Africa."

"Africa," said Caroline. "Everyone has an uncle who's been there. Or am I thinking of India?"

"I wouldn't know," said Emma. "My uncle never set foot out of Roehampton."

"But what made you go to Africa in the first place?" Caroline asked.

"I went with Alfred."

Caroline turned to Munday and said, "Well?"

"For my research," said Munday. "But I never wondered why. At the time I would have been more surprised by someone who said he *didn't* want to go. The name was always magic to me. Africa, Africa— and the Mountains of the Moon. I thiught of lions and craters and people whom no one had set eyes on before. It's infantile, I suppose, but there it is. If a chap told me he wanted to go to Istanbul or Java, I wouldn't ask why."

"I've been to Istanbul," said Caroline. "On that vastly overrated train. I'd never do it again."

"It's a bewitching name," said Munday.

"That's why my first husband went to Dubrovnik," said Caroline. "He hated it, and a Jug picked his pocket."

"I found Africa disappointing," said Emma. "Such sad people."

"The Africans," said Caroline.

"Well, I was thinking of the expatriates," said Emma. "But the Africans as well. There was nothing one could do."

"You had your painting," said Munday.

"Humped Cattle, Tea Harvesting," said Emma. "I've tried that here. It doesn't work. I'm afraid I've become a television bug. Alfred hates it. I watch the news and those awful discussions. The Irish business, the miners. It's like one of those third-rate serials with a complicated plot, in endless installments. You have to keep up with it, all the new developments and characters." She reached for a dish. "Will you have some more meat? And there's lots more Yorkshire pudding."

"I'm doing fine with this," said Caroline. "It's delicious."

"I'm not much of a cook," said Emma. "I never got any practice in Africa. We always had help, fetching and carrying, cooking, anything you can name."

"It sounds idyllic."

"It was beastly," said Emma. "Have you read Eliot? *The Cocktail Party?* 'When these people have done with a European, he is, as a rule, no longer fit to eat.'"

"Tripe," said Munday.

"But you must have loved it to have stayed so long there," said Caroline to Munday.

"It began to wear a bit thin," said Munday. "I sometimes feel I could have discovered all I needed to know about isolation and perhaps even tribalism right here in Four Ashes."

"Not witchcraft surely?"

"And witchcraft," said Munday, "of a sort. Anyway, that love of Africa or the exotic anywhere is like sexual voyeurism. You go on watching and you think you're perfectly detached. But you're involved in a rather pathetic way. It changes you. You're violated by just seeing it."

"So you stopped being a voyeur," said Caroline.

"I never started."

Emma coughed. She passed the salad to Caroline and said, "There are avocados in it. I hope they're ripe."

"Who is Mrs. Branch?" asked Caroline.

"She used to do for us," said Emma. "Alfred was forever scaring her half to death with African stories."

"*My* idea of an African story," said Munday, "is talking about one's servants."

But Emma ignored him: "Once, Mrs. Branch said, 'They must be so savage,' and Alfred said, 'Well, they wash their hands before they eat—that's pretty civilized.' He's full of remarks like that. You were at his talk, so you know."

"You notice she took the hint," said Munday.

"I must remember that," said Caroline.

"Alfred uses Africans to reproach the English," said Emma. She smiled. "Incredible isn't it? But that's anthropology."

"I always think of anthropologists as having these jungle helmets and shorts, and becoming honorary chiefs of obscure tribes, and hiking for days with little native guides," said Caroline. She had affected a stagey manner; she was acting. How strange it was to see her behaving like this, Munday thought; to see them both, Emma and Caroline, playing parts in company, assigning him his trivial part, because the role of lover was unplayable. "Oh, yes," Caroline said, "and being terribly interested in arrowheads and blunt daggers."

"You've just described my husband," said Emma.

"Not exactly," said Munday.

Emma leaned towards Caroline, and said, "You should see Alfred's weapons."

"I'll open that second bottle of wine," said Munday. He went to the sideboard and pulled the cork, and filling the glasses he said, "I think you're going to like this one. It's rather better than that Spanish number."

Caroline smiled and said, "This has been a lovely evening."

"I'm enjoying myself," said Emma. "We see so few people. We don't do much in the way of entertaining. It's a treat for us having you over."

"Yes," said Munday. "But you must have lots of friends in the area."

"Not really," said Caroline. "Like you, I'm a stranger here—though I've lived here for quite a number of years. The local people aren't very easy to know. And the others are too easy, if you know what I mean. I live a quiet life."

"So do we," said Emma. "But not by choice. There are so many plays on in London I'd like to see."

"That's an expatriate remark if I've ever heard one," said Munday.

"It's true," said Emma.

"My husband and I used to go up to London for the plays," said Caroline.

"And you don't go now?" said Munday.

"Well, I lost him you see."

"I'm sorry," said Emma.

"It takes some getting used to."

"You're managing, though," said Munday.

"Just," said Caroline. "I had to give up my dogs."

"Dogs?" Munday reached for his glass of wine, but

he saw his hand was trembling, and he didn't pick it up. He moved the glass in circles on the table. He said, "What did you do with them?"

"I bred them," said Caroline. "Alsatians—beautiful creatures."

"That must have been a lot of work," said Emma.

"I had help. Mr. Awdry found me a wonderful chap," said Caroline. "Local. But awfully sweet."

"Was it Hosmer, by any chance?" asked Munday.

"Why yes, but how did you know that?"

"I see him at The Yew Tree from time to time," said Munday.

"You're very brave," said Emma. "It must be hard for a widow here."

"It can be," said Caroline. "But the day after my husband died, I overslept. I hadn't done that for years. Perhaps that tells you something about our marriage."

At that moment the lights went out. "Power cut," said Emma. But it had been announced as a possibility, and they were prepared for it. There were candles on the window sill. "Just a moment," said Munday. He struck a match, but in the spurt of flame he saw the rigid corpses of two dogs, their skin peeled off, their white muscles showing a thin foam of decay. And another, more vivid image, his dagger in the throat of the foxhound. Munday found the candles and brought them to the table. The conversation continued, but in candlelight, with their faces half-hidden and their bodies in shadow, it was more confidential, with an intensity that the harshly-lit room had restrained.

"They whisper about me," said Caroline into her fiery sherbet.

"Who does?" asked Emma.

"The locals," said Caroline. "You must have heard the talk. They say terrible things about me. They tell stories."

"I've heard nothing," said Emma.

"What sort of stories?" asked Munday.

"Oh, you know the kind of thing," said Caroline.

She paused. The bones and hollows in her face were set off by shadows; her eyes held two candle flames. She finally said, "I didn't give up my dogs—they were stolen. One morning I went to the kennel and they were gone. It's dreadful when something you care about disappears—you can't help thinking you're next."

"It is dreadful," said Emma. "That makes me angry." She was breathing hard with her mouth shut. She said, "They talk about us, too."

"Do they?"

"They object to our visitors," said Emma.

Caroline said, "They can be very cruel."

Munday said, "In Africa—"

But Emma had leaned forward and was saying, "We don't intend to stay here." Her panting made the candle flame dance near her face.

"That's not true," said Munday.

"It is!"

"Why not?" Caroline put the question to Emma.

"We're just renting this house—it's not permanent. I've never liked it here, and I don't want to stay."

Munday said, "We haven't made any firm decision. We haven't even discussed it."

"I've made up my mind," said Emma. "This house! At first I thought it was England, everything I've always disliked about England I found here—the damp, the cold, the shabbiness. That awful trap that appalled me even when I was a girl. So I thought it was me. But it wasn't. No, it's something else, something much worse. There are rooms in this house that Mrs. Branch refused to clean—I've *seen* things! Alfred laughs, but it's so terrifying for me sometimes. You have no idea."

"Calm yourself," said Munday. "I love this house."

"I can't help it," said Emma. She blinked and started again, "This house—"

"You'll have to forgive Emma," said Munday. "She's not well."

"No," said Caroline. She looked at Emma as an

adult at a child quieted by terror; Emma was very pale and small—she might have been stunned by a slap in the face. "I know what you mean," said Caroline. "My house is no better. I'm alone, and when you're alone in a room even a toast rack can look like an instrument of torture."

"I'm often alone," said Emma. "Alfred doesn't know."

"She paints," said Munday. "And there's the garden. Emma's always had green fingers."

"A crack in the wall or a mirror—even that can look very threatening," said Caroline. "And the furniture seems to sit in judgment upon you."

"Yes," said Emma eagerly. "Yes, that's exactly how I've felt."

"And the noises," said Caroline.

"The noises!" said Emma. "It's worse during the day, much worse when the sun is shining, as if you're being mocked by the light. That's so sinister."

"My house is empty," said Caroline. "I shall go back there tonight and turn on all the lights. Do you know how it is, entering an empty house?"

"I do," said Emma. "It's the feeling I had when we came here, and it has never left me, not for a single moment! It doesn't bother Alfred at all."

"I don't see why it should," said Munday, but he had known the fear, and Emma's outburst had reminded him of how keenly he had felt it.

"But it would be better if you did," Emma said. "Then you'd know how I felt it, as Caroline does."

Munday was struck by how easily this first time Emma said his lover's name.

"It just occurred to me," said Caroline. She touched at her throat with misgiving.

"What's wrong?" said Munday.

"I won't be able to turn on the lights tonight. The house will be dark. These damned power cuts!"

"What a shame," said Emma. "You see, I know just what's going through your mind. It's late, it's dark— do you have very far to go?"

"I'll see you home," said Munday. "If it'll make you feel any better."

"That's awfully kind of you," said Caroline.

Munday tried to find an emotion in her eyes, but he could not see past the candle flames flickering there, two narrow blossoms of light that gave her cat's eyes.

"Yes," said Emma. Her face fell. "Then I'll be here alone."

"I won't be long," said Munday. He had visualized something like this happening, though he had not guessed that Caroline and Emma would get on so well. The darkness helped, and seeing them together he had become aware of their similarities: Caroline wasn't glamorous, nor was Emma so plain. They both had strengths he needed and an attraction he valued. But he knew he would have to choose; it was the worst of love, the excluding choice, and he had delayed it for too long.

"It's selfish of me," said Emma.

"Not at all," said Caroline.

"I wish there were something we could do," said Munday.

"But there is!" said Emma. She turned to Caroline. "Why not sleep here—stay the night?"

"I couldn't," said Caroline.

"It's no trouble. We have masses of room. That's what people do in the country, the way I imagined it. I can lend you a nightdress."

"Emma—"

"See to the coffee, Alfred."

"I really could go straight home on my own," said Caroline.

"But there's no one there," said Emma. "You're not expected."

"No," said Caroline. "That quite true."

"I want you to stay."

"You're sure?"

"Absolutely," said Emma. "Do it for my sake. So it's settled. Now, take this candle and go into the other room, and we'll bring in the coffee."

Caroline left the room, carrying the candle. The light wavered, a liquid glimmering on the walls, as she glided down the passage.

"I'm glad she's staying," said Emma. "I feel I've been so unfair to her. I don't like to think of the things I've said about her."

"I'll put some wood on the fire," said Munday.

"Such a sad woman," said Emma. "Be kind to her, Alfred."

19

CAROLINE WAS CROUCHED on the sofa, her knees tucked beneath her. She hugged a cushion to her stomach and said, "I like her. Perhaps that's the reason I stayed."

"Really," said Munday, but he made it a murmur of disinterest and doubt.

"You know very little about your wife."

"I know she's lonely, and her heart bothers her. She's had a bad time of it." He lit the candles in the wall holders over the hearth. "We're partly to blame."

"Partly?" said Caroline. She smiled and flicked one of the tassles on the cushion with her fingers. "Are you going to leave her?"

Munday thought a moment. He said, "Wouldn't it be perfect if we could live like this, the three of us."

"You don't mean that," she said.

Then Emma walked in with the coffee. She served it and took a chair before the fire, between Caroline and Munday. "I'm not having any coffee," she said. "It would only keep me awake. I've put a nightdress and clean towel on your bed. It's the back bedroom. I hope you'll be comfortable."

"You're very kind," said Caroline.

There was complete peacefulness on Emma's face. She said, "It would be lovely if every evening was like this. The candlelight, the fire, good company. I think I could actually bear it here." She let her head fall back and she seemed to sleep, still smiling quietly. Her repose excited Munday; he felt a stirring of desire for her, thumbs and fingers within him warming his grave pulse to a weightless dance. The desire he felt for Emma became a yearning for Caroline—it was intense, bearing on one, then the other, a sexual blessing Emma inspired that he would bestow on Caroline. He savored the speed and impatience, the flutter in his blood.

He said, "Emma's had a long day. Cooking's quite an effort for her."

"I'm awake," said Emma. Her eyes were nearly shut. "Just."

"I'd like to help with the washing-up," said Caroline.

"It's too dark for that—this blackout," said Emma. "I've piled the dishes in the sink. Alfred and I can tackle them tomorrow."

"It's easier in the morning," said Munday.

Emma rolled her head to one side and said to Caroline, "I feel as if you've rescued me."

"It's *you* who's rescued *me,*" said Caroline.

"No," said Emma. "I didn't realize until tonight I could be happy here. It's your doing."

Munday said, "You look tired, Emma."

"I *am* tired." Her voice was thick with fatigue. "That fire always makes me so sleepy." She sat up straight and said, "I'm nodding off. You must forgive me. I'm going to bed. Alfred, will you lock up and make sure Caroline has everything she needs?"

"Of course," said Munday.

Emma got to her feet. She was somewhat unsteady. Caroline came over to her and said, "Sleep well," and raised her hands. Emma reached and took them, and the women drew together, an action of unexpected grace, like that of two trained dancers beginning to music. They faced each other and touched cheeks, and then they kissed with great naturalness. It was a swift sisterly gesture, with a mute sigh in it, and their bodies met, their loose lips grazed. But Munday saw them hold it a fraction too long, and he was a gaping witness to a moment of intimacy. He sat back and squinted—he did not want to look away, though he felt he should, it was only proper.

And without saying more to him, Emma went out of the room. He heard her on the stairs, the light stamps rising up the other side of the wall. The sound faded and stopped. Then there was the wind in the chimney, the soft pop of the fire.

"Now," said Munday, and he got up from his chair and made a move towards Caroline.

"Aren't you afraid she'll hear?" Caroline whispered.

"She'll be asleep soon," said Munday. He went over to her and brushed her ear with his mouth, and kissing her he received a faint sweet fragrance of Emma's cologne. He inhaled it and said, "I can taste her on you."

"You're so slow."

"Why do you say that?"

"I could always taste her on you," said Caroline. "She helped us. We need her. It would be awful, you know, just you and I—living here in this place, dishes in the sink."

"It would be different somewhere else."

"Where?"

"Anywhere," said Munday. "At your house."

"*This* is my house!" she said. She saw his bewilderment and added, "You didn't know that. I think she does, in her way. You know very little. You barely know me."

"I know I love you," he said. He took her by the waist and drew her towards him. She struggled, but remained in his loose grip.

"You invented me," said Caroline.

There was a scrape on the ceiling, Emma's foot-steps. They both looked up. Munday listened for more, and Caroline said, "She did too."

"No."

"I needed it. I'm grateful to you for that," said Caroline. "She's beautiful." Caroline faced him and said, "But you're a desperate man."

He took one of her breasts and worked his thumb over the nipple. "What are you?"

"The same," she said. "I'm like you. Why else would I be here?"

"So you see, we belong together, you and I."

"And Emma," she said.

There were sounds of bedsprings just above their heads, the low ceiling creaked. It was plaster, rough-ened in patches where the stain had made it peel, and it was slumping and cracked in enough places to give the impression that if it was jolted too hard it would divide at its severest crack and collapse and cover them. The thick beam which ran along the center would splinter as well and add weight to the chunks of stone, the shower of dust. The sight of the ceiling cav-ing in was vivid to Munday because the strain of the creaking and the five-note song of the bedsprings con-tinued like music from the finger-harp which set Afri-cans in motion.

"She's in bed," said Munday.

"She can't sleep." Caroline reached up and ran her fingers dreamily along a crack. She said, "She's right there."

As she was looking up Munday stood close to her and pressed his face into her neck. The bedsprings seemed to respond to the pressure of her fingers, touch-ing and following the crack. She moved in Munday's embrace, stroking the ceiling, until her back was turned to him and he was pressed against her shoulders. She took his hands and lifted them from her waist to her breasts and cupping the backs of his hands in her own she slid them over her breasts—she was languidly fondling her body using his hands. Then she planted her feet apart, opening her legs and lifting her buttocks against him, scalding his groin.

They stayed like this, pressed together, as if she was carrying him, like a swimmer rising with a victim on her back from a deep firelit pool. The room had darkened, the heat was hers, not that of the dying fire that ceased to blow with any force into the chimney. He remained on her back, holding to her breasts, and he was aroused, for although she was facing away, her hands kept his over her breasts and the gentle switching of her soft buttocks he found a wonderful caress. She pulled at the neck of her dress, and he heard the sigh at her teeth as her nipples rode through his fingers.

The bedsprings still sounded, but he didn't hear them. He embraced a stifling heat and remembered Africa, a memory of bursting blossoms that surged in his body and reddened the backs of his eyes with fire. She was jungle, moving against him, trapping him in the rufous dark of her heat, weakening him but making his penis into a club. She took his right hand and moved it down her stomach, bumping his wrist on her hip, and pressed the pad of hair, gripping herself with his tickling hand and rolling the other over her breast. She pitched and came alive, plant flashing into animal, feathery and damp, but with muscles working under all that warmth.

She was a creature from an amorous bestiary, as if she had clawed her way out of a voluptuous myth, a long-legged heron or swan, with horny yellow feet, a woman's head and hunger and eager winged hands, and the cries of a child in her throat. Briefly, Munday imagined he was subduing her; but that was illusion— he was no hunter, the subduing was hers, she gripped him and bore him as if driven by the scratching on the ceiling, the sound of the bed. With her stroking buttocks she brought him almost to the point of orgasm. He flew, clinging to her back, seeming to rise on the quivering light and shadow of the room that was like a passage through a forest of dense trees. And her shrugging insistent speed was like a reminder that he must obey her and follow her to the end. She dropped to her knees, and Munday went down, pulling cushions from the chairs, kicking his shoes off.

"Let me do it," she said. She helped him off with his clothes, but slowly, undoing each button. He reached for her dress, but she was quicker: she squirmed and stepped out of it and then knelt over him in a pair of tight lacy pants.

"Listen," she said.

The bed spoke through the ceiling, and the ceiling itself seemed to tremble with the sound.

"She can hear us," he said.

"No," she said, and worked her pants down with her thumbs. In the whiteness of her body he saw a peculiar savagery: she was a huntress clasping a ferret between her legs. She got on all fours and then face down on the floor, on her knees and lifted her yellow buttocks at him. He hugged her from behind and entered her, but she complained and took his erect penis and fixed it at the tightness of her arse. He prodded it into her feeling her roughness squeeze him, and he opened her until he could lie across her back. He sodomized her in pumping strokes while he ran his fingers over her cunt, and it seemed to him as if, straddling her in this way, his mouth at the back of her ear, he was crawling over a dank forest floor.

"I love you," he said. "Please, God—"

"Don't stop," she said, much calmer than he.

He felt an orgasm approach, pinching his ankles and calves, climbing to his thighs and concentrating on that sawing prod that was pushed so deep into her it felt as if it was wearing away.

She acted quickly. She moved from under him and pushed him over, and holding his penis like a truncheon she licked at his inner thigh, rolling her head between his legs and lapping at him. She jerked on him, blinding him with pleasure, and her mouth slipping over him and her tight grip made him feel he was being carried upside-down. She had captured him and carried him into this heat and now his arms lay on the floor and she, the marauder, was dragging him to a destination not far off. He put his hands over his face and groaned, and he felt her draw him to her to feed on. There was no sound from him; he shivered, his shoulders going cold, and now a chill, like a wind starting in the still room breathed frailty on him. Caroline swallowed and ran her arm across her mouth. Munday was going to speak, but he hesitated, and he realized he was listening for the ceiling and the bedsprings. There was nothing, except that so quiet the ceiling was emptied of cracks and even the beam looked powerful.

"I love you," he said at last.

Caroline went over to the fire and threw some split pieces of wood on the fire. She hit them with the poker and drew light from beneath them. Flames jumped at splinters. But Munday was cold; he put his shirt on as, naked, Caroline built up the fire.

"That first time," she said, "here, in front of the fire, after we'd finished I sat beside you. You were sleeping. And I was thinking—" She broke off and smiled and shook her head.

"That you loved me," he said.

"No," she said.

"What, then?"

"That I loved myself," she said. "It was—I can't describe it—euphoria—the way I feel now. It's so marvelous. I wonder if other people feel that way, that overwhelming affection for their body after sex. I was so happy I wanted to cry and touch myself. It was real love."

He said, "Narcissism."

"Yes, yes," she said. "But not the ugly kind, posturing, preening yourself before other people, making them acknowledge you."

"Nothing to do with sex, then," he said.

"Everything," she said.

"What a selfish view of sex."

"I admit it," she said. But I can't help it. Sex can

make you feel so strong you don't need anyone. After I make love, I think I could go to a desert island or a forest and live for the rest of my life. And this feeling lasts for ages."

"Then why don't you go to your forest?"

"God, to be away from here!" she said. She looked at Munday and said, "As soon as I start to go, I want to make love again. Then I look for you."

"You don't have to look far."

"It's not that easy," she said.

"We could make it easy," he said. He reached for her hand. "I want to live with you."

"You'd hate me," she said, pulling her hand away.

"Never," he said, and clutched her. She allowed it, but she was staring at the ceiling. He said, "I know what you're thinking. I could live without her."

"But *we* couldn't," she said.

He touched at her face, like a blind man reading braille for an answer. Sex had emptied him and made him speedily innocent; there was nothing of desire in his touching—it was curiosity.

She said, "Don't give her up. I couldn't love you that way. And you'd despise me."

"You're making it impossible," he said.

"It's been possible up to now," she said. "We can go on like this. She matters more than you know."

"Poor Emma," he said.

"Don't pity her."

"What is it you want me to do?"

"*Keep her,*" she said. "If you want me, keep her in this house—stay with her, please."

Munday said, "That's crueler than leaving her."

"It is the only way."

"Is it the village?" he asked. "Are you afraid of them thinking you drove her away?"

Caroline said, "You don't understand."

"But I *do,*" said Munday. "Africa prepared me for this."

"This isn't Africa."

"Villages are my subject," he said. "I know how they operate. You don't know and so you're afraid."

She took her dress from the floor and made a shawl of it for her shoulders, and then she stared at the fire and said, "You know nothing."

The accusation maddened him. He said, "You want to make a fool of her so that you'll seem innocent."

"No," she said.

"That's why you met me secretly—to hide me, from *them!*" But he didn't press the point; he remembered, as he said it, how he had hidden Silvano. "You'll keep on using her, inhabiting her mind."

"I care for her," she said. "Nothing must happen to Emma. You don't know what they'd do if it got around that Emma left. They've already stolen my dogs."

"But that happened before you knew me."

"Yes, how did you know? It doesn't matter—don't tell me. They've hated me for a long time. They drove me out of this house. They have no mercy."

"I can handle them."

"They wouldn't leave you alone," she said. "Look what they did with your dagger. That was deliberate. There'd be more of that."

"I'm willing to risk it," he said.

"I'm not," she said. "But that's only part of it. If you want me you must keep her."

"I won't do that for them—or you," he said. "Emma is mine. She loves me. And isn't it strange? It's because of her love that I could live without her."

"But don't you see *I* couldn't!" she cried.

He was silent. He closed his eyes.

"And you couldn't," she said. "They wouldn't let you."

"Where does it end?"

He fell asleep after that, then opened his eyes on a smaller fire and dead candles, and the new order of the room and Caroline's absence suggested that time had passed. He picked up his clothes and went upstairs in the dark, feeling his way along the hall and listening to the boards creak under his feet as he entered the bedroom. He looked around the room and remembered Caroline's last muffled reply, "That's up to Emma."

The curtains were drawn; what he could make out were the shadowy tops of the bed, the wardrobe, the dresser—and the darkness gave them a heavy solidity, as if they were rooted there and yet half-missing, like tree stumps. From the dresser mirror came a glimmer of silver light, and all around him in the room hung webs and veils of black. He tugged his pajamas from under the pillow and silently put them on, careful not to disturb Emma. But when he slipped into bed he wanted her to wake up and ask him where he had been, what doing—no, he wouldn't tell; but if she asked a question he had been unable to frame, an answer might occur to him.

On other occasions, that first night he had made love to Caroline, or when he had met her furtively in the barn or in the church, he had come back to Emma and felt a kind of revulsion. Touched by lust, he could not bear to be near her. But tonight he wanted to hold her; he was wide awake and he wanted her to hear him and throw her arms about him and pull him to her. It had happened—on nights when she had, half-awake, seen his sleeplessness and believed he was troubled; in Africa, where the moon was so large and clear it lighted the curtains, and the air in the room was heated like accusation, preventing sleep: she had comforted him then.

Now, he nearly shook her. But he would be gentle. Resting would calm him. Sex had starved him of sleep, and he envisioned a life without sleep, being awake to each moment, snared in nerves—that horror of having to endure without rest what one rested to forget. He lay on his back, next to Emma for comfort, feeling the heat of his bruises, the teethmarks like stitches Caroline had left on his flesh. He tried to seize sleep with his eyes and draw it into his head.

He craved a simpler world, one he had a hand in

inventing and could inhabit easily. For an hour or more in his wakefulness he imagined such a world, of order and sunlight, where neat huts were ringed by fences of flowers and people hoed in hillside terraces of vegetables; where the pattern of life, approved by the anthropologist, was unalterable, and all around were mountains, white cliff-faces, and forest, and secured by jungle too dense to admit any adventurer. But he saw that it was not of his imagination; it was an actual place he had cast himself away from, and it was not so peaceful: some nights, sleeping in their rickety huts, children had their faces chewed by hyenas, and he had been unhappy at times—but never afraid or desperate. He had traded it for the shadowy menace of the Black House, but in this mockery of home there was no danger except fear: the menace was the shadow, and one was made free by risking fear, choosing a way through it.

He got up on one elbow and shook Emma lightly. She was turned away. He put his face close to her ear. He had lain there so long and wide awake that his voice had an unfamiliar clarity. "You were right," he said. "We can still go."

His words didn't wake her. He said, "I want you to forgive me, please. It was her doing. You don't have to say anything now—just trust me. I love you, Emma, I always have. I want to stay with you."

He leaned over and took her shoulder in his hand and pulled her towards him. She seemed to object; the stiffness in her he took to be deep sleep was like resistance, her flesh had the feel of clay, and she was heavy. When he let her go she rolled back to her original slumbering position. He kissed her hair and said, *"Emma—"* Her arm was tightly crooked against her stomach. He wanted her to wake so that he could tell her they were saved. But her sleep was perfect; he could not rouse her gently; he would not rouse her at all.

There was the other to tell. He could face her now

with his refusal. He got out of bed and went down the hall to the last bedroom.

"Caroline?"

He kicked the door open and saw the empty bed, and at the window the first of dawn, a frosty yellow-blue light on the glass. He sprang to the closet and opened it. An old black coat turned on a hanger and under it were dusty misshapen shoes.

Methodically, in the feeble light, he searched for her, knowing that as he did so he was ridding himself of the Black House, room by room. He looked again down the hallway with its long carpet and he saw enormous footprints, a giantress's tread, where it was worn. He listened to the silence until his ears roared. He opened the door to the box room (a trunk, cartons, a crippled chair) and a tide of cold air paused on his skin and shrank it. He went into the two other bedrooms, the one with the child's religious picture in a frame on the wall, the larger one, where Silvano had slept—an aroma of the African's perfumed soap still floated in a narrow layer. Each room Munday noticed had its own distinct hum, and the whole house murmured. He crept in his bare feet down the stairs to the kitchen. A light that had come on when the power was restored burned uselessly over the sink of dirty dishes. He looked in the back hall among the rubber boots and walking sticks, and in the bathroom with its wet streaming windows. He was anxious to find her, to put her to flight, but a foretaste of disgust kept him from taking any pleasure in it.

He threw open the door to the living room, but saw only the empty chairs, the vicious cushions, the shelves of decaying books. The fire was out, ashes were heaped on the irons and spilled from these mounds into the fire screen. The wrinkled plaster, the stained walls and split beam and the stale odors of wax and wood-smoke, gave the room a feel of senility; it was something he had never seen in the house before—fragile and harmless, propped there over his head, the house was revealed in the morning light with all its cracks apparent. He could pull it to pieces.

Someone was watching him. He glimpsed a movement and turned to face a pale intruder with wild hair entering from a side room, startled in the posture of being caught, with terrified eyes and lined cheeks. It was a trespasser, an awful portrait of one; then as he went closer, he saw the flaw in the mirror, the ripple of his pajamas, the flaw scarring his face, the chimney behind his head.

He made his way to the study. But he stopped; she would not be there, and he did not want to see his weapons, his notebook, his unfinished work. She was gone, there was no doubt of that. The Black House was empty, and for seconds he imagined that not even he was there—that it remained for him to admit it with some final act. It was a despair he had heard of in Africa, where a man might rise one morning, send his houseboy to market with a long detailed shopping list, lock the door and shoot himself. But he had never felt that despair, he had never feared any village, and now he knew that no matter how remote he was he would survive, for here in a village where there was no sheltering fabric of jungle, where birdsong took the place of locusts' whines, and church bells drums, which had at times appeared to him stranger than any African outpost, he had mastered solitude.

He had been haunted, and though Emma had slept through it all, put to sleep by her injured heart— a heart she had once given him to fail and burn at his own lungs—she had always been with him. He had never been alone. He said her name softly, then louder, then broke off and left himself with the echo.

The room grew dark, and he felt a chill, his feet prickled with cold, as the sunrise was eclipsed by cloud. Sleeping in bed, he might have missed those early minutes of sun that had helped him search the house, the warmth of the early-morning dazzle that had appeared only to recede under the eaves of sky. He sat down and warmed his hands under his thighs and saw Africa, green and burning, people scattering as if stampeded by the sun. Then the dark fire spread, the Black House matched Africa, and it was alight, cracking with heat and fire and falling in upon itself, crushed by its own weight and size.

But that was another anxious dream. The Black House was indestructible; only its tenants could be destroyed—if they didn't know their time was up and stayed too long. Caroline had taught him that, but he would leave with Emma. It puzzled him that she was still in bed. An early riser, she had always been up before him; but it was some satisfaction that on this morning he was first. He sat in the empty room, studying the dead fire, and waited for Emma to wake.

Bedside.
Beachside.
All around the town.

▶ **Available at your local bookstore or mail the coupon below** ◀